LOVE... AND SLEEPLESS NIGHTS

LOVE... AND SLEEPLESS NIGHTS

Nick Spalding

LAKE UNION
PUBLISHING

The characters and events portrayed in this book are fictitious. Any similarity to real persons, living or dead, is coincidental and not intended by the authors.

Printed in the United States of America.

Published by Lake Union Publishing, Seattle

www.apub.com

ISBN-13: 9781477849873
ISBN-10: 1477849874
Library of Congress Control Number: 2013916321

For Judy. The best mum in the world.

CHAPTERS

LAURA'S DIARY
Monday, April 1

Dear Mum,

Well, it's finally happened. I've achieved my lifelong ambition. The one thing I knew I wanted to accomplish from an early age.

It's been many years in the making, but I can now honestly say that I, Laura Newman, have successfully thrown my guts up in front of a group of men at a crucial job interview.

It's a modest achievement in the grand scheme of things, I know. Others have sought to climb Mount Everest or cure cancer. Me? I just wanted to embarrass myself in front of important and influential people in the most spectacular way possible.

Oh my yes. When my time on God's green earth is done, I'll have many, *many* fond memories to look back on—including the day I attended an interview at the Hotel Chocolat central offices in London and did the Technicolor yawn all over three company senior executives.

The timing was, of course, *perfect.*

Rather than the sudden and overwhelming urge to be sick hitting me at a more opportune time—while watching *The X Factor*, or listening to another one of Jamie's office anecdotes, for instance—it happened at the precise moment I was impressing the hell out of potential employers with my unrivalled knowledge of chocolate production and marketing.

Until the time of the upchuck, everything had been going quite well. The interview had come at precisely the right time for my nerves, Jamie's sanity, and our joint bank account.

The stress of having to close the shop thanks to the recession was just about killing both of us, so having the chance to interview for a highly paid role with one of the largest chocolate companies in the country was a major lifeline. Needless to say, this isn't what I'd planned for when I first opened the shop—before the downturn hit and running your own independent business suddenly became about as sensible as juggling flaming hand grenades. To tell the truth, I probably limped on for longer than I really should have. If I had been thinking purely logically, I would have sold up two years ago and gotten out with minimal fuss. As it is, though, I'd invested so much of myself in that shop that simply boarding up the windows and handing back the keys felt like a betrayal of my dreams.

Dreams don't pay the bills, however, so the inevitable happened three months ago and Laura McIntyre's ambitious plans for chocolate-based world domination went by the wayside.

To be honest with you, by the end it was something of a relief to be free of the stress, although replacing the stress of shop ownership with the stress of finding a new job isn't the greatest of exchanges when you get right down to it. You can imagine how pleased and excited I was to find an advertisement for a senior position at Hotel Chocolat. This was a job I had the skills, experience, and qualifications to do standing on my head.

So off I go to London—tottering along on my blackest, shiniest, most authoritarian high heels; wearing my most businesslike black pencil skirt and jacket, my hair in the tightest, most professional ponytail I could endure without my eyes permanently watering. I'm more prepared for this interview than they were for the bloody D-Day landings. My poor, overtaxed brain is chock-a-block with every detail it can hold regarding the company's business practises and methods.

Tucked under one arm is my portfolio, which includes various new chocolate designs and flavours I've come up with, along with the receipts from the shop—right up until just before the crunch came along and ruined everything. I am *determined* to get this job. I am a modern, powerful, creative woman who will not be denied!

Sadly, I'm also feeling a wee bit queasy as I board the 8:15 to Waterloo from a drizzle-soaked Southampton. I put the unpleasant feeling down to Saturday night, and the excesses of Charlie's birthday party. It's never taken me two whole days to recover before, but I figure I'm in my thirties now, so it's probably only going to get worse.

The journey by train is spent revising and trying to ignore the two chavs at the back of the carriage. Both are clearly already drunk, and one is probably mentally challenged to boot. He has that irritating song "Fuckin' Perfect" by Pink playing at full volume from his mobile phone and keeps singing along with the chorus, making a particular effort to scream the line, "You're fucking perfect to me-ee!" at the top of his lungs. There must be a class somewhere that these people join to learn how to be as annoying to other members of the public as possible. I imagine the first lesson is how to stop in the middle of a busy street to hit your kids, up to a final lecture about how to most effectively drive your immediate neighbours insane with parties that go on to three in the morning and aggressive, smelly pit bull terriers. The two I'm stuck with owning must have excelled in the session devoted to antisocial behaviour on public transport. Thankfully, the annoyance disappears when a muscular train guard, who looks in no mood for hijinks of this sort, stalks past my seat and neatly ejects both of the little sods at Woking before they can vandalise the train.

Once in London, the cab ride to the Hotel Chocolat offices costs an arm, a leg, and part of my lower intestine—but I arrive good and early, ready to dazzle and wow my prospective employers to the point of them needing sunglasses.

First is the half-an-hour wait in front of the receptionist. This seems to be a compulsory part of job interviewing these days. There must be some sort of manual for employers that suggests a good way to soften up applicants is to have them sit directly across from your receptionist in uncomfortable silence for thirty minutes.

This one is about twenty-two and wearing more make-up than the bloody Joker. I'm hoping for a loud noise off to one side, just to see if the slap she's wearing falls off her face if her head moves too quickly.

The phone on her desk rings and the clown princess of crime picks it up. "They're ready for you now, Mrs. Newman," she tells me through her four layers of foundation.

"Thanks," I reply, getting up and worrying at my skirt, which has inexplicably developed several large creases despite the fact I've been sitting still for half an hour. My heart is hammering in my chest like a caffeine-injected blacksmith as I pick up the portfolio beside me. I wobble past Heath Ledger towards an expensive mahogany door. It's opened by a shiny young man in a dapper grey suit. He offers me the kind of smile I've only seen before on the face of a used car salesman.

"Good morning, Mrs. Newman," he says. "Please take a seat." He gestures to a chair in front of an expensive mahogany desk. There must be a mahogany salesman in the city somewhere with a gold-plated toilet.

"God morning," I reply.

God morning? What the hell does *God morning* mean? I meant to say *good morning* of course, but my nerves got the better of me. He's going to think I'm some kind of weirdo, God-bothering religious fruitcake now!

"Good morning," I say. He smiles at me again in a slightly confused fashion and walks round to join his two colleagues behind the desk. One of these is a thin, pleasant-looking black man in a crisp blue suit, and the other is the actor Christopher Biggins.

I blink a couple of times. How is this possible? Since when did Biggins—portly comedian and star of many a bawdy television romp in the 1980s—change careers and become an executive for a chocolate company?

I blink again. It's not him, thank God. He just looks uncannily *like* Christopher Biggins. Relief washes over me. I don't do well in the presence of celebrities—even minor ones. I once saw Brian from *Big Brother* in Best Buy and nearly peed myself. The thought of having to conduct myself professionally under the level gaze of a pantomime dame chills me to the bone.

Hang on a minute. Isn't Christopher Biggins dead anyway? I'm sure I read that somewhere . . . *Oh God. How long have I been standing here thinking about Christopher Biggins?*

"Please sit down," not-Christopher Biggins tells me. He's got a look on his face that suggests I was standing stock-still trying to remember if Christopher Biggins is dead or not for an uncomfortably long period of time.

Stop thinking about Christopher Biggins, you mad bitch!

I sit down, grateful that the desk hides the cavernous creases in my skirt. The nausea from earlier has returned stronger than ever, but I put it down to a combination of nerves and the Saturday hangover and do my best to ignore it.

"My name is Charles Lipman," says the nice black man. "These are my colleagues David Presley." He indicates the slick car salesman. "And Roger McDougal." He points at not-Biggins.

"I'm very pleased to meet you all," I say, lying through my teeth.

"As are we, Mrs. Newman," Lipman continues. "From reading your CV, it appears you may well have the qualities we're after for the position of southern area creative manager." He pulls out a copy. "Tell us all about your previous experience."

And with that, the interview is underway. I put thoughts of camp television stars (who may or may not be dead, the jury is still out at this point), wrinkled skirts, and *Batman* villains out of my head, and begin the job of dazzling these three men with my suitability for this fabulous job.

It all goes swimmingly. For about twenty minutes. They nod their heads appreciatively as I tell them about their business. They smile approvingly as I suggest ways to increase productivity and profit margins. They even chuckle at my carefully honed jokes about running my own business in a recession-hit economy. Jamie had fed me these last night during a last-minute flurry of revision. I wasn't sure about using them, but he said they'd go a long way to proving I had a sparkling personality.

It wasn't all that pleasant detailing the collapse of the shop. Nobody likes to talk about something that ends in failure. The main thing is for them to know that the shop went under thanks only to the bad economy—not because I have the business acumen of a dazed camel. They seem to readily accept my well-crafted point of view, so I move on swiftly to other matters, relieved to have gotten that explanation out of the way.

I'm in the middle of explaining the marketing strategy I'd like to employ for next Easter, when the nausea I've been keeping at bay all morning breaks through my carefully constructed mental dam and washes over me like a sickly tidal wave.

"Are you alright, Mrs. Newman?" not-Biggins asks, seeing I've suddenly gone a whiter shade of pale.

"Yes," I squeak. I take a couple of deep breaths and continue. "As I was saying, the campaign needs to focus on parents, so I've devised a few straplines I believe would—"

My mouth is full of sick. One minute it's empty, the next it's full. I've never known anything like it.

In my previous experiences, I've had more warning signs: the rolling of the stomach, that horrible coppery taste, the feeling of your throat muscles constricting . . . This time, though, it's like a magic trick, and not a good one like the kind David Copperfield performs in aircraft hangars, or the type David Blaine inflicts on innocent passers-by in the middle of a city street.

The vomit simply appears in my mouth in a split second. I shut my lips tight trying to prevent its exit into the world. My cheeks puff out, and I begin to resemble Alvin the bloody Chipmunk.

"My word. Are you feeling sick?" Charles Lipman asks.

Alvin can't reply. If Alvin tries to say anything, a stream of warm vomit will be the only answer. Some might say this would actually be an improvement over the high-pitched, squeaking stupidity that usually comes out of Alvin's mouth, but I'd cheerfully listen to a whole album of that crap right now rather than be sitting here with a gob full of my own stomach lining.

Then horrifyingly, like a fat commuter boarding an underground train during rush hour, more sick jostles its way into my already overfilled mouth. My hand flies up to cover my lips, but the inevitable is already happening. My gob can't take anymore. The barrier is breached. The walls of Jericho have well and truly fallen.

From between my fingers, a fountain of vomit sprays forth, happy to be free of its enforced imprisonment. It's like putting your hand over a hose—only smellier and involving more dry cleaning.

All three of my interviewers back away in horror. Charles Lipman and David Presley are out of their chairs in an instant, but poor old portly not-Biggins is less limber, and instead of jumping out of his chair to avoid my upchuck, he simply falls backwards in a slapstick tumble his famous doppelgänger would have been proud to execute in any matinee performance of *Jack and the Beanstalk*.

I'm up out of my seat as well, one hand still clasped to my face. With the other, I try to indicate that I need the nearest toilet. I waggle my finger around feverishly while skipping backwards out of range. It looks like I've invented a new dance, some kind of finger waggling, puffy-cheeked update on the Charleston . . . with added stomach broth.

Thankfully, Charles Lipman divines the import of my interpretive dance. "There's a bathroom through that door!" he screeches, pointing maniacally at another expensive mahogany door to my right.

I rush towards it and bang the door open. Inside is one of those executive washrooms that I have no doubt no one has thrown up in previously. It's just not designed for that kind of thing. This washroom has seen many rich hairy men's arses in its time, but I bet I'm the first woman in history to come in here and lose her giblets. I happily christen the facilities in the toilet stall at one end of the room.

Most of the sick has already made its way up from my stomach, so I'm spared the hideous dry heaves. These are always the worst part of being sick. You sound like a power-lifter trying to get four hundred pounds over their head, and look like a dog trying to bring up a stuck bone.

After only a couple of minutes I'm able to move away from the toilet bowl to clean myself up. There are some flecks of vomit on my jacket, but on the whole things could be worse. My face is that of a heroin-addled prostitute, but my clothes are in a fairly respectable state of repair considering what's just happened.

Of course I can never leave this bathroom again. This is my home now. They will have to send in food, drink, and other supplies. I'm glad my mobile phone is in my pocket so I can still communicate with loved ones. They'll miss me no doubt, but perhaps the people at Hotel Chocolat can arrange visiting hours. I'll have to bed down in the toilet stall, and I'll need some books to while away the coming decades, but on the whole staying in here is far better than opening the door and facing the three men I've just been sick in front of.

"Mrs. Newman?"

It's fucking not-Biggins. He wants me out. He wants to bask in my shame, to delight in my embarrassment, the bastard. I *hate* you, not-Christopher Biggins, and everything you stand for.

"Are you alright, Mrs. Newman?" Presley also pipes up.

Of course I'm not alright you colossal pillock. I've just completely ruined my chances of getting a job with your company.

"Yes, I'm fine!" I shout through the door a little too loudly. "I'm going to come out now."

The door swings open and I'm greeted by three worried faces. Not-Biggins looks the most concerned, to his credit.

"I do apologise gentlemen. I can't explain how that happened. I assume I must be sick."

Charles Lipman's eyes narrow. "You're not . . . *pregnant* are you?" he asks tentatively.

Me? Pregnant? Don't be so flaming silly!

"Oh, I very much doubt it, Mr. Lipman. My husband and I are always careful with our contraception."

And there we have it. I'm now discussing my sexual health with three men I met less than half an hour ago. The bright red of shame flushes my face.

"Oh." Lipman looks horrified. Presley looks like a deer in the headlights. McDougal continues to inexplicably look like Christopher Biggins.

"Well, Mrs. Newman," Lipman carries on, "perhaps we should end the interview there, given what's just happened? We wouldn't want you to have to continue in your present state."

You mean the feeling of bloated nausea? Or the drying vomit now forming an unsightly crust on my lapel?

"Perhaps you're right Mr. Lipman." My face takes on its most hangdog expression. "Thank you for seeing me today. I apologise for the sickness."

"That's quite alright, Mrs. Newman. My wife suffered with morning sickness with our first child," not-Biggins points out.

I'm not pregnant. Fuck you, not-Biggins!

I go over and pick up my portfolio.

"You're welcome to leave that here if you like, Mrs. Newman, I'd like to read through it," Charles Lipman says. A glimmer of hope breaks through the clouds of abject mortification.

"Thank you, Mr. Lipman, I will." I'm surprised by the way my voice is shaking. With sudden unvarnished terror I realise I'm close to tears. Lipman's simple offer to read my portfolio is about to make me cry like a five-year-old girl.

What the hell is the matter with me?

With shining eye and trembling lip I go to shake hands with Charlie-boy. He looks down at the hand I proffer, no doubt examining it for signs of my stomach contents. I smile like an arsonist holding a match and withdraw the hand, swallowing the hard lump I've got in my throat.

"Well, good-bye gentlemen," I say in a rush. "I hope you all have a very pleasant day."

All three offer me an equally polite farewell.

For an instant, not-Biggins looks like he's going to hug me. I don't think I could stand that. If he tries it, I will burst into tears. How could I not? He has the friendly, open face of a pantomime legend. Thankfully he doesn't go for an embarrassing clinch, and without another word I scurry out of the room. As I pass the Joker, I can hear her on the phone asking for a cleaner to come up to Mr. Lipman's office as quickly as possible. I couldn't feel worse about myself right now if you told me I had dengue fever . . .

Of course, there is no way I'm actually *pregnant*. No way in hell! It's just the result of the hangover from Saturday—and probably the Thai takeaway we had last night. Yes, that must be it! Just a combination of too many vodkas and some bad chicken pad thai noodles.

The visit I make to a nearby Boots on my way back to the train station is *entirely* coincidental. I merely go in to purchase some Pepto-Bismol to settle my stomach. Quite how the pregnancy test finds its way onto the counter in front of the sales assistant is beyond me, but for some reason I buy it anyway and stick it in my jacket pocket. I may—or may not—take the test later, just out of idle curiosity. Only because I've never taken one before and am interested on a purely academic level as to how they work.

After all, there's no way I'm pregnant. Oh goodness gracious me no!

Oh good God, I'm pregnant. Knocked up. Up the duff. In the first blossom of motherhood. Carrying the first few cells of an unborn human being that will one day soon expect to squeeze itself out of my vagina, which can't happen, of course. It's *impossible.* Squeeze a human being from my prim, healthy lady garden? Don't be so ridiculous!

Oh, Mum, I really wish you were here. I'm *terrified.*

Love and miss you,

Your soon to be enormous daughter, Laura

xxx

JAMIE'S BLOG

Tuesday 2 April

"Don't worry, I'll pull it out before I come and finish up on your back."

As far as I can tell, with the above words my life as I knew it came to an end. Not the most apocalyptic, erudite, or quoteworthy of statements to mark the end of existence itself, I admit. Nevertheless, this was indeed the utterance that signalled the death knell of Jamie Newman's carefree and frolicsome existence. I've put a lot of thought into this, and I'm sure I'm right.

It was a month ago.

No . . . let's go back a bit further than that, to last autumn, when Laura had to come off the pill because it was giving her migraines. That was fine, though. The family planning clinic wasn't far from the office, so I was happy to pop down and pick up a free supply of condoms until such time she found another pill to take—one that wouldn't leave her needing a darkened room for the rest of the day. Either that, or until we agreed on an alternative form of contraception.

It was only supposed to be for a few weeks, but if there's one criticism you could level at Laura and me as a couple, it's that we can procrastinate to absurd lengths if we want to. Testament to this fact is the eight-year-old couch we're still sitting on. No matter how many times that bloody DFS advert comes on the TV, we still can't get our arses in gear to go and have a look at their latest collection of sofas in their never-ending sale.

Anyway, fast-forward to a few weeks ago—and a mesmerisingly dull Sunday evening in March. Frankly, I'm going to blame Simon Cowell for this entire thing. If the selection of lunatics on *The X Factor* had been of a higher standard, they might have held our attention for longer and I wouldn't have suggested a quick screw before *Top Gear* started.

I'm aware that sounds about as romantic as herpes, but it's not actually so bad. Laura and I have a very healthy sex life—where long, sensual, and romantic lovemaking sessions are very much in evidence. But the universe thrives on variation, and as such we also enjoy the occasional quickie when we have a spare bit of time. As two people with long work hours, these quickies have sadly become more common than the sweaty, lengthy, candlelit sessions—a big drawback to living in twenty-first-century Britain if ever there was one.

We've really perfected it over the past few months. We can have sex in the morning before work, in the evening while the chicken is defrosting, in the bathroom just before heading out to Walmart—and on one memorable occasion when we were both feeling uncommonly horny, in the disabled lift *at* Walmart. Don't worry, we felt awful about it afterwards.

Suffice it to say, if there was a speed-shagging championships, we'd make a good showing.

And thus it was that Jamie Newman positioned his lovely, graceful, and inordinately beautiful wife on her knees on the aforementioned eight-year-old couch and prepared to administer a good, hard, quick pounding.

But, *disaster*!

"Oh shit. I haven't got any condoms," I tell her, pumping little Jamie rapidly in order to maintain an erect state while we consider this dilemma.

"Really?" my gorgeous wife replies, bum aloft and arms gripping the sofa cushions. "I haven't got any either!"

"Stay right there," I order. "I'll go have a look in my bedside cabinet."

Off I trot, penis waggling gaily in front of me like a divining rod, leaving Laura to rest her head in her hands—the perfect globe of her peachy little behind still pointing upwards, making her back arch in that way I find so irresistible.

Sadly, there are no condoms in evidence in the bedside cabinet. I move on to the bathroom to check the cabinet in there, still pumping away at little Jamie to ensure that should I find any of the little rubber lifesavers, I will be standing proud and ready. Thus begins a five-minute search of every cupboard and drawer I can think of—all conducted with one hand. I resemble some kind of sex pervert with a fetish for household storage facilities.

"Come on Jamie!" Laura shouts, the impatience in her voice unmistakable.

"Sorry! Just, er . . . play with yourself for a while. I'll be there as soon as I can!" Yes, indeed, the romance is well and truly alive on this very special night.

So there we are, me frantically pulling drawers with one hand and penis with the other while Laura is left to her own devices with Simon Cowell in the background, chatting to a contestant who's just sung "Camptown Races" to Nicole Sherzinger in full scuba gear. (The contestant is the one in scuba gear, by the way.)

"It's no good," I say, wandering back into the lounge. "There're no condoms in the house."

"Shit," Laura replies. "We'll have to leave it, then."

She's right, we should stop. It's the sensible course of action. But here's my problem: my wife is a *very* attractive woman, and right now she's kneeling on the couch, her legs apart and her bum in the air. This is when Jamie Newman utters the words that seal his fate:

"Don't worry. I'll pull it out before I come and finish up on your back."

There's a part of Laura—the romantic, soft, demure lady inside her—that is no doubt disgusted by this pronouncement. Fatally, the part of Laura firmly in charge of her faculties right now is the animalistic, filthy, sex kitten that every woman *also* has inside her—if you look hard enough and poke her in the right places.

"Okay, but make sure you do it right," she breathes in a husky voice.

I do indeed *do it right*, in my defence. I exhibit what at the time I believe to be *superhuman* levels of self-control and succeed in not arriving at my destination until I've successfully made Laura's toes curl and removed myself from the equation.

The aim with which I dispatch my manly exuberance at the conclusion of events isn't particularly good, so at least we now have a *very* good reason to get off our arses and buy another couch.

The problem is that this particular method of ad hoc contraception isn't good enough. Pulling out early *doesn't* mean you're safe even if you think you are. This is something that teenagers with no common sense whatsoever know, but is a fact we had both conveniently chosen to forget until yesterday: April Fool's Day.

And what a crappy April 1st it had been for me already, before I even walked in the door at 6:00 p.m. I'd spent the entire day arguing with a subeditor over the advertising space at the rear of the paper. I say *arguing*, but it had mostly been a series of passive-aggressive emails culminating in a testy five-minute "chat" outside the Reprographics Department.

This isn't the kind of fun-filled day at work I'd envisaged when I'd struck out on my career as a writer. I thought it would be all about sitting in a whirlwind of creativity, knocking out brilliant and insightful articles about whatever important topic I felt needed Newman's expert opinion. It was my destiny to write the best press releases, news articles, and advertising copy that had ever been committed to paper.

Sadly, the universe hasn't humoured me thus far, so I find myself killing time at the local paper, arguing over an extremely trivial three inches of column space. It was an argument I'd lost, so my mood was blacker than the soul of an adult Justin Bieber fan by the time I got home.

"Evening, baby," I say morosely to my wife when I see her standing in the kitchen.

"Evening," she replies in a very small voice after I administer my usual hello kiss.

Had my mood not been quite so bad, I would have noticed the signs right there. As it was, I pulled off my tie, ambled into the lounge, and parked myself on the semen-stained sofa cushion (turned upside down), intent on watching people less fortunate than myself on the news for half an hour or so. This is an aspect of human nature I've never really liked, but when you've had a shitty day at work, it does often make you feel better to come home and find out all about somebody whose day has been so bad they've wound up talking to Jeremy Thompson about it. I'm completely oblivious to the emotional state of my nervous, fidgety wife as she comes and sits next to me.

"Good day?" I ask her, hoping she'll just say yes, and then ask me how mine went so I can launch into an epic diatribe on how much of a wanker Colin Forbes, the subeditor, is.

"Umm. Not . . . not so great, I suppose." She picks at one corner of a cushion.

"Really? That sucks," I reply, eager to use this point in the conversation to steer it towards my own woes. "I can sympathise. I've had a ball ache of a day. You know that twat Forbes? The one with the squinty eye? Yeah, well, he's been a right prick today. I had to get an extra half-page spread sorted for the Easter promo, but *oh no* . . . he says he needs it to run the rugby report. Bloody rugby report. Who cares about rugby, eh? Stupid sport. I tell you, baby, sometimes this job does my head in. I really wish I could leave it, but I can't be arsed to look for anything else at the moment. Going through all that interviewing rubbish makes my blood run—*oh shit*."

My blood runs cold. I've forgotten about Laura's job interview. Today was the day she went to London to see the Hotel Chocolat people. (It's chocolate with an *e*, by the way. This is Britain, for crying out loud. The day I start spelling things in French is the day they can come and lock me up for general insanity.) How could I bloody forget such an important thing? I even wished her good luck this morning before I left for work. Nine hours later and I've forgotten about it completely. I'm going to blame Colin Forbes and the dry chicken sandwich I had for lunch.

A tiny mewl escapes my lips as I try to get my head around the utter catastrophe I've just brought on my own head. I know that the next few minutes of my life are going to be *awful*. I also know I'm likely to be sleeping on the semen-stained couch tonight.

I begin to apologise . . . and stop. I simply cannot think of an adequate way to express my sheer, unbridled regret. There aren't enough words to appease the wrath that I know is coming my way—like a dark harbinger of the Jamie Newman apocalypse. If I thought hacking off one hand might do the trick, I'd do it. Hell, I'd gnaw the bloody thing off.

I look at Laura. It's even worse than I thought.

I was expecting a vicious scowl—a vision of pent-up female fury, ready to be unleashed on my stupid, forgetful man-face. But no. This is far, far worse. She just looks pale, upset, and very, very confused.

Oh God! The raging animal I can deal with. But Laura just looks deeply hurt by my oversight. This makes me feel a million times worse. I haven't made her angry, just sad. I wish I could kill myself by choking on a sofa cushion.

"I'm so sorry, honey," I say and take her hand. "Tell me how the job interview went." I look at her downcast face. "Did it go well?"

Which is about as silly as asking a Jewish person in 1939 if they're going to vote for Hitler at the next election. She looks at me with those glorious blue eyes, her mouth trembling. I gird my loins and start mentally compiling a shopping list of Häagen Dazs ice cream, flowers—and possibly a brand-new car. Her hand squeezes mine. I take a deep breath and prepare myself for whatever she has to say.

"I'm pregnant."

"Well, never mind," I begin. "I'm sure something else will come up, and this won't—"

Hmmm. Something's wrong. My brain is sure Laura just told me the interview didn't go well, but my ears are insisting she said something completely different. Best to rewind the last few seconds and re-evaluate . . .

Nope, she definitely didn't say anything about the job interview.

But what was the strange and alien sentence she *did* come out with? It sounded like *I'm pregnant* . . . but that is, of course, impossible. That is a sentence Laura must *never* utter, at least not for the next six or seven years while we're still building our careers and there are far-off holiday destinations to be visited. It's probably a good time to ask her to repeat herself so we can put to rest the silly idea that she said something about being pregnant.

"Sorry? What did you say?"

"I said I'm pregnant."

Oh my—

My ears don't appear to be functioning properly at all today. It still sounds like she's saying she's pregnant. I'd better ask one more time just to get to the bottom of it once and for all.

"What?"

"I said I'm bloody pregnant, Jamie. Are you deaf?"

I try to respond, "Blurben hurmen?"

It now sounds like the speech centre of my brain has short-circuited. I am no longer able to form proper words and will spend the rest of my days communicating in a way that only the people of Sweden will understand.

"What?" Laura says.

This time I can only produce a sound like a tyre deflating. My mind is going a hundred miles a second, yet is also inexplicably frozen solid. How can this be happening? How can today have started with me straining to release last night's Thai (I really need to cut down on the unhealthy takeaways), continue with a terrible chicken sandwich at lunch, peak during an afternoon argument with Colin Forbes, and end with my wife telling me she's pregnant? How can this happen today? On the first day of Apri—

Aha! Now I get it! It all becomes abundantly clear. It's the first of April! Laura—the little scamp that she is—is playing an April Fool's joke on me. How very clever and funny my wife is!

I love a good April fool. I've been on the receiving end of a few crackers in my time. For instance, there was the one back in university when my classmate Carlo changed the submission date on my creative writing assignment to April the second. Oh how he laughed as I spent the next six hours working at the keyboard like a chimp on amphetamines, trying to knock out three thousand words before his fake deadline. It was my fault really. He knew how bad I was at paying attention to deadline dates and exploited my lack of concentration in expert fashion.

Then there was Superglue Thursday. I was eleven, my brother Chris was thirteen, and he thought it an excellent idea to coat the inside of my Spock ears with superglue. How he laughed as I spent the afternoon in the emergency room with Mum while the acetone gently melted the glue and slightly burned the tops of my ears. He wasn't laughing by the time we got home and he found himself grounded for the next two months. I took great delight in wearing my brand-new set of Spock ears as I cycled past his bedroom window whenever I had the chance.

Laura's particular choice of April fool on this occasion is more prosaic and required less thought behind it, but I have to give her props for the commitment she's putting into the performance.

"Yeah . . . good one, Laura!" I exclaim happily.

I'm so pleased I've managed to work out the joke. She had the wool pulled over my eyes for a while there, but now I've seen the light!

"What?"

That's funny. She should be smiling now, happy in the knowledge that her little ruse has been discovered. I jump out of my chair, releasing some of that pent-up nervous tension.

"I said good one! You really had me going there baby. You . . . pregnant! *Brilliant*!"

For some reason she still isn't smiling. My feet, having a far better grasp on the reality of the situation than my mind, take me swiftly out into the kitchen to make a cup of tea. Laura follows me. She stands and watches me banging cups and the kettle around for a moment before speaking.

"Jamie, this isn't an April fool. I'm being serious. I'm pregnant!"

See, this is the problem with my wife: she never knows when to let a joke go. It's all about the timing and I've seen through her duplicity, so there's no real reason to keep it up.

"Come on baby, you can stop now. I know you're mucking about."

Her face like thunder, Laura stomps over to me and pulls the tea towel out of my hand. She hits me with it. Twice.

"I'm not bloody joking, you idiot!" She hits me with the towel again to emphasise her point. "I"—*whack*!—"am"—*whack*!—"pregnant!" *Whack*! *Whack*! *Whack*!

"Please stop assaulting me with the bloody tea towel!" I wail.

Her arm drops. I put the cup I'm holding back onto the counter with trembling fingers. Silence . . . terrible, terrible silence descends.

I look at my wife's exhausted face. "How?" I ask.

The look of exhaustion turns to disgust. "It might have had something to do with you humping me like a sex-starved rhinoceros. That's generally the way these things happen."

"But . . . but we're *careful*."

It will be one hour before I remember the night of the frantic wank search for condoms.

"Not careful enough."

I breathe in and out a few times. I can't think of anything to say, but I *must* say something. I can't spend the rest of this marriage communicating via clicks and grunts.

Unable to utter anything more about the pregnancy, I give her a half-hearted smile and say, "So, how did the job interview go?"

She gives me a look of pure, unadulterated misery, her eyes welling with tears. "I was sick all over Christopher Biggins!"

"Isn't Christopher Biggins dead?"

Laura starts to cry in great hitching sobs, and I throw my arms around her. I have to as my legs are about to give out on me.

An hour later, I've consumed two beers from the fridge and am feeling a touch calmer. Laura went to pour herself a glass of wine, but remembered the reason why she needed a glass of wine in the first place and put the bottle back. Instead, she nurses a cup of sweet tea—because that's what you do when you've had a shock: drink sweet tea. Quite how a sugar rush and caffeine injection is supposed to calm your nerves is beyond me, but what do I know? I can't even screw my missus without putting a baby in her belly.

"What are we going to do, Jamie?" Laura asks, staring at the television, where the reporter is standing outside Number Ten telling us all about the new tax breaks for working families. The coincidence is eye-watering.

"I don't know, baby. I really don't."

Now, there is *one* suggestion I could put forward . . . but it is a *horrible* suggestion. The kind of suggestion you hope never to make in all the days of your life. Sometimes, though, necessity trumps all other considerations—and this is one of those times.

"Do you . . . do you want to have it?" I ask. "Because, you know, you don't have to." The words are like ashes in my mouth. I can't believe I even said them.

"Do you mean a . . . a . . ."

"Yes," I say, cutting her off. "It is an option." An awful, *awful* option.

"I don't know. What do you think?"

The logical, sensible part of me says: *Yes, oh God yes. We don't have enough money or time or money to have a baby right now.* But looking at Laura, her beautiful blue eyes glistening with tears, I just can't imagine ever putting her through that kind of . . . *procedure.*

This is the woman I love. The reason why she's now pregnant is because I love her. Because I *made* love to her. This baby is a product of that love. Alright, it wasn't the most romantic bunk up in history, but it wasn't a casual, meaningless shag either.

"No," I say emphatically. "I don't want that." I take her hand. "I love you baby, no matter what. And if you're going to have my baby, then you *are* going to have my baby." I sit back a bit. "Unless you don't want to have it, of course."

She laughs. It's a short, brittle sound, but a laugh nonetheless. "I hadn't even thought about not having it, to be honest. All I've been thinking about is how big my arse is going to get."

"Don't forget your tits," I say, smiling for the first time in what feels like a century. "They're going to be *massive.*" I waggle my eyebrows at my tired wife and make obscene grabbing gestures with my hands, making her giggle.

She wipes her eyes and sniffs. "It's going to be bloody hard, honey," she says. "Me without a job, I mean. The money from the sell-off isn't going to last long."

I put my arm around her. "We'll be alright. I can grab some extra freelance stuff. Maybe you could find some too."

She gives me a withering look. "What? Like a freelance chocolate maker?"

"Yeah! Why not? That kind of thing exists, yeah?"

Of course things like that don't bloody exist. I'm clutching at straws, but I'll say anything right now to keep the mood away from abject misery.

"Maybe," she replies, and giggles again. "I could go to people's houses and cook a shitload of chocolate for them."

"There you go, then! I could do the marketing for you." I put a hand out. "Laura Newman: She'll cook you a shitload of chocolate."

This makes her collapse with laughter, which makes me laugh, too. I guess if you can get the shock of your life and be laughing your arse off an hour later, it must mean the situation can't be all *that* bad.

Right?

LAURA'S DIARY
Wednesday, May 22

Dear Mum,

Looking at one's insides via the medium of a computer screen is disconcerting to say the least. What's going on in your body is about as private a matter as you can think of. Having it splashed across a monitor—even in the shape of an ultrasound scan—leaves you feeling strangely vulnerable, even if the only people watching are your husband and the sonographer.

It's been nearly two months since I found out I was up the duff. In that time my emotional state has swung around more erratically than a weather vane in a hurricane. One minute I'm excited and looking forward to bringing new life in the world, the next I'm virtually shaking with terror and wishing I had been born a celibate monk—or should that be monkess?

I spent a good thirty minutes mulling that one over the other day just to avoid thinking about being so bloody pregnant. I usually start to panic whenever I think about the responsibility of bringing new life into the world. It's hard enough managing my own existence—adding the job of steering another human being through the vagaries of this world seems, quite frankly, impossible. It'll be a miracle if I can get the bugger through to its eighteenth year without it either ending up incarcerated, institutionalised, or maimed.

And before you can even start worrying about all that blather, you've got to successfully carry the poor thing in your body, and then push it out with no problems after nine months.

With all this in mind, it was with some trepidation that I booked the ultrasound at the local hospital. I mean, there are so many questions, aren't there? What if there's something wrong with the baby? What if it doesn't move? What if we can't hear the heartbeat? What if it's got two heads? What if it bursts from my stomach like that thing from *Alien*?

Ah, *Alien*. A movie I saw once in the early nineties and have never dared to watch again. At the time I was mortally terrified and remained so for weeks afterwards. Little did I know that the memory of it would rear its ugly, acid-spitting head again when I fell pregnant. There's nothing quite like a movie about a parasitical alien organism that grows inside a human body to really make you feel good about having a tiny human living inside you.

Trying not to think of such things, Jamie and I jumped in the car and made our way to Queen Alexandra Hospital for our appointment. Our first shock was being told the doctor wouldn't actually be the one administering the scan. Instead, it would be carried out by someone called a sonographer. This sounded to Jamie and me like a submariner's specialism, and we were both slightly disappointed when a dumpy Asian woman walked in and introduced herself.

We were rather hoping for a bespectacled young man in a navy blue sweater and glasses, wearing a pair of those enormous World War II earphones, and speaking in a broad Brooklyn accent. Instead, Narinda took us through to a room in the X-ray Department.

"Do you know how a sonogram works, Mrs. Newman?"

I used to run a chocolate shop, Narinda. I wouldn't know a sonogram from a Sony PlayStation.

"No, sorry."

"And how about you, Mr. Newman?"

"Well, I guess it's an X-ray analysis of the inside of the human body . . ."

This is where I generally zone out—when Jamie takes on *that* tone of voice. For some reason he, like a majority of the males of the species, finds it impossible to admit that he knows little to nothing about a given topic. Instead of admitting it, he'll try to sound like he knows what he's talking about by piecing together random bits of information floating around his head that may or may not have something to do with the subject in question.

". . . and you hold a thing that looks like a bar code scanner at Walmart, and you run it over Laura's belly. In fact, it's a similar technology to the bar code scanner, isn't it?"

Oh good God. Now he's comparing the method by which we can study our unborn baby to the way you buy a tin of beans and a fruit cake. What does he expect is going to happen? Narinda here runs the scanner over me, it beeps, and the price of the baby pops up on the flaming screen?

Narinda gives Jamie a look that one usually aims at the mentally challenged. "Um, no, Mr. Newman, it's not like a bar code scanner. A sonogram is based on sound waves. High-frequency sound waves that pass harmlessly through Laura's body, producing an image of the baby on the screen."

"Ah," Jamie replies, affecting a look of studied intelligence. "So it's much like the sonar systems found on a submarine? They use it to detect enemy ships and large animals in the water. Like whales."

Oh, fabulous, now he's equating me with a bloody humpback.

"Well, let's get started, shall we?" Narinda says chirpily, completely ignoring my moronic husband. "Sit down, Mrs. Newman, while I check the machine."

I sit down on a chair that looks uncomfortably like it belongs at the dentist's. This does not help to alleviate my sense of unease. Narinda presses a few switches on a rather antiquated-looking machine next to the chair (it's got a white plastic surround, and white plastic surrounds were unfashionable even in the late eighties) and looks back at me with the same chirpy smile. She obviously practises it in front of the mirror every morning. It's a smile that says: *Relax, nervous first-time mother. I've done this a million times, and while it may be a big deal to you, I'm already thinking about the tuna pasta salad I'm going to buy from the cafeteria for my lunch.*

"Just lift your shirt for me, Mrs. Newman."

Unbelievably, Jamie giggles at this. I know what's happening. He's nervous about the scan as well, and whenever my husband feels uptight he reverts to childhood sensibilities. I shoot him a look filled with sharp daggers. He shifts in his seat to cover his embarrassment.

"This is the transducer," Narinda tells us. I thought that was the movie where the robots change into cars, but I keep my mouth shut because that's obviously not right.

"I'm going to run this over your belly, and we'll see what pops up," Narinda exclaims cheerfully.

I don't know what's going to "pop up," Narinda. But if it even slightly *resembles an Alien facehugger, you're going to have to get out of the way of an exploding Laura Newman as quickly as you can.*

Narinda then squirts cold lubricant over my stomach. The tube makes a dispirited farting noise as it empties itself. I deliberately don't look at my husband beside me, as there's every chance he's trying to suppress a look of childish glee.

"Off we go then," Narinda says, as if we're all going on a jolly outing to the seaside rather than examining the alien life-form currently taking up residence in my uterus. For a while there's not a lot to see on the screen. Just a static cloud of white against a dark background. Narinda runs the transducer across my belly again, this time a bit slower. This is obviously taking longer than usual as she's starting to look like one of those lunatics you see on the beach with a metal detector. A few more seconds go by and she still can't seem to find the pot of gold she's looking for.

Jamie's hand tightens on mine. We're both feeling the tension now. Either my baby has developed superhuman powers of invisibility—which will bode well for him or her in later life—or there's a problem. Heart rates increasing, we watch Narinda take another pass. Finally, she lets out a short laugh of satisfaction and focuses on one point. "There we go, there's your baby."

And, indeed, there it is. The child growing inside me. The blob that will one day become a child, anyway.

"Is it a boy or a girl?" Jamie asks in a dreamy voice.

"Too early to say, Mr. Newman," Narinda tells him.

It's wobbling. The tiny peanut-shaped foetus is moving about. Aaaaargggh! There's a person inside me moving around! Aaaaargggh! Why did no one bloody warn me? All you ever hear about is doe-eyed mothers listening to the heartbeat for the first time and getting all misty while they gaze at a fuzzy image of the creature lurking in their womb. They don't mention the bizarre feeling that comes with realising there's a living thing floating around inside your body, taking up valuable real estate and nicking half your food. There's a word for things that do that: *parasite*. Aaaaargggh!

"Wow. That's so cool," Jamie says.

Well, he bloody *would* think that, wouldn't he? It's not him that has to push the bloody thing out of his body. Oh, no. He'll be standing gormlessly to one side watching while my body is systematically destroyed by the creature as it claws its way into the outside world. With any luck it will get him before he has a chance to take off down the corridor like a bat out of hell. Then it'll turn on me . . . the poor sap that brought it into this cruel, cold world. And I won't be able to run, will I? Oh, no. I'll probably be strapped into those stirrup things and unable to defend myself as it works its way up my body and . . .

Okay. I have to get a grip here. I'm just having a pregnancy panic. This isn't the first and I'm sure it won't be the last. I'm giving birth to a baby, not a monster. A lovely, pink, squidgy little baby that I will fall in love with the second I see it, I'm sure. There's every chance Jamie will *still* take one look at it and be off down the corridor like a bat out of hell, but I'm sure they'll bring him back in a net if I ask nicely enough.

I take a few deep breaths as I study the blurry image on the screen. The foetus jiggles again, making my heart race. But the more I look at it, the more used I become to the concept that I have a living, breathing human being inside me. I look down at my belly and back up at the screen, trying to connect the two.

"Would you like to hear the heartbeat?" Narinda asks, knowing full well what the answer will be. Jamie and I both nod—he a little more enthusiastically than me, if I'm being honest.

"This is the part I love the most," the sonographer says happily, turning up the volume.

It's like listening to the sound of the universe. The measured *thump-thump, thump-thump* is almost hypnotic. It fills the room—and it fills my entire body. I look at Jamie. This time the childlike expression on his face is beautiful. He looks completely awestruck. I'm sure I look exactly the same way.

"Wonderful, isn't it?" Narinda says in a calm voice.

It takes me a few moments to form words. "Yes," I tell her, mouth as dry as the Sahara. "It's incredible."

All thoughts of horror movie monsters are banished from my mind by that consistent *thump-thump* of my baby's heart. I could listen to it forever.

"It sounds like the start of an AC/DC song," Jamie says, doing his usual brilliant job of ruining a perfect moment.

"What?" both Narinda and I say at the same time.

"Yeah! You know . . . da-dah, da da-dah, da-dah, da da-dah." He starts miming playing the drums. I start to consider divorce proceedings. Then, to compound matters, he starts to sing.

"The video game says play me . . ." It's an awful screeching voice, like a cat having its testicles squeezed in a vice. "Face it on a level, but it takes you every time on a one-on-one . . ." he continues, until he realises we're both staring at him. "You know . . . it's "Who Made Who," isn't it? Great song." Jamie points at the ultrasound screen. "Even the kid likes it."

I look back at the screen, and, yes—oh, good God in heaven, yes—it looks like one tiny arm is raised above the rest of the body. My unborn foetus, still too small to even have an identifiable gender, has one arm aloft in a fist pump. I'm going to give birth to a heavy metal fan.

Narinda turns the volume back down with a huff. I can't blame her change of attitude. She's probably not used to having what she obviously perceives to be a magical moment reduced to an excuse for a fully grown man to play air drums.

"Your baby looks perfectly healthy at this stage, Mr. and Mrs. Newman. The heartbeat is strong and regular." And in the key of C apparently. "I detect no problems and am happy to book you in for your next scan in a few weeks, when we should be able to identify the gender, if you want to know it."

Don't bother, Narinda. It's obvious from the fist pump I'm having a boy.

"Thank you very much. It's very nice to have our minds set at rest, isn't it Jamie?"

Jamie doesn't answer. He's sitting there with his eyes closed, humming the first few chords of "Who Made Who" under his breath, fingers twitching rhythmically in his lap.

"Jamie!"

"What?" he exclaims, startled out of the rock concert going on in his head. "Oh, yeah, er . . . *yeah.* Minds definitely set at rest. Thanks very much for your time." He beams at Narinda, then looks back at me. "Hey, Laura," he says, pointing at my stomach. "That stuff looks just like the gloop from the *Alien* movies doesn't it?"

Somehow, Jamie manages to make it out of the room without the transducer inserted into his backside. This once again displays my sometimes superhuman levels of tolerance.

The drive home is a thoughtful one, for me at least. Rather inevitably, I'm subjected to AC/DC's greatest hits at full blast. I'm sure it's just my imagination, but I think I can feel my tiny baby moshing around my womb in time to the music. I just hope the little bugger doesn't go for a stage dive and crash into my pelvis.

As Jamie headbangs along to the caterwauling coming from the car stereo, I sit back and think about what's just happened. My hand involuntarily moves to my stomach as I remember the sound of the baby's heartbeat. I wish I'd gotten Narinda to record it for me so I could listen to it whenever I liked. A wonderful feeling of contentment passes through me. Don't get me wrong, I'm still absolutely terrified about the whole thing. We can't afford a baby, I can't imagine the damage it's going to do to my vagina, and having a child changes your life in ways you can't even begin to contemplate. But that heartbeat is undeniable . . . and *amazing*.

This is going to be a roller coaster ride that I won't be able to get off. And like a roller coaster ride, it'll involve a lot of vomit and will end with me screaming my head off.

Love you, miss you, and have a newfound appreciation for the twelve hours of labour you went through with me, Mum.

Your contemplative daughter, Laura

xxx

JAMIE'S BLOG

Tuesday 11 June

In recent days I have been thinking only of the things I will now never be able to afford, thanks to my inability to control my semen distribution. I read a horrifying statistic once—back when I was young, single, and didn't care about such things—that a child costs upwards of two hundred grand to bring to adulthood. *Two hundred grand.* That's a three-bed semi-detached, people. Or a Lamborghini Diablo for the weekends and a second-hand Porsche 911 for the drive to work. Or several luxury cruises around the world, a year-long cocaine binge, and a daily blow job from a high-class escort girl for several months.

I'm not saying I would ever have actually *purchased* any of these wonderful things, but just the mere fact I no longer *can* makes me sick. I'm trying my hardest to be positive about the pregnancy, I really am. But when your offspring is still a couple of inches of cells inside your wife's uterus, it's a little hard to focus on how adorable, intelligent, or good at mowing the lawn they are likely to be in years to come.

All I can dwell on is the downside. Mainly the raping my bank account is going to continually endure, but also the fact I'm going to have to take on the responsibility of bringing up a child in this strange, challenging, and R-rated world. If you've been reading my blog for a while now, you'll know that Jamie Newman and considered, thoughtful, adult behaviour are about as far apart as Kim Kardashian's legs. How the hell am I supposed to convince a child that I have anything worthwhile to contribute to their existence?

Laura is the exact opposite of me, of course. She's built for this stuff. Running her own shop for years has built an innate ability to plan and organise; skills she's putting to good use with the pregnancy. There must be some German in her family background, as the Teutonic way she's going about this thing is hair-raising to say the least. She's already booked the midwife months in advance, and she can recite the timeline of a pregnancy down to the nanosecond and has started putting together an overnight bag for the trip to the hospital. She also likes to regale me with graphic, stomach-churning descriptions of what's happening to her body. It's putting me off sex good and proper.

I have a feeling this is deliberate. Laura positively glows with all those hormones floating about inside her body, making her look about as sexy as it's possible to be without a soft-focus lens and a Barry White soundtrack. I basically want to fuck her every second she's awake.

The stories about giving birth she likes to terrify and disgust me with (accompanied by the God-awful pictures she's pulled off the Internet) are her way of quelling the Newman horn long enough for her to get on with her day without me hanging off her leg like a rutting hound.

Pregnancy (thus far anyway) definitely agrees with my wife. She's bouncing through the world right now with a healthy exuberance I find quite disconcerting. It's a great deal of fun to be around though, if I'm honest. It's as if falling pregnant has brought out a new bubbly side to Laura's personality that I'm very much enjoying being around. In many ways she's like she was when we first met and our relationship was brand-new—which I guess is quite understandable when you think about it. Something brand-new is about to enter our lives, so why wouldn't we be excited and a little nervous about it? Having a baby is kind of like falling in love all over again. Who'd have thought it?

We're now way past twelve weeks into the pregnancy, which means the threat of miscarriage has diminished considerably. I didn't even know this until Laura happily announced it a few days ago. The fact that she could have miscarried hadn't occurred to me. I'm terrible at this, aren't I?

It's customary after that particular milestone to start telling friends and relatives about the newest member of the human population. This avoids potential calls to the authorities when we turn up on their doorstep in a few months with a new baby. It also means people won't think Laura is just getting really fat. I can't be sure, but I think she'd prefer twenty years in prison for child kidnapping than to have her best friends think she's developed an addiction to KFC and has really let herself go.

We thought the best way to break the news would be to arrange a couple of impromptu get-togethers at our house on consecutive nights—one for friends and one for relatives. Anyone who couldn't attend would be told via Facebook.

I can thank Laura's pregnancy for providing me with the first genuinely *useful* reason in my life to use the stupid social network. I'm not inclined to post pictures of happy pensioners with some asinine phrase about everlasting love underneath it. Nor have I ever been tempted to engage in the largely pointless pastime of building an imaginary farm populated with nonexistent sheep. And I most certainly have *never* thought it necessary to inform everyone I know via status update that I am in the local Burger King having a piss in the disabled toilet.

Having said all of this, there's no denying the fact that it's very convenient to tell your friends and relations that you're going to be a father in your status. This means you don't actually have to communicate with *any* of them face-to-face or over the phone to tell them the good news. Let's face it. There are a limited number of people you actually care about enough to tell them the big news stories in your life. I feel no urge to tell Kathy Wilkins—a girl I got off with once at a school disco—that I'm going to be a dad. Nor do I feel it necessary to pick up the phone and call my cousin Alan, given that he lives in Canada, has questionable personal hygiene, and a disturbing tendency to marry women a lot (really, *a lot*) younger than him. I occasionally check the Montreal online newspapers . . . you know, just in case.

Facebook makes everything a damn sight easier. In previous decades you'd have to spend time, money, and effort to tell the world that you have healthy semen. Now it's just thirty seconds of typing and a mouse click.

The first announcement came on Friday evening. We invited just about every friend we wanted to break the news to. Laura asked Tim and Dan along (we made sure to buy plenty of man-size tissues, because those boys can cry like an Oscar-winning actress when they want to), as well as her best friend Melina, her ex-flatmate Charlie, and a few other randoms I frankly don't get on well enough with to mention here in more detail.

That sounds a bit harsh, I know, but I have enough trouble keeping track of my friends without adding to the load. Besides, I know which of her friends Laura is really close to, and I've made an effort to get to know them. I love Tim and Dan (in a purely hetero way, of course). They're like the epitome of what a gay couple should be like: loud, proud, and preferably clothed in expensive designer labels. They also happen to have the kind of committed and dedicated relationship most straight people can only dream about. Dan even enjoys PlayStation games. Many a happy evening is pissed away with me and him trying to murder each other on Call of Duty while Laura and Tim sit in the kitchen holding mugs of hot chocolate topped off with marshmallows, moaning about how childish we are.

I steer well clear of trying to understand the bond that Laura has with Melina. The nature of a best-friends-forever relationship between two women seems to be profoundly complex. Melina is the sister Laura never had—with everything that entails. Whenever they have an argument, I tend to hide under the duvet and hold my breath. I *certainly* don't get involved. I tried it once and just about escaped with all my limbs intact.

Charlie once sold me a load of really good cannabis for half price, so she's alright in my book.

I elected to keep my side of the guest list a little smaller, knowing full well that the gossip machine and Facebook would largely do most of the announcing for me. Still, Ryan would have killed me if I didn't tell him to his face, so I invite him—even if it does mean having to spend a couple of hours in Isobel's company. I was hoping those two would have split months ago, but it appears true love blossoms in the strangest of relationships. At least she seems to make him happy. This makes me worry for the very sanctity of his mortal soul, but I tend not to think about it too much, providing Isobel stands downwind and keeps her hands in her pockets.

I'm more than happy to invite Dave and Katherine, and even happier when they tell me Angela and Mitchell are out of the country skiing, so there's no need to conveniently "forget" to ask them along.

Our guests have no idea why we've decided to throw this little shindig, so Laura and I have twinkly little smiles on our faces for the first hour of the evening. There's something quite excellent about sharing a secret no other bugger knows about. I can understand why people think spies are cool. At about nine o'clock, we both get up and shush everyone into silence.

"Guys, we have an announcement to make," I say, taking a deep breath.

"Oh God, you're getting a divorce!" squeals Tim.

"What?" I scowl. "What makes you say that?"

Tim contrives to look extremely sheepish. "Oh, I don't know. Little signs . . ."

"Little signs? What bloody *little signs*? There haven't been any signs. We're perfectly happ—"

"Jamie!" Laura butts in before I can launch into a proper tirade. "We're not getting a divorce, Tim," she tells him.

"Are you getting that sex change you've been on about?" asks Ryan, sending Isobel into a fit of drunken cackling. I'm pretty sure she's already polished off a whole bottle of Chardonnay. The way she keeps shoving Ryan's hand between her legs is a dead giveaway.

"Very funny, cock-features," I retort with rapier-like wit.

"Come on, tell us what it is," Dave shouts, earning a dig in the ribs from Katherine.

I keep expecting one of them to guess what we're about to say and ruin the surprise, but none of them have so far. I suppose Laura and I have never given off the signals that we would even contemplate having kids, so why would any of them make that connection? I decide to concentrate on their faces as Laura gives them the big news to see what reactions it gets. Laura takes a deep breath.

"I'm pregnant," she says matter-of-factly. "Nearly fifteen weeks."

Right, then, here're the reactions:

Tim and Dan: Pretty much what you'd expect. Two little high-pitched gay whoops, followed by furious hand flapping in front of faces.

Dave and Katherine: Dave dumbfounded, jaw wide open. Katherine wide-eyed, but pleased.

Melina: Delighted. Hands clapping and smiling broadly. She's up from the couch in a microsecond and hugging Laura.

Charlie: Somewhat confused. This is no surprise. Charlie is a lovely girl but not overblessed in the brains department. There's every chance she's still working out the meaning of the word *pregnant.* There's also every chance she's stoned, which probably isn't helping matters.

Ryan: Pissing himself laughing. This is also not unexpected. The number of conversations we've had about never, *ever* having children is in double figures at least. He will dine out on this for months, if not years, to come.

Isobel: Hmmm. Not sure about this one. The cross-eyed, glazed expression may be a sign of happiness, but it could equally be just the wine. I don't think massaging Ryan's groin has much to do with her feelings about my upcoming fatherhood. Nor does the thin line of drool coming from one corner of her mouth . . . I hope.

"That's so, so fantastic!" Tim squeals, this time in happiness. Dan's hands have gone to his face in delight. I love these two, but sometimes I do wish they'd dial down the camp just a bit. "Ooh! Ooh! I want to be a godparent!" Tim wails.

Dan gives him a playful clout. "You bitch. I was going to say that."

"Well paint me bright yellow and call me a fucking banana," Dave says. "You're the last couple on earth I would have expected this from!"

"Dave!" Katherine says in a horrified voice.

"It's alright, Katherine. We felt exactly the same way," Laura says. "It's taken us weeks to get used to the idea."

. . . *of never buying a Lamborghini*, I think in the dark recesses of the pettiest parts of my brain.

It seems that the general reaction is a good one. I note that Katherine and Isobel have both got their smart phones out and are probably changing their status updates. There will be tweets and retweets happening as well, I have no doubt.

God bless the social network revolution. My cousin Alan will be up to speed in no time, provided he's not been banged up for inappropriate touching by the Montreal police.

The rest of the evening is awash with the usual questions. The one I've been dreading is asked by Isobel: "So, did you plan to knock 'er up, Jamie? I hope there were no pictures of Jesus nearby!" This sends her into another gale of drunken laughter. Laura gives me a look that screams, *you'll be explaining that one to me in bed later, mister.*

I've managed to keep the explicit details of my night of terror with Isobel to myself for two years now, but no longer, it appears.

"It wasn't planned Isobel, no." I tell her.

"But we're happy about it nonetheless," Laura interjects, just to make everybody clear. I feel like she's trying to convince herself more than anyone else, but I put the thought out of my head. The horny leer Isobel is aiming in my direction is helping to do this magnificently.

Other than that little embarrassment (thankfully Laura was so tired by the time everyone left she'd forgotten all about Isobel's cryptic utterance) the evening went well. We sent our friends off armed with all the information they'd need about the pregnancy to spread the story across the Internet, and we both sat down to do our own Facebook status updates. Laura's received ten times more likes from her largely female friends than I did from my predominantly male friends—which just goes to show who's really paying attention, doesn't it?

I'd like to say that the following evening with the relatives went well, but families (mine anyway) have a distinct and never-ending ability to fuck up even the happiest of occasions.

LAURA'S DIARY
Wednesday, June 12

Dear Mum,

There are many times I wish you'd squeezed out more siblings for me to fight with over the bathroom. I always feel I missed out somewhat because I never had a large family. But Saturday night convinced me that on the whole, I was actually better off with just you.

Friday evening went brilliantly. Tim and Dan were beside themselves, Melina immediately wanted to tell me everything she'd learned during her pregnancy, and Ryan and Isobel had sex in the closet while the rest of us were downstairs wondering what they were up to. I'd only just washed those sheets, too.

Jamie and I talked long into the night after they'd all left. The announcement made the pregnancy more real for the both of us, I think, and our level of excitement has gone through the roof now that the truth is out. It was a very encouraging evening, so I went into Saturday night in a positive frame of mind.

Ha! More fool me. It's not that I don't like my husband's family, it's just that I sometimes feel decidedly ganged up on when Jamie and I are at odds. If I had you, my useless dad, or any of the aforementioned bathroom-hogging siblings to back me up, it might not be so bad.

Oh, and on the subject of my shitbag of a father, I spent a fairly unpleasant hour the other day talking to Jamie about whether we should contact him to let him know he's going to be a grandfather. The last I'd heard he was still in India somewhere—probably Goa—wearing a kaftan and smoking his own body weight in cannabis. Even if I did want to tell him, the chances of getting hold of the feckless idiot are slim to none. He bounces around most of Southeast Asia like a multicoloured pinball, high as a kite on marijuana 90 percent of the time.

It still baffles me how a sensible, down-to-earth lady like yourself could have shacked up with a man like that, Mum. Don't get me wrong—I'm glad you did, otherwise I wouldn't be here. All I can imagine is that he was a lot more straight-laced in his earlier years—or that you were a lot more bohemian. I think I like the latter idea better. The thought of you decked out in a long dress made of hemp with flowers in your hair, dancing around a campfire and waving your hands in the air singing about being stardust is one that fills me with mischievous delight.

One of you certainly changed a great deal by the time I hit five years old, that's quite obvious given the speed with which your marriage broke down. It's plain to see you grew up, Mum. Dad apparently didn't.

Jamie was dead set against telling him about the baby. "All he'll do is tell you to call it Moonbeam Sunrise or some other hippy shit, and ask if he can borrow £500 to fix his motorbike."

He's probably right. It would have been nice to have a father who is actually an adult, but we can't always get what we want—as Mick Jagger insists on telling us.

You're the one I really miss being here, Mum. That goes without saying. Every time I remember I won't be able to show you your new grandchild, it makes me blub like a schoolgirl. It's all these bloody hormones. I seem to cry at the drop of a hat these days. I'm even starting to fill up now as I write this diary entry. It's quite pathetic.

Still, getting a few wet spots on a diary page is far better than breaking down in front of your husband's relatives, which is what happened on Saturday.

Jamie doesn't have a huge family, but he's got two more parents and two more siblings than I do, so we'll call that a win for his side. I get on pretty well with Jamie's sister Sarah, and brother Chris. I would get on better with his dad, Michael, if he didn't look at my tits whenever he gets the chance. He's very sly about it, and I very much doubt I'm the only woman in the world he does this to, but my God it can be annoying. It's quite disconcerting to be out on a family picnic and catch your father-in-law gazing at your boobs over his pickled onion.

The relationship I have with Jamie's mother Jane, has always been distant, but it's always been cordial—ever since that first chat I had with her just before the wedding when I showed her I wasn't a pushover. Yes, Jane has never entirely approved of Jamie's decision to marry a girl without a high social standing, but she's just about accepted me into the family, with a degree of good grace most of the time. I've never thought we'd be all that close, but at least it looked like there was some kind of bond between us thanks to our mutual love for her son. Tonight showed me there was more bubbling under the surface than I realised, however.

As on Friday, we elected to keep the surprise on hold until about nine o'clock. I cooked a spaghetti bolognese for all of us (I don't let Jamie near the kitchen if I can help it—and we certainly never have fajitas if I do), which I took my time over to impress the in-laws. Thankfully Jane isn't a particularly good cook herself. I once found three dog hairs in one of her casseroles.

Side note: Does anybody actually *like* casserole? I've never come across anyone who does. I mean, what is it exactly? Really, really thick soup? Only that's broth isn't it? Either that or it's a runny roast dinner. As far as I'm concerned you can tart the bugger up as much as you like with sprigs of coriander and mint, it's still going to look like dog sick in a bowl when you get right down to it.

Anyway, back to the point. The bolognese went down well. Even Jane polished off her entire plate, which amazed me. No one seemed to notice I wasn't filling my glass from the bottles of white we'd opened for the occasion. I'd just surreptitiously leave the dining room every half an hour or so to recharge my glass with a carefully concealed bottle of lemonade.

I wasn't feeling the excitement of a withheld secret like I was the previous night, and I could tell Jamie was more nervous about revealing the existence of the baby as well. Telling your mates is one thing, letting the family know—the people whose opinions really matter in the grand scheme of things—is *entirely* another.

By nine, the atmosphere in the room was decidedly convivial. Michael had told his third golden anecdote of the evening to a chorus of polite laughter, Jane had bored everyone with how much she was loving her new gym and how her instructor was really helping with her thighs, Chris had successfully steered his mother away from sensitive questions regarding his new relationship with Helena the Portuguese barmaid, and Sarah was pleased to announce she'd lost eight pounds in the last month. It seemed like the appropriate time to drop the bombshell.

Jamie tinks a fork on the side of his glass. I don't know why he does this as there are only six of us present, but he likes to obey these little customs from time to time.

"Stop doing that, Jamie," his mother says. "You'll set off my tinnitus."

"Sorry, Mum." He coughs and takes the legendary deep breath. "Laura and I have an announcement to make."

"Oh God. You're getting a divorce, aren't you?" Sarah says from around the bread roll she is stuffing into her mouth.

Jamie's face crumples. "No, we are not getting a divorce. Why does everyone think we're getting a bloody divorce? Do we give off divorcey vibes? Are you lot privy to some highly advanced precognitive abilities I'm not aware of?" He takes a massive swig of wine in disgust and folds his arms. "Honestly, you try to tell people something important and they just make groundless assumptions," he mutters under his breath.

"Don't slouch, Jamie," Jane tells him. "It makes you look like a naughty schoolboy. Sit up straight."

"Mum! I'm thirty-two years old, for crying out loud. Don't tell me how to sit!"

"Don't speak to your mother like that, son," Michael pipes up.

"You do slouch a lot, Jamie," Sarah adds. "You always have."

"Yeah? Well you've got an idiot for a face," Jamie sneers at her.

"You're such a badger's sack, Jamie!" Sarah wails and the conversation descends into the kind of bickering only family members can have perfected through decades of practice. It's giving me a headache, though, so I decide to nip things in the bud.

"I'm pregnant!" I say over the tumult.

Everyone stops talking at once. Silence—*pregnant* silence, you might say—descends. Then Jane, looking squarely at my husband, says something that gives me a *really* good idea of her true feelings for me.

"Is it yours?" she says in a level tone. I've never stepped into a walk-in freezer, but I imagine the experience is much like our dining room at that moment.

"Of course it's mine!" Jamie is livid. I just struggle not to burst into tears. "What the hell kind of shit is that to say, mother?"

"Don't swear, Jamie!" Michael says.

Jamie gives him daggers. "Oh sod off, Dad. You swear like a paralytic docker when Mum's not around. You even did it when we were kids, so knock off the responsible parent act, okay?"

Jane swings around to stare at her husband. "Michael Newman!"

Michael swigs his beer. "Oh fucking hell woman, calm down. A bit of swearing never hurt anyone."

"Apologise to Laura," Jamie orders his mother in a cold voice.

Chris, who has wisely stayed silent, slowly moves his chair backwards and removes his glass of wine from the table. There's an air of resignation about his movements that suggest he's been in the middle of one of these squabbles on many occasions.

"Well . . ." Jane begins and then pauses with a look of severe consternation on her face. You can see how hard it is for her to even contemplate the idea of apologising to another human being. Jamie has told me stories in the past that have made her out to be a harridan of the highest order. I've always taken them with a pinch of salt, knowing how he likes to embellish for the sake of a good yarn—but now I'm starting to realise he may have been telling the truth after all. The woman's pretty much just intimated that I go around shagging other men.

"Say sorry!" Jamie snaps, and for added emphasis bangs his hand on the table. Sadly his fist hits the fork still on his plate, neatly catapulting a healthy amount of bolognese at my head.

Within the space of a minute I've been called a slut and had food thrown at me. This usually doesn't happen to people outside terrible American soap operas.

Jamie looks mortified. "I'm so sorry, honey!"

I look down at the lovely cream blouse I'd elected to wear, knowing it will be going in the bin later.

"I love this blouse," I tell the table. "It was on offer in Jane Norman."

Then the tears—held back thus far by my indignation—begin their onslaught on my eyeballs. Try as I might to avoid crying in front of my adopted family, I just can't help it.

And it's snotty. That's always the worst, isn't it? Water leaking from your eyes is bad enough, but add mucus dripping from your nose to the equation and you're presenting an image to the world a hagfish would find unattractive. I feel a little light-headed. Bolognese sauce drips off my ear. Jamie grabs a napkin and starts dabbing at my face with it. I look up at him.

"Your mum thinks I'm a slag, Jamie. Why does she think I'm a slag?"

"I never said you were a slag, Laura," Jane remarks haughtily.

"Indeed," Michael agrees.

"You pretty much did, Mum," Sarah argues.

Chris remains silent and looks at his watch.

"I'm sorry if that's how it came across," Jane says. "I'm just very surprised. Jamie has always been dead against having children, so I thought—"

"You thought my wife would go and kick her heels up in front of the first passing provider of fresh semen?" Jamie finishes.

"That's not what I meant."

I hold out a conciliatory hand. There's a blob of sauce on it. "It's okay, Jane," I say in a slightly sing-song voice. I think the stress of the evening has been a bit too much for me. I'm not sure I'm completely in control of my faculties. "I'm not bothered."

"Thank you, Laura," she says with a nod of her head.

"After all," I smile sweetly, "it's not your fault you're a bitch, is it?"

I've never dipped my whole head into a jar of freezing liquid nitrogen Mum, but I imagine the experience is much like our dining room at that moment. Jane looks like someone's stuffed a lemon up her arse. Sarah is stunned. Chris is concentrating very hard on the table cloth, and Michael is looking at my tits.

Jamie, sensing that the only way out of this horrifying situation is to act very calmly, clearly, and with authority says, "I think maybe this is a good time to end the meal." He stands me up. "I'll go help Laura clean herself off." He gives his mother an apologetic smile. "I'm sure it's the pregnancy hormones, Mum. You probably remember, don't you?"

"Yes," she says, trying to keep any emotion out of her voice. "I don't recall insulting anyone like that, though!"

Trying to retain some dignity I wave off Jamie's arm and stand straight. My hair is matted with sauce and there's a strand of spaghetti waggling off the end of my nose, but I still intend to exit the room with the final word.

"Thank you for coming, everyone," I tell them. "I'm sorry if things got a bit testy there at the end, but I hope that you're happy for us. We're going to be parents and we're very pleased about it." I look directly at Jane. "Unless of course the baby is Fernando's, the Mexican delivery boy I screwed last month in the chair you're sitting in, Jane."

I've never visited the crushing, ice-cold depths of the ocean floor, Mum . . . I'm sure you know the rest of that by now.

Jamie's family departs pronto. Jane is out the door slightly faster than a cat with its tail on fire. Michael gets in one last sneaky stare at my chest before following his irate wife out into the night. Sarah kisses both of us and congratulates us on the pregnancy. Chris looks at me with what I think is a newfound sense of respect, before asking where we bought our tablecloth. He leaves with the name John Lewis on his lips.

Jamie closes the front door very slowly. I gulp. This could go badly. I've just insulted the woman who brought him into the world.

"That," he says, "was absolutely brilliant!" He gives me a huge hug.

"Really? Your mum is going to hate me."

"Meh, she wasn't keen on you to start with. Don't take it to heart, though. She's never liked any of my women." His eyes gleam with merriment. "None of the others ever told her she was a bitch, though. Priceless!"

He kisses me through the sheen of bolognese sauce I still haven't managed to clean off.

"I am delighted to be married to you," he says. "And even more delighted that you're having my baby."

I don't know if I'd call that a win, Mum, but if a man says he loves you even when you've just mortally insulted his mother, and you look like an Italian restaurant has thrown up over your head, I guess you must be doing something right.

Love you, miss you, and wish Jane could take a leaf out of your book!

Your still slightly light-headed daughter, Laura

xxx

JAMIE'S BLOG
Wednesday 10 July

Yawn. Out of bed again . . .

I can't sleep because of Laura's thrashing so thought I'd update the blog. I'll get onto the reasons why she's thrashing around in bed like a landed turbot shortly, but first:

I've never been to the hospital so much in my bloody life. I'm thinking of paying for a permanent parking space. I'm sure it'll end up being cheaper in the long run than having to pay the extortionate parking fees. It seems like barely five minutes have passed since the last time we drove away before I'm once again sitting with the driver's side window open, bashing the stupid ticket machine and swearing sulphurously when it doesn't spit out the ticket quickly enough.

I hate hospitals. They're full of sick people. Corridors and corridors of people suffering either from things I can catch, or things I don't want to look at. Every time I enter one I have to constantly suppress the mild panic attack that threatens to claw its way up my throat and embarrass me in public.

Imagine my delight, therefore, at having to more or less live in the maternity wing thanks to my wife's pregnancy. I've seen some of the nurses so many times now I'm seriously considering adding them on Facebook. We're also getting very familiar with our doctor, a short, timid-looking man called Abbotson. He has a facial tic. He winks. A *lot*. It's very disconcerting.

I can't tell whether he's being serious about the pregnancy or not when he speaks to us. "You have to keep up your vitamin intake, Mrs. Newman," he'll say. "A healthy immune system is vital to a baby's development." *Wink*. "It's advisable to take multivitamins right up until you give birth." *Wink wink*.

Do you mean that squire, or are you mucking about? You sound quite serious, but the winking is making me think this is one big practical joke at our expense. Do we need the bloody vitamins or not?

Other than the tic, Dr Abbotson is a congenial sort of bloke. The same cannot be said for Marigold Ubantu, our midwife. Marigold is originally from Namibia and has forgotten more about delivering babies than the rest of the human population will ever know. She's terrifying. Marigold came to the UK over twenty years ago from a country about to tear itself apart through civil war.

One of the first things she said to us was: "I have helped deliver babies with gunfire going on over my head. Don't you worry about it at all. Marigold will see you right."

I think this was meant to soothe our nerves, but Marigold is over six feet tall, has forearms like hams, and survived half her life in a country where sudden death was an ever-present threat. She's impressive and scary in equal measure. Frankly, I don't envy Laura one little bit. She's the one who gets manhandled by Marigold on a regular basis.

"She's very gentle when she needs to be, don't get me wrong," Laura told me after one visit. "But if you do anything to annoy her—like, say, you haven't been keeping to your pregnancy diet—she turns into this mighty Zulu warrior and gives you the flintiest, eyeball-straining look of displeasure I've ever seen. It makes me wee myself a bit every time."

"You want to change midwife?" I asked her.

"Are you kidding?" she replied. "This woman has successfully helped give birth to children in a bloody war zone. Even if she does shout at me, she's perfect!"

It's not just Laura who gets criticized. The other day Marigold wanted a one-to-one with my wife on how she felt the pregnancy was going. I objected, not least because there's very little to do in a hospital other than kick the chocolate machine repeatedly until a Twix falls out, but also on the grounds that I was the father and had a right to be there.

"You go away now, you stupid man!" Marigold hollered at me. "She's the important one here, not you and your dangly penis. It did its job months ago, now let me do mine." And with that, the door was closed on me for an hour, and I had no hope of re-entry.

On this particular day though, Marigold is in a very good mood.

"We can tell the sex of the baby today, Newmans," she beams. "We'll see whether you're having a sweet little girl, or one of those nasty, smelly little boys." Marigold throws her head back and laughs to the heavens. It's like being around a force of nature imprisoned in a human body. "You want to know what the sex is?"

This is something Laura and I have discussed at length. While there is a certain thrill to remaining in the dark until such time as the child is squeezed from the womb, it comes with an inability to plan ahead properly.

Other couples may have the time and money to shop for both a baby boy and girl, but Mrs. Newman and I are on a tight budget right now, with her working as part-time manager of the local Morton & Slacks chocolate shop, and me languishing in the bowels of the newspaper's marketing division. Also, we're both testy buggers when kept in the dark, so we decide it's best to know the gender of our unborn child as soon as possible to avoid stress, arguments, and an ever so slight feeling of disappointment if it ends up being the sex we don't want.

"Yes, we'd like to know," Laura says.

"Aha!" Marigold grins. "Good for you! I hate these wishy-washy bastards who can't decide or want to wait until the baby comes out. The sooner you know, the sooner you can start worrying about what colour to paint everything. Am I right?" I get the feeling that if I disagree she'll smack me on the head until I'm permanently cross-eyed, so I nod vigorously.

"Right, let's go see Narinda." Marigold strides out and we follow along like the good little expectant parents we are.

Narinda is pleased to see us. I'm not sure if she's happy to see Marigold or not. Everyone has the same stunned expression on their face when the Namibian woman appears, so it's quite impossible to say how they're feeling about the situation.

In short order, Narinda has the ultrasound going and finds the kid where it's supposed to be, swimming around in utero and blissfully unaware of the insane world it's going to be thrust into in a few months.

"Okay, then," says Narinda. "I can tell you the baby's gender now. Are you sure you want to know?"

"Yes," Laura and I say together.

Narinda smiles and shakes her head. "*Absolutely* sure?"

"Yes."

"Because once I tell you, there's no going back!"

I get the impression Narinda is one for the big birth moments. It's obvious she thinks it's better to find out if your kid's an innie or an outie when it escapes from between its mothers legs.

"Oh, for the sake of the good Lord, woman!" booms Marigold. "Tell these poor buggers whether they have a boy or a girl!" she says, giving Narinda the eyeball.

Narinda looks ever so slightly terrified and looks back at me and Laura. My heart skips a beat.

"You're having a girl," she tells us.

A girl. Visions flash through my head: pink ribbons, Barbie dolls, ponies, hair clips, teenage boyfriends with acne, the shotgun I'm going to have to buy to keep said teenage boyfriends on the external side of my daughter's underwear, make-up boxes, sleepovers, a fridge full of ice cream, posters of boy bands, the arguments about skirt length, perfume bottles on every bathroom surface . . . and, worst of all, living with *two* women on their period. *Gah.*

A minefield of experience unravels in front of me. Eighteen years of putting up with not one but two completely insane creatures who I'll never understand—who will take over my house with soft, frilly things that smell of jasmine and ylang-ylang. All of this sounds dreadful, but for some reason I'm smiling like an absolute goon.

"A girl," Laura says, her eyes filling with tears for what's probably the fifth time that day. "I'm having a little girl."

"Yes, you are!" Marigold bellows. "Good for you! Girls are much nicer and don't start wars that get your village burned to the ground."

There's a moment's silence while we digest this.

"Yeah," I say. "That's a good reason to have a girl, alright."

Marigold doesn't throttle me, so I guess I didn't say anything that offensive . . .

The rest of the day's appointment is the usual question and answer session, with Marigold getting through all the important health matters related to this stage of a pregnancy. I've zoned out to tell the truth. The big news of the day has come and gone and it's all I can think about. More accurately, all I can think about is names. Now we know it's a girl, we can get down to the tricky business of slapping an identifier on her.

"What about Kayla?" I suggest to Laura in the car on the way home.

"Kayla? That sounds like it's skirting dangerously close to Kylie, Newman."

"Is it? Doesn't sound like it to me."

"I'm not calling my child Kayla."

"Ariadne?"

"Are you fucking mental?"

"What about Jacinda? Jacinda's a nice name." Jacinda is in fact a bloody *horrible* name, but I'm having fun winding Laura up now.

"You're kidding?"

"No, I'm not," I lie. "I think it's a lovely name."

"It sounds like someone who has sex with her horse."

"Maybe something a bit more original, then. How about naming her after somewhere nice?" I fake a look of intense concentration. "I know! Syria. That's got a good ring to it."

There's every chance Laura will see through my ruse with that one. Even I shouldn't be dumb enough to suggest naming a baby after a country that's been bathing in the blood of its own people for the past few years.

"Syria! You're seriously suggesting we name our baby Sy—" Laura looks like she's just sucked a lemon. "You're winding me up, aren't you?"

I smirk the smirkiest smirk that's ever been smirked. "Of course not, darling."

"You, Jamie Newman," she says, pointing a finger at me in no uncertain terms, "are a baboon's warty scrotum."

I can tell when Laura is irate with me, her insults get very creative.

"Perhaps we should think about the name another time," I suggest.

"Agreed," she replies acidly.

I give it just the right amount of silence before saying: "Bulimia's a nice name as well, you know," in a cheery voice.

It's a miracle I make it home in one piece.

Yawn. I guess at some point I should try to crash out on the couch.

Whether I'll be able to sleep or not is debatable, though. I can't get girls' names and images of tattooed teenage boys with their arms around my equally teenage daughter out of my head.

Going back to bed is certainly out of the question. Sleeping next to Laura is almost impossible at the moment. The baby has reached that stage in her development where she's able to move around properly and has started making her presence felt in no uncertain terms.

Her. I just described my baby as a *her*.

What an exquisitely strange and wonderful feeling. Typing that three letter word has cemented my unborn daughter's existence once and for all in my head. She's no longer a collection of cells, or a foetus to be referred to as it. She's a person now. A her. My baby Bulimia is a real person!

The first time the baby kicked Laura was while we were watching *The Walking Dead*.

It seems my daughter is as big a fan of zombies as I am. This is just as well, as it will give us something to bond over later in life. Nothing spells out the love between a man and his daughter than hordes of the moaning undead stumbling towards you, ravenous for human flesh.

It was in a particularly tense moment of the episode—the dour American chap in the cowboy hat and his family are hiding under a truck as a herd of zombies walks past, trying to remain completely still and silent buggers—so you can imagine my reaction when Laura shouts "*Fuck me!*" and grabs the swell of her belly.

"Jesus Christ!" I wail, sending the contents of my wine glass on a collision course with the already semen-stained couch. "What? What's the matter?"

"The baby!" Laura squeals. "I felt it kick." Her eyes go wide. "There it goes again!" Her face contorts. "Oooww! You little sod, give it a rest!"

"That's fantastic!" I crow.

I'd read that some babies start kicking from pretty early in the pregnancy, and we're a few months into ours by now, so I was starting to get worried that Laura might be carrying a right lazy cow. This wasn't a good sign for my far-reaching plans for the front garden. All is well, it appears, and the baby is making up for lost time.

Laura makes a face again. "Fantastic for you, pal. You're not the one who's got somebody practising kung fu in your uterus."

I'll never be able to watch that episode of *The Walking Dead* again without a feeling of immense happiness and excitement. Which is extremely weird as they're not the emotions you usually associate with hapless individuals being ripped to pieces by rotting, animated corpses . . . unless you're sixteen and don't get out much.

That was over two weeks ago now, and the baby has fallen into the habit of smacking her mother around like a nightclub bouncer every evening. Sometimes the fun and games carry on right through a large portion of the night as well. Luckily for Laura, she's a deep sleeper. Even baby Newman's high-kicking exploits can't keep her awake for long. The same can't be said for her father, who has always been a very *light* sleeper. While Laura is off and sawing logs, any sudden movement the baby makes translates its way into my wife's sleeping form. When the baby jerks about, so does Laura—sometimes violently.

I've been slapped awake on more than one occasion recently. Similarly, my testicles have made friends with Laura's knee three times, and my shoulder blades now know what it's like to have a pointy female elbow smacked into them at three in the morning. I've taken to sleeping on the couch when these episodes occur. It's either that or have everyone think I'm suffering severe spousal abuse.

I have to stop being annoyed at my unborn child for this forced move to the uncomfortable sofa. She can't help it, after all, being an unborn foetus. I'm sure there will be countless opportunities for me to be irritated with the little cow over the next twenty years, so I have to let this one slide on account of the fact she has no eyebrows yet.

I'm going to curl up on the couch now and try to get some sleep. I don't know whether I'll be successful, but at least I can be 100 percent sure I won't wake up with a bruised scrotum.

LAURA'S DIARY

Saturday, August 17

Dear Mum,

I still have the fashion sense of a demented chimpanzee. Only now I'm a *chubby* demented chimpanzee.

Last week over coffee Melina suggested we hit the town with a couple of friends. I enthusiastically agreed. I haven't been out for months now and am well aware that my chances to go clubbing in the future are going to be severely curtailed by the simple fact that they don't allow newborn babies into nightclubs. The more this pregnancy develops, the more I'm coming to realise that I'm going to have to give an awful lot up when the baby comes.

Please don't misunderstand me. The thought of holding my pink little baby sends shivers of delight through my whole body whenever I picture it in my head, but that doesn't take away from the fact that my days of carefree nights out are rapidly coming to end.

Mel knows all this, of course. She's been through all this already with Hayley. I am extremely lucky to have a best friend who's already navigated the tricky course of first-time motherhood and can offer up the kind of sage advice I'd happily pay for if I could afford it. Thinking about it, this dynamic has been the backbone of my friendship with Mel ever since we met in the first year of secondary school.

She's always been the one to do things first. She kissed a boy before me, lost her virginity before me, had a painful breakup before me . . .

"In some ways you're like my canary," I told her once when we were both a little the worse for wear.

"What? What d'you mean by that, McIntyre?"

"You know. Canaries. They die first when there's gas in the mine."

"What? Are you sayin' you wanna gas me? You . . . you comple' bitch."

"No, no. I mean . . . you do stuff before me so I know whether I should do it or not."

"I'm norra soddin' canary, McIntyre!" Mel screamed, before falling off her stool and covering herself in vodka.

From that point on I made a point of buying as many stuffed toy canaries as I could find—giving them to her as presents. As running jokes go, it's a rather good one, I think.

For our girls' night out on the town, Melina said she'd bring along her ditzy friend Rachel from work, and I thought it'd be nice to invite Shelley, the woman I've shared the manager's job with for the past few months at the local Morton & Slacks in town. The idea of a night out is all well and good, but now I have to come up with something to wear that will accommodate the rapidly increasing size of my belly.

I'm starting to resemble the world's skinniest Buddha. Until now I would have happily described my belly as being pot-like. Now it's more like a tureen—and it's not going to get smaller any time soon. Nothing I have in my wardrobe fits anymore. *Useless* are my tight little black dresses. I tried to squeeze one over the baby to see if I could get away with it but just ended up looking like a black snake that had swallowed a football. Jeans are right out for obvious reasons—and as a duvet cover won't let me cut much of a glamorous figure on the dance floor, I'm going to have to bite the bullet and wear maternity clothing.

Melina, knowing this day would come, handed over some of her more stylish maternity clothes from when she was pregnant with

Hayley. "I kept them because Travis and I want another one in the next couple of years. But your need is more immediate than mine!"

I thanked her for the bag of clothes, put them in the cupboard, and tried very hard to forget about them . . . successfully, until tonight. Now the bag is open, the clothes are laid out on the bed and my heart has sunk to the depths.

Don't get me wrong. The maternity clothing companies try hard. Every effort has been made to accommodate the distended belly into the cut and line of their products. They try their best to make you still feel feminine and sexy. They fail *utterly*, of course, but we should give them marks for making an effort.

I can't escape the mental image of a squeezed sausage as I yank on a pink-and-black number that's gathered below the breasts before flaring out over little Miss Newman in a cascade of material. Without the additional cloth it would be a lovely little dress, but as it is I just feel like a big fat cow trying to fit into an outfit that would be far too small for her were it not for the additional yard or so of cotton.

Still, it fits, which is more than can be said for my LBDs. I may never wear them again—curse Jamie and his overactive penis!

The crying fit lasts only five minutes this time. I'm very pleased they're getting shorter now. My hormones must be settling down at last. With the dress on I sit down to put on some make-up. I look like a haggard witch at the moment, so it's going to be a difficult and time-consuming operation to bring me up to snuff. Thanks to my unborn child I haven't been sleeping well at all. I don't have eye bags, I have eye hammocks. Still, that's what concealer was invented for . . . and foundation. Lots and *lots* of foundation. It'll make me look like a cheap Eastern European prostitute, but that's still better than Princess Panda Face in my book.

So there we have it. Bump on display to the world and covered in slap, I'm ready for my first night out on the town in months! It's seven thirty, I'm knackered already and won't even be able to drink my cares away—thanks to my stupid body's inability to consume alcohol and give birth to a healthy child at the same time.

A sober fat git I shall remain all evening. Woo-hoo. I can barely contain my excitement.

No, no. I mustn't go into this evening with that kind of attitude. This may well be the last time I get to do this kind of thing, so I'm determined to have a good time, come hell or high water! Tonight will be a celebration of my imminent passage into motherhood, not an excuse to wallow in self-pity over the loss of my carefree youth.

The only thing Mel's friend Rachel was losing by the end of the evening was the contents of her stomach. I have never been on a night out with the girls and not been falling down drunk by the end of it—therefore tonight has been a real eye-opener for me. It comes as a great shock to discover that people, when they have consumed a large amount of alcohol, turn into what can only be described as utter twats. It really isn't easy to maintain a happy mood when the people around you are becoming more inebriated by the minute and more irritating by the second.

Not drinking meant I became the taxi service for the evening. I picked up Melina and Rachel at Mel's house, then went over to grab Shelley from work. Shelley and I have become firm friends in the past few months, since we started the job share. A mutual hatred of Morton & Slacks has been the cornerstone of our relationship.

She's worked for them for eight years, while I was forced into the job share thanks to a dwindling bank account and Jamie's lack of penis control. I had hoped Hotel Chocolat might see past my vomitous exploits at my interview and still offer me a job, but so far—nada.

When the part-time manager's position at Morton & Slacks came up, I had no choice but to take it. At least it gives me the chance to work with chocolate—even if it is the mass-produced stuff. Besides, when you've fallen pregnant, working for a large organisation certainly has its benefits.

"Bleed the bastards for every penny," Shelley said to me a while back, when I confided in her that I was knocked up and would need to tell our bosses about it sooner or later. "I'd get myself pregnant again too, if I wasn't thirty-eight and a chain smoker."

Back to tonight: Shelley puts out her cigarette before getting into the car, and we're off towards town for what will be an evening I'd happily consign to the dustbin of my memory if I could.

Things start off okay. They always tend to, as nobody is shit-faced at eight thirty—unless you're in Ireland, of course. We begin proceedings at the Bog and Trellis in the high street. I have no idea why anyone would willfully give a pub a name like that, but it's one of the national chains, so there's every chance a computer somewhere is spitting out random words that get combined with one another before being slapped up on the front of what used to be a bank. I look forward to one day visiting the Fetlock and Nazi, or the Vomit and Biggins.

The pub is packed, and I awkwardly have to manoeuvre my bump through the throng. I'm not all that comfortable carrying it around in front of me yet. Even though the baby's still got a lot of growing to do, she's already started to put my centre of gravity off. I think this is the *real* reason they tell you not to drink while pregnant. The combination of alcohol and centrifugal force would be enough to throw you on your arse every thirty seconds. Also, it happens that a pregnancy bump has hitherto unforeseen magical powers: it makes you completely invisible to members of the opposite sex!

I'd like to think I scrub up pretty well when I make an effort, and I've always attracted the appreciative stares of many a man when out clubbing in the past—particularly if I'm wearing a ridiculously short dress and heels that show off my long legs. This evening though, I could have been wandering around in a see-through latex jumpsuit, wearing a hat with the words I'LL FUCK YOU FOR A JELLY SHOT written across it in neon letters, and I'm convinced not one man would have so much as glanced at me.

It's a depressing realisation. The bump is like a brand. It means I'm definitely off the market. Not that I'm looking or anything, but a woman likes to think she can turn heads even when she's happily married.

I'd have to sexually molest the fruit machine in the corner to get anyone's attention in my present state. What makes it worse is that Melina, a woman I'd cheerfully have sex with if I leant that way, is getting all the attention I'm not.

Still, at least having a big bump in front of me does get me to the bar and over to the toilet quicker. A swift cry of "Mind your backs! Pregnant woman coming through!" is usually enough to part the crowd faster than a bullhorn and a salivating German shepherd. This is the second unforeseen magical power of the bump—and one I will find a lot more useful in the near future. People will climb over themselves to get out of the way of a pregnant woman if she scowls at them long enough.

We leave the Bog and Trellis at nine forty-five. I'm stone-cold sober thanks to my three Diet Cokes, but Melina and the girls are already in a warm, happy haze of light drunkenness following several glasses of wine. As we walk towards the nightclubs, I get my first inkling of what being drunk involves—when viewed from an objective standpoint.

For some reason the other three girls have all gone deaf. At least I assume this is the case, as they've all started shouting. Consumption of alcohol squares with volume it appears.

"What club you wanna go to?" Melina says loudly, only a few inches from my face.

"I'm not bothered, to tell the truth," I reply.

"Let's go to Mother Kelly's!" shouts Rachel.

"Yeah. Mother Kelly's is great!" agrees Shelley.

Mother Kelly's is *not* great. Mother Kelly's is a shit hole with a sticky floor and stickier toilets. The road behind it is affectionately known as stab alley.

"Off to Mother Kelly's we go then!" screams Mel.

I sigh, knowing they'll brook no argument from the pregnant, sober one, and consign myself to a night of having my shoes sucked off my feet.

Once past the muscular bouncers we enter the nightclub and make our sticky way over to the bar. The girls order a round of shots. I have a lime and soda water. I can't have another Diet Coke as the caffeine will keep me up all night, and I frankly need a decent night's sleep. I just *love* being pregnant!

The others knock back their drinks with gusto and proceed to order another round. I suck on my straw and begin to think of ways I can take this out on Jamie's penis. It's to blame for my current displeasure and will pay for its crimes.

I spend most of the next hour sitting in a booth at the side of the dance floor. I get up and have a half-hearted go at dancing, but I can feel the baby kicking every time I do so much as a sideways shimmy, and my legs are as heavy as lead weights after five minutes.

My friends are way past the legal limit now and are having no such problems. There they are: three otherwise sensible, professional ladies, whirling round on a sparkly dance floor like a trio of overexcited baboons with electrodes up their arses. Consumption of alcohol also takes away your ability to dance, it would seem. Mel is hopping around with her arms stuck out in front of her, resembling a confused Dalek.

Shelley is doing some kind of grinding thing that's making me wish my eyes would spontaneously cease to function, and Rachel has found one of the dancing poles near the stage. I rather wish she hadn't, as any minute now I'm likely to get a really good look at her vagina.

To her, I'm sure she looks like a professional stripper, sexually arousing every man in the nightclub with her suggestive, energetic dance moves. To me (and anyone else not drinking), she looks like a mental patient trying to fuck a lamp post. Her legs flail in every direction, her head whips round like a prizefighter about to go down in the tenth. I'm thinking of going over to pull her away from the bloody thing before she hurts herself, when the inevitable happens.

Trying the old legs-clamped-around-the-pole-and-back-arched-seductively pose, Rachel loses her footing and goes crashing to the dance floor with an audible screech. We now discover yet *more* interesting aspects of the drunken state: the inability to feel either pain or embarrassment. Rachel is up in seconds, laughing like a loon. She's going to have an enormous bruise on her backside tomorrow, but for now she brushes off the accident as if it never happened.

Amazingly, many of the men on the dance floor are still regarding her with animal curiosity. *Great* . . . so you can gyrate around a pole like a rutting hyena before falling on your arse in a heap and *still* get more attention from the male of the species than if you're just a tiny bit pregnant. *Fantastic.*

I sigh and get up to go for my seventeenth wee of the evening. Mother Kelly's is just the place you want to be when your bladder is weaker than the British economy. How truly delightful it is to repeatedly hold a graffiti-covered door closed with my hand while squatting over half a toilet seat to go about my business. What really caps off the experience this time round are the two people having ugly sex in the stall next to me.

"Give it to me!" she growls. Given the state of the place, I can only assume she means dysentery, as the chances of achieving orgasm through the miasma of piss and cheap perfume are small to say the least.

I hope he gets her pregnant, I mutter under my breath.

It's only when I look round to see there's no toilet paper that I decide the evening is well and truly *over.*

"I'm going," I shout at Melina, who is still bouncing around looking for Doctor Who so she can exterminate him.

"It's only midnight!" she wails back.

"I've got a headache and the baby's giving me hell!"

Mel looks understandably disappointed. This is her first night out without her own child for a long time, and I guess she wants to make the most of it. I would feel guilty, but I already need another wee and if I drink any more lime and soda water, I'm going to be sick in a very green manner. Mel tells Shelley the bad news, and we all troop off to find Rachel.

We eventually discover her locked in a death struggle with a drunk soccer fan. At least it looks like a death struggle initially. As we get closer, it becomes apparent they are kissing . . .and touching. Oh good God, there is so much *touching.* If we don't do something soon, touching is likely to move on to *insertion* and then we're in real trouble.

I pull the two lovebirds apart. The Arsenal fan looks angry for a second, then utterly nonplussed. Somebody completely invisible has just broken up the advanced necking session, so his confusion is entirely understandable. Rachel isn't any happier, but she can see me just fine so is a lot clearer on what just happened. My face is like thunder, so she doesn't put up much of a fight when I tell her we're evacuating the premises.

"I'll just get Gavin's number," she says.

"Fuck Gavin," I tell her. "You'll thank me in the morning," I add, dragging her away by an arm.

We're nearly at the car when Rachel goes three different shades of green and runs behind a row of wheelie bins. Melina staggers over to help hold her hair back while Shelley deposits herself on the nearest car bonnet and sparks up a cigarette. For my part, I ignore the fact I need the toilet and prop myself up next to her. As Rachel strains behind me and Shelley hacks up a lung, I reflect that being sober and healthy due to pregnancy might not be such a bad thing after all.

It's funny. Before tonight I was dreading the idea of having a baby and not being able to go out clubbing where and when I wanted to. Following everything I've just witnessed, though, I have to say that I'm extremely glad to be leaving it all behind. This is a wonderful feeling. I hated the idea that being pregnant meant the end of my life. Now I realise it just means the end of parts of my life I'm probably getting too old and cynical to enjoy anyway.

The more I stop thinking that having a baby is changing my life for the worse—and the more I realise it's actually changing my life for the better—the more I get excited about what is to come.

"Good night?" Jamie asks sleepily from the couch when I get in the door.

"Let's put it this way. If I'm going to throw up a lot, have no centre of balance, and look deeply unattractive, I'd rather have a baby at the end to show for it."

He gives me a confused look. I wave it off, smile to myself . . . and go for another sodding wee.

Love you and miss you, Mum.

Your stone-cold sober daughter, Laura

xxx

JAMIE'S BLOG
Tuesday 10 September

"I want bacon," the monster growls at me from her duvet cocoon in the centre of our bed. "Get me bacon."

"Yes, mistress," I say humbly, tugging my forelock as I back out of the room in fear for my life.

"Bacon and chocolate. I want bacon and chocolate," it tells me, cold, hard eyes boring their way into my mortal soul. "Together!"

I must serve the creature. I must do as it says. For six months now I have been locked in this terrible bondage of my own making. And each day the monster grows worse. Its demands now border on insanity. I don't know how long I can continue to please its every bizarre whim. There must come a time soon when my usefulness will be over and it will bite the top of my head off.

I should leave. Run now while I still have a chance. But I am the one responsible for the creature. I must stay and placate it for the sake of all humanity. For were I to leave, were I to cease my constant, lonely vigil, it may decide to turn its unholy gaze on the innocents beyond this forsaken house. I cannot allow that to happen. I *must* stay and serve the monster!

I stumble down the stairs, the sound of its ragged breathing following me to the ground floor. In the kitchen, I get out the frying pan and place three rashers of bacon into it.

"Make sure it's fucking crispy!" it screeches, and I quail over the cooktop, praying that one day soon this hell will be over and that sweet death will take me in its warm embrace. I fry the bacon until it is as crispy as I can make it.

Placing the dead pig flesh on a plate, I remove the chocolate from the fridge and begin to grate it over the bacon. I don't know why!

Why? Why would anyone want bacon and chocolate together? It's a culinary travesty, a meal fit only for demons that inhabit the lowest reaches of the underworld. But . . . I must not say anything to the creature. Must not let it know my thoughts. It will eat me alive if it knows.

The chocolate melts over the bacon. The smell is horrible, a combination of pig meat and dairy milk that makes my stomach revolve like a hotel door. Slowly, I make my way back upstairs, the plate held out in front of me like an offering to one of the elder gods. In the bedroom it stirs. One beady eye stares at me from the duvet cocoon, bidding me enter.

"Is it crispy?" the monster demands.

"Yes, yes it is indeed crispy," I reply in the voice of the smallest mouse, "and covered in chocolate, as you requested."

"The Bournville Dark?"

My heart sinks, my palsied hands begin to shake. This is it. My time is up. Once I speak, it will reach out and pluck my heart from its cage, showing it to me as I expire noisily on the carpet.

"No, mistress," I say, gulping back the terror. "It is the dairy milk. You finished the Bournville last night." I cower, knowing the death blow may come at any time. For a second it stares. I gaze back into its eyes and feel my sanity teetering on the brink of an abyss. The monster considers my fate, and I feel my bowels begin to loosen.

Then, it snatches the plate from me, exposing one taloned hand for the briefest of moments.

"Begone foul slave!" it tells me . . . and my soul sings. Today will not be the day I am eaten alive. It spares me for another. *Praise the Lord!*

Once more I tug my forelock and back away as it slobbers and stuffs the chocolate-covered meat into its ravenous maw. My heavens, I do not know how much longer I can go on. The suffering.

Oh, the *suffering*!

The bacon and chocolate surprise is just the latest in the list of cravings that Laura has developed during the pregnancy. However disgusting the combination of bacon and chocolate may sound, at least it's edible.

A few weeks ago we were shopping in Walmart, when I realise I've lost my wife.

I search for five minutes before I find her in the detergent aisle with an open box of Tide. She's sneakily popping one wet finger into the powder and licking it off, a look of ecstasy on her face.

"No!" I cry, and rush to snatch the box from her hand.

"Give it back, Jamie! I want to eat it!"

"You can't eat detergent, woman!" . . . which is a phrase no sane, reasonable person should ever have to utter.

I've done a bit of research about pregnancy, and I know that these weird cravings happen. Something to do with the body lacking minerals and vitamins the baby needs. It all sounds perfectly reasonable. But *detergent*? In what way does it benefit mother and baby to suck down a load of washing powder? What is there in a box of Tide that my unborn daughter thinks she needs? Is she perhaps worried that the womb is getting a bit dirty? Does she think it could do with a good spring clean? If so, it doesn't bode well for her ability to keep her bedroom tidy in the future, does it?

Detergent isn't the only cleaning product Laura has inexplicably craved. I walked into the bathroom a couple of days after the Walmart incident to find her contentedly sucking on a bar of soap like it was a lollipop. There she was, laid out in the bath, her big belly breaking the surface of the water—with a big bar of Dove stuck in her gob. The frothing made it look uncomfortably like she'd caught rabies.

I think she's secretly training me for when the baby comes along. I'll be an expert at snatching foreign objects from my daughter's mouth, as I will have spent several months beforehand doing the same with her mother.

The longer this pregnancy goes on, the more I'm starting to realise that having a baby makes a woman lose her mind. Laura is usually the sensible, clever, down-to-earth half of our relationship. I'm the one prone to flights of fancy, lack of common sense, and moments of blinding idiocy. Having the dynamic turned upside down is deeply distressing.

The mood swings are the worst.

Case in point: I decided last week that what we both needed was a good, hearty meal. One conducted out in public at a restaurant, rather than on our laps in front of *The Biggest Loser* repeats. I'd just been paid, so it seemed like a good excuse for us to spend some quality time together in a relaxed atmosphere. We've both been working like dogs recently, along with dealing with the ups and downs of the pregnancy, so I thought it would be good for us.

"Oh Jamie! That sounds like a wonderful idea," Laura exclaims when I tell her the plan. She then bursts into tears like I'd just shot her dog. A couple of months ago I would have been concerned and asked her what was wrong. By this stage, though, I'm well used to her bouts of uncontrolled emotions and simply let her cry on my shoulder for a few minutes until she pulls herself together.

"I thought we could go for Italian."

This brings on fresh waves of eye water. "Oh Jamie! You're so thoughtful!"

What?

"It's just like the date we had. When you made the Piazza Navona in the lounge!"

"Oh . . . er, yeah. That's right."

That wasn't the reason I'd actually suggested pizza. I just fancied a quattro formaggi and garlic bread. But if Laura wants to believe I've suddenly become Captain Thoughtful Pants, then who am I to let her down?

I look at my now sodden shirt. "I'll just go change this and we'll pop out, then."

"Excellent!" Laura beams, and we both go upstairs.

I put on a fresh shirt and go for a wee in the bathroom. Laura is out of my sight for no more than twenty seconds. In that time, though, she has gone from ecstatic about our impromptu night out to suicidal.

"I can't go out!" she wails from her perch at the end of the bed, in front of the mirror.

"Why not?"

"Because I'm an elephant!"

What?

Has it finally happened? Has my wife completely succumbed to the pressure of giving birth and lost her mind completely? Will I have to spend the rest of my days feeding her buns and mucking out her pen?

"I'm so fat!"

Ah. Now I understand.

I come over and sit next to her. "You're not fat, baby. You're gorgeous."

"No! No, look at me! I'm a big, squishy lard monster!" As if to demonstrate, she pokes herself in the belly.

"Don't poke the baby, dear," I tell her.

"Sorry."

There's a moment of silence.

"I'm fatter than a bloody sumo wrestler!"

"No you're not. You look absolutely wonderful!" I'm skating on very thin ice here. "You're having our baby and because of that I'd say you look beautiful."

Laura smiles. I do a mental backflip of self-congratulation.

"I do?"

"You do." I kiss her on the forehead. "And you'll keep looking beautiful. It doesn't matter that you're going to get even bigger—"

Oh, fuck it. And I was doing so well.

Laura looks at me with abject misery, puts her head in her hands and blubbers. I stand up. There is nothing—literally *nothing*—I can do to improve this situation. So I take the coward's way out and leave.

"I'm just going to check the restaurant opening times on the laptop, baby."

Downstairs, I sit hunched over the laptop wondering who will walk down the stairs next. Laura could stay in the realms of self-pity for the rest of the night, or she could turn into an axe murderer craving my blood. I simply have no idea. I've never been so terrified in my life. When I hear footsteps on the stairs, I cringe a bit. It's hard to look at the doorway as Laura enters. But when I do . . .

Oh my.

She looks amazing. Laura has changed into the blue maternity dress she picked up last week in town. Her hair is up, showing off her neckline, and the make-up she's wearing simply accentuates what I consider to be the most beautiful face in the world. On top of all that, I can see the perfect round globe of her belly beneath the dress. My daughter lies there—beneath her mother's breast, slowly growing stronger and heading towards the day when she'll look at the world with her own eyes.

Laura has never been more beautiful.

"You look incredible," I tell her.

"Really?" she says, unsure of herself.

"Of course."

"I'm sorry I keep flying off the handle. I just can't seem to control myself."

"It's okay." I go over and place a hand on her stomach. "It's all going to be worth it, gorgeous. You just wait and see."

Laura smiles and we kiss. Looks like I'm going to get my quattro formaggi after all!

The happy mood lasts about an hour and a half—which is quite good these days. Unfortunately, the restaurant is *very* busy and our order takes a long time to come. *Too* long for my pregnant wife, whose temporary good nature is slipping away faster than a greasy squirrel on a frozen slide.

"How bloody long is this going to take?" she mutters, tearing a bread roll and stuffing one half in her mouth.

"Relax baby. They're busy."

"I know they're busy, Jamie, I've got eyes, haven't I?" Her head whips round. "This is bloody ridiculous though. We've been sitting here nearly an hour."

"I'm sure they're coming."

And come they do about five minutes later, just as Laura is starting to stab her fork into the tablecloth. I breathe a sigh of relief, thinking the worst may have been averted.

"Sorry for the delay folks," the waiter says. "Here are your pizzas." He deposits two plates of round, cheesy goodness in front of us and prepares to leave.

"What exactly do you call this?" Laura says, steel running through every syllable.

"Your pizza, madam."

"This isn't my pizza. I ordered a margherita. This is quite plainly a Vesuvio." She glares at the waiter, fork hovering over the table in one white knuckle. "Do I *look* like I want a Vesuvio?"

"I'm pretty sure you ordered a Vesuvio, madam."

Oh God. Somebody kill me. Kill me now.

"Really?" A few heads turn to look at us. "I'm a pregnant woman, you *cock*. Do you think a pregnant woman would want to eat something really *spicy*?"

"I have no idea, madam." The poor man is now looking decidedly scared.

"Oh, you have no idea? Tell me, did your mother have any children who lived?"

Ouch. That's a bad one, even for angry Laura.

"I'm sorry, madam," he says, trying to recover the situation. "I will take this away and get you what you wanted."

"Too late!" she screams and stabs the fork into the middle of the Vesuvio, narrowly missing the waiter's hand as he goes to pick it up. "My husband and I are leaving."

"We are? But I wanted a pizza."

The look Laura gives me contains daggers, swords, machine guns, land mines and at least one intercontinental ballistic nuclear missile. I get up, resigned to eating sodding toast again for dinner.

Laura storms out of the restaurant, pausing only to lean over a young couple near the window who are waiting for their meals as well. "You won't get what you ordered you know!" she barks at them, tearing them both from the romantic reverie they'd obviously been enjoying. "If you ordered a quattro stagioni, don't be surprised if he brings out a plate of fucking vermicelli!"

I grab one of Laura's arms and usher her quickly out the front door. I have a feeling we won't be returning to this particular restaurant any time in the near future.

We ended up traipsing around the twenty-four-hour Walmart looking for frozen pizzas.

I picked up a pepperoni for me and a ham and cheese for Laura. Both look like they're made of cardboard and will probably taste much the same. It's only when I get to the self-service counter that I realise my wife is no longer with me. When I do find her ten minutes later, I have to chase her up the aisle to get the bottle of bleach out of her hand before she takes a swig and earns herself a night in the emergency room.

LAURA'S DIARY
Friday, October 4

Dear Mum,

It's impossible. Completely and utterly *impossible.*

I look down at the enormous bump in front of me, and there is no way I can squeeze its contents out of my vagina. It's ridiculous! What am I, a reticulated python?

Intellectually I know it's perfectly possible, otherwise the human race wouldn't exist, but there's a gigantic mental block in my head that simply can't accept it on a visceral level. I can see why so many women elect to have a caesarean. In the last few days I've started to have not what I'd call panic attacks—but definitely panic "incidents" that come and go quite at random.

I'll be behind the counter at work thinking about nothing in particular, when this little voice will pipe up: *that baby's head is going to wreck your undercarriage.* And I'll spend the next ten minutes frozen in fear until a customer snaps me out of it with a question about mint thins.

On top of that there's the whole bringing-up-another-human-being-for-the-next-twenty-years part of the equation. The sheer responsibility of it threatens to crush the life out of me. How the hell do these women squeeze out four or five of the little sods? I know that some of them (the housing authority kind, who look up to Kim Kardashian and believe everything they read in the tabloids) have babies so they can get benefits from the government—and thus never have to trouble themselves with finding a job. I just can't get my head around that. No amount of government handouts could ever persuade me that it's worth having my lady garden stretched to the breaking point, and my life completely taken over by a miniature person with incontinence and no volume control. I spoke of my concerns (oh, alright, I cried like a bitch) to my midwife, Marigold.

"You need prenatal classes, you stupid girl," she said in her usual caring manner. "I keep telling you to go. It'll help you with all this stuff when I'm not around."

I admit I've been putting off prenatal classes. I have enough night terrors thinking about the birth, thanks to the information I *do* have—I don't need my worst fears confirmed in a public setting. I say as much to Marigold. She shakes her head and regards me with the eyeball.

"I never heard such girly rubbish in all my days. You think you're the first to have these worries? Get your skinny white backside to classes and don't talk such cow shit to me anymore!"

With this sage advice ringing in my ears, last night Jamie and I attended our first prenatal class. I'll give you three guesses how it went. The first two don't count.

"Really?" whines my husband when I tell him what we're doing.

"Yes, Jamie. We need to go. I'm thirty weeks in now. There's stuff we have to learn about."

"It won't be any fun, you know."

"It isn't supposed to be fun. It's supposed to be educational."

Jamie groans even louder. "But it'll be a room full of idiots like us."

"Look, Marigold's recommended this class to me at the leisure centre. It's private, so there are fewer people. It won't be that bad."

I should learn to never say *it won't be that bad* before entering into an activity for the first time. It's like I'm putting a curse on myself.

We arrive at the leisure centre at six thirty to find four other couples waiting outside one of the smaller activity rooms towards the back of the building.

"Evening," I say, waddling up to them. I get a few obligatory British nods of heads and muttered return greetings.

One woman, a petite Asian girl, gives me a toothy grin. "Hello to you! I'm Lolly! This first time?" she says in that clipped, efficient manner Asians have when English isn't their first language.

"Yes," I reply.

"Ah . . . good! Good!" she turns to a white guy in his fifties standing next to her. "They like us two week ago, Brian!"

"Looks like it," Brian replies. The dynamic between the two of them is fairly obvious. I have to wonder whether he paid for her up front or on inspection of the goods at the airport.

"Why are we all standing out here then?" Jamie asks the small crowd of expectant parents.

"She's late again," sneers a tall, rangy-looking individual in a brown sports coat near the door—one arm wrapped round his much shorter wife's neck. Body language can be such a dead giveaway sometimes. He rolls his eyes.

"I'm sure she'll be here soon." This much friendlier response comes from a lady a good few years past forty standing with her equally friendly-looking husband of about the same age. "Nice to meet you love," she says and extends a hand, which I'm happy to take. "I'm Susan and this is Clive."

"Hello. I'm Laura and this is Jamie."

"Lovely." She regards my belly. "How far gone are you?"

This is a question I've been asked more times than any other recently. A pattern has formed in most of my conversations, which revolves exclusively around how my pregnancy is progressing . . . and very little else.

"I'm thirty weeks."

"Thirty-five for me. First time?"

"Yes. You?"

"Yep. Decided it was about time we produced offspring. Couldn't have left it much later!"

She's going to ask me if I know the sex of my baby next.

"Boy or girl?"

"Girl."

I have to finish the ritual, to do otherwise would be rude. "Yours?"

"We don't know yet. We wanted to keep it a surprise."

Yes, and by the look of the clothes you're wearing you can probably afford it.

The predictable conversation is interrupted by a stick insect in a yellow jumpsuit. At least this is my first impression of the woman who runs the prenatal class.

"Sorry I'm late, everyone."

"Not a problem Trisha," a thickset woman sporting a close-cropped haircut says from where she's standing next to a pregnant girl covered in tattoos. They might as well have a sign above them saying LESBIANS in big, black letters.

The stick insect unlocks the door. "Come in everyone!" There's a nervous energy about this skinny woman that's already setting my teeth on edge.

We file into the room. The four other couples take up position in a semicircle around Trisha in front of some large sponge mats. Jamie and I slot ourselves in on one end in front of a spare mat and try to look inconspicuous. It doesn't work.

"Welcome, my friends!" Trisha says to us, clapping her bony hands together in delight. "You must be Laura and Jamie."

"Yep, that's us," Jamie confirms.

"Excellent. We run quite an informal class here. The best thing to do is just listen, watch, and join in as you pick things up, okay?"

We both nod a little uncertainly.

"Goody, goody gumdrops!" Trisha exclaims happily.

The phrase *goody, goody gumdrops* is not one you want to hear spouting from the mouth of someone who's supposed to be a health-care professional. I turn to look at Jamie. He looks like somebody has just flicked him on the testicle, so I assume he feels much the same way. Trisha goes to an iPod dock on a table at the back of the room. She puts her iPhone into it and plays with it for a moment. The room is suddenly filled with what sounds like Free Willy being raped.

"What the bloody hell is that?" Jamie cries.

"Oh, don't worry!" Trisha says. "I like to get the mood for the class right with a little whale song." She looks at the thickset lesbian. "Could you get the lights for me, Ashley?"

The woman does as she is bid, while Trisha produces another black electronic device from her bag and deposits it on the table next to the iPod dock, switching it on as Ashley flicks the lights off. Beams of light erupt from the spherical black device, bathing the room in fake starlight.

"Oh Jesus Christ," I hear Jamie say under his breath.

Free Willy is still being sexually molested, but now the assault is being conducted in the icy depths of space. The other couples deposit themselves on the floor. We reluctantly follow suit. Trisha starts to speak, her words punctuated by the aquatic sex crime going on in the background.

"Welcome once again all of you." *Beeeeeooowwwwww.* "I'm pleased to see you all back, along with some lovely new faces." *Beeeeeooowwwwww booo.* "In this evening's class, we're going to concentrate on labour breathing." *Ikky ikky ikky beeeeeoooowwwwww.* "Then we'll move on to discuss postlabour pain management." *Beooow beooow beooow booooooooooo beeooowww.* "Any questions so far?"

Jamie raises a hand.

"Yes, Jamie?"

"Any chance we could lose the whales and the stars? I can't decide whether I should be beaming down to the planet or trying to fuck a humpback."

That put the both of us in Trisha's bad books for the rest of the evening. She did turn off the whales but insisted the stars stay on. What got me was that the others in attendance didn't seem to bat an eyelid at this strangeness. They obviously felt that it was a perfectly normal part of preparing to give birth. Unless they were all *Star Trek* fans who worked at SeaWorld I failed to see how this could be the case.

We willingly take part in the breathing exercises to show we aren't complete outsiders. Jamie is told to help me keep a rhythm by talking calmly and holding my hand, squeezing it in time with my breaths while I puff and blow like a malfunctioning steam engine.

Next to us are Lolly and Brian. Brian has one hand on his wife's back, the other on her upper thigh. He keeps squeezing her leg every time she breathes out in a manner that sounds almost orgasmic. It's quite nauseating.

"And now, please change places," Trisha tells us.

"Excuse me?" Jamie says.

"You need to change places, Mr. Newman." Trisha's disgust at his dislike of her whale music has pushed him into surname territory. "You need to know what your wife is going to experience as much as she does."

Jamie stands up and puts his hands on his hips. "Do I? I mean, *really*?"

"Indeed."

I decide to join in the lively discussion. "Er . . . I kinda think Jamie's right here, Trish."

For the first time, Trisha looks properly displeased with us.

Her narrow face gets even narrower. "Please Mr. and Mrs. Newman, I am a trained professional. These techniques will help you a great deal through the pregnancy, but only if you allow them to."

"Alright, alright," Jamie says and flaps his hands. He pulls me up and takes my place on the mat, grumbling to himself.

"Now then, gentlemen and lady," Trisha says, her soothing tone returning. "Please repeat what your wives were doing. Deep, rhythmic breathing while your spouse helps you."

Jamie reluctantly starts the exercise, while I try very hard not to laugh as I grip his hand and watch his face turn purple.

"And faster gentlemen and lady please," Trisha bids them. The three men and one lesbian all speed up their breathing rate.

The room now sounds like it's been invaded by a crowd of horny walruses. I wasn't prepared for how much aquatic mammal life you encounter during an prenatal class.

"Faster please!" Trisha commands again.

Now Jamie is really going for it. It feels like an air of competition has filled the room: who can breathe the loudest, fastest, and hardest? Typical boy (and apparently lesbian) behaviour.

I grip my husband's hand for dear life as he takes it up another notch. The collective grunting has reached a crescendo when Jamie, having built up enough air pressure in his body to float a hot air balloon, emits a loud, sharp fart that cuts across the grunting like a knife through butter. Or should that be cheese?

Immediately he stops the exercise and goes crimson. I try so, so *very* hard not to burst out laughing. In my efforts not to further compound Jamie's embarrassment, I slam one hand over my mouth to stop a bray of laughter from escaping. Usually that would be the end of it, but I'm over thirty weeks pregnant and my body is no longer entirely under my control. This goes double for my bladder.

In short, I pee my pants. Not a lot, mind you. We're not talking Niagara Falls here—but it's certainly enough to make my knickers good and wet. Thank God I'm wearing a dark pair of maternity jeans.

"Oh, Christ, I've wet myself," I tell Jamie under my breath. Unfortunately the whole room has gone silent in response to Jamie's bottom trumpet and the statement carries to everyone.

"Are . . . are you both well?" Trisha asks hesitantly.

Oh yes, Trisha. We're just peachy, *thank you. My husband's about to follow through and I already have. This evening is right up there with our wedding night.*

"I think we'll be going now," I say in a bland voice.

"Oh really?" Trisha sounds downcast. "But we haven't got to the chanting yet."

"Another time perhaps."

I help Jamie to his feet. He's being uncharacteristically silent, which probably isn't the worst thing in the world right now. Steering him with one arm, I waddle in the direction of the door.

"No worry, Laura!" Lolly pipes up. "I piss myself too the other day!" She snorts with laughter and points at Brian. "And he fart in front of my father at wedding!"

I know she's trying to make us feel better, but surprisingly enough, it's not working. With as much speed as a woman in her third trimester can summon, I propel my mortified husband out into the corridor and bustle towards the main entrance. I don't risk a look back, just in case Trisha is following us with a couple of adult nappies and half the continent of Antarctica.

That night I had a dream I was giving birth to a dolphin in a Chinese restaurant. I woke up drenched in sweat and with a pounding heart. If that's what private prenatal classes do to you, then I'd rather go without, thanks very much.

I'm going—alone—to one of the free classes run at the health centre this week. It'll be boring, run-of-the-mill, and packed with mothers-to-be, but at least I won't have to worry about incontinence or space whales from another dimension.

Love you and miss you, Mum.

Your incredulous daughter, Laura

xxx

JAMIE'S BLOG
Sunday 10 November

Like Salt–N-Pepa once requested in song, let's talk about sex. More specifically, sex with a pregnant woman. *Oh my.*

It goes through stages. During the first few weeks of the pregnancy, I was more likely to have sex with the entire Australian women's volleyball team than I was with my wife. I couldn't really blame her, though. In that period of time, when she wasn't peeing in the bathroom she was throwing up in it, and when she wasn't doing either of those she was fast asleep. Slipping her a length would have been virtually impossible. The one occasion she gamely tried to give me a blow job ended with her head in the toilet bowl and me nursing a freshly squeezed penis.

I resigned myself to a few months of healthy masturbation. It wasn't too bad all things considered, especially because Laura knew full well what I was doing and condoned it. There's something decidedly appealing about being given permission by your other half to wank yourself into insensibility on a regular basis.

Then as Laura went into the second trimester, things changed for the better. With the nausea and fatigue subsiding, she suddenly perked up and turned into what I can only describe accurately as a total fuck monster. Even in the first fledgling weeks of our relationship (when I wasn't poisoning her with bad chicken and she wasn't dumping me for her ex) Laura was never this rampant.

The pregnancy hormones may have made her more emotional than a thirteen-year-old One Direction fan, but they also gave her sex drive a kick up the arse that I was barely able to cope with. After about a week, my cock looked like battered salami. She looked adorable at that stage, though. The growing bump adding to what I consider to be the best curves in the world. Plus, I had the bonus that for the first time in our relationship Laura preferred it on her knees doggy-style, because it was the most comfortable position for her. *Woo-hoo!*

Then we entered the third trimester, and things understandably started going downhill again. I'm not all that good at reading the minds of women, but even I can appreciate that swollen breasts, piles, a bad back, and a massive belly aren't exactly conducive to sexual arousal. I resigned myself to once again beating it like Michael Jackson—this time with some fresh wank bank material from our recent second trimester exploits.

Colour me every shade of surprised, then, when last night Laura turns to me on the couch in the middle of a particularly dull episode of *Four Weddings* and puts her hand over my sleeping penis.

"Baby, I'm horny," she says into my ear in a husky voice.

What's this? Little Jamie wonders, stirring from his malaise.

Laura squeezes him gently, waking him further. *Blimey, and there I was thinking I'd have to settle for you ringing my neck tonight after Laura has gone to bed. Now it looks like I may get to fulfill my true purpose in life. Wahaay!*

"Are you?" I reply, incredulous.

"Yeah. Have been all day. I have no idea why."

"But what about . . . you know . . . that." I point at the enormous dome sitting in front of her.

"That's just fine where it is," she whispers in my ear. "I want your cock in me, baby."

And I want to be in you, Laura, little Jamie exults, setting off on one of his legendary laps around the metaphorical track.

For some reason my heart is beating like crazy. Laura and I have had sex more times than it's possible to count, but because she's heavily pregnant it feels like something completely new—and just a wee bit *strange*.

"Shall we go into the bedroom?" I say.

"Yeah," she says and squeezes my groin one more time.

I'm up like a shot and out the lounge door with my jeans already unzipped. I notice I'm alone. On previous occasions my wife would have either been right behind me, or just ahead, wiggling her tight little bum as we hurry upstairs. Now, though, I look back to the couch to see her still trying to get up. It's rather like watching a tortoise stuck on its back. I shake the mental image before it ruins the moment and hurry back to assist her off the couch.

"Give me your hand, sweetheart," I tell her, and together we manage to heave her onto her feet. I'm off again, out the door and up to the—

Still no Laura. Back I go, and now she's leaning against the TV, one hand on her back, an agonised expression on her face.

"You okay, baby?" I say, hurrying back again. I've now covered the entire length of the lounge three times, and my cock is starting to display signs of chaffing.

"Yeah, I'm fine."

I place a warm hand on the small of her back and give it a rub.

"Oh, that's lovely," she says. To maintain the sexy mood she once again gives my genitals a squeeze, reaffirming little Jamie's belief that he's going to see action this evening come what may.

Together—slowly—we make our way out of the lounge and up the stairs. In the bedroom I rip my clothes off in nanoseconds. Five minutes later we manage to remove the last of Laura's, and she collapses on the bed like a beached minke whale. I must find whales sexy as my penis is ramrod straight and ready to go. I don't know what it is about Laura being pregnant, but it drives me crazy. Perhaps it's how lovely and curvy she is, perhaps it's how soft and creamy her skin has become, perhaps it's the knowledge that my child lies inside her, an affirmation of our love, sexual compatibility, and my virility.

Nah, it's the humungous tits, isn't it?

"How do you want to do this?" I enquire, in the manner of a removals man asking a colleague how they should get a three-seater couch through the front door.

"Spoon me," Laura replies and rolls herself to one side with an audible grunt.

She's not left me much room on the edge of the bed but I don't want to make her roll over again. I don't have a block and tackle handy to help her with it. I lie down behind her and nibble her neck. She takes little Jamie in one hand and starts to administer a slow hand job, the likes of which I try to achieve on my own all the time, but never quite accomplish.

"Right then, let's take this slowly," she says and guides me between her legs, sticking her bum back for ease of access. "Slowly . . . slowly . . ."

"Left a bit, up a bit," I continue.

The removals firm of Newman & Newman eventually achieves a successful entry, after a few moments of careful movement. I reach one hand around my wife and caress her belly as we make love. Everything is going swimmingly until my daughter decides she's had enough of this shit for one night and delivers a karate kick to Laura's abdomen that Steven Seagal would have been proud of.

"Oooww!" Laura shrieks and bucks her hips. My position on the bed is already precarious thanks to the way she's lying, and having her thrust herself backwards turns precarious into untenable.

"Fuck a duck!" I wail and fall off the bed.

In an effort to prevent injury to my still erect penis I twist in midair like a champion diver so that little Jamie is pointing skywards. Unfortunately this means that my back is the first part of my anatomy to come in contact with the carpet. The air is driven from my lungs, winding me painfully. Meanwhile, back on the bed, Laura has rolled onto her back to settle the baby down. She does this a little too quickly and tweaks her already complaining spine.

"Oooww!" she cries with a sharp intake of breath.

"Damn it!" I shout in pain, one hand going to my own back.

There we both lie, writhing in our respective agonies, one on the bed, one on the floor. It's like the worst advert for Advil you've ever seen in your life. Looking down from above, we could be partners in a very strange synchronised dance competition for sadomasochists.

"Are you okay, honey?" Laura asks.

"I think I've done my back in."

"Let me have a look," she says with concern, and begins to roll towards the edge of the bed. Looking up, the first thing I see appearing from the bed covers is the looming bulge of our unborn child. It's like watching a pink sun come up, only sideways. Laura's face comes into view shortly afterwards, a strained expression writ large across it.

"Can you move?" she enquires, voice somewhat muffled by the duvet.

"I don't know," I respond, still wincing as I rub the small of my back.

"Let me try and help you," she suggests and moves even closer to the edge of the bed.

I realise this already disastrous evening could get a lot worse in very short order if Laura loses her balance right now. Concern for my own well-being is paramount, but even that is trumped by my concern for the baby if Laura falls off the bed, drops the intervening two feet between us, and pins me like André the Giant.

My arms go out. One grasps Laura's belly to steady it, the other flies in the direction of her head—the only other part of her anatomy I can see. I'm sure she appreciates me stopping her tipping over, but her gratitude is lost in the screech of distress that arises due to the thumb I've just stuck in her eye.

"Christ Jamie!"

"Sorry! I was trying to stop your fall!" I jump to my feet in concern for her welfare.

If this didn't already look like a Three Stooges routine minus Curly, it certainly resembles one when I stub my toe on the side of the bed in a hasty effort to provide first aid to my partially blinded wife. I sit down with a sharp hiss of agony, one hand still on my back, the other now grabbing my throbbing toe. Likewise, Laura has a hand on her back while the other is now covering her left eye.

Episodes of *ER* have gone by with fewer injuries than this aborted sex session in the Newman household. Inexplicably, my penis still thinks it's party time and is standing proud awaiting further instructions. I look at Laura for a moment thrashing around next to me and decide she's probably not in the mood anymore. Still, I'm probably going to be laid up with a bad back for the next few days, so I'll have plenty of time to wank myself into a stupour, won't I?

"I'm sorry honey," I say, leaning over. Laura tentatively removes her hand from her eye, as if she's not completely sure I'm not going to smack her around the head with the table lamp.

"Why did you poke me in the bloody eye?"

"Why did you throw me off the bed?"

"I didn't. The baby kicked. You know how I react sometimes when she does it." She looks at my toe. "What did you do?"

"Stubbed it on the bed."

Laura actually gives me a look of sympathy, which once again reinforces my opinion that she really must love me. How else could someone brush off being assaulted with a thumb while naked and pregnant? Laura looks down at little Jamie, who still doesn't know when he's done for the night.

"You're still hard after all that? Blimey."

I shrug my shoulders. "What can I say? You do it for me even with mild spinal injuries."

With one eye still twitching and weeping copiously, Laura pats the bed next to her.

"Lie down, sexy. Let's see if I can still do something about that."

Her twitching, watery eye is a bit disconcerting. I feel like I'm being seduced by a stroke victim. I've become very adept at brushing off these disturbing thoughts recently though, so I position myself accordingly and await further developments. The relief on my aching back is fantastic, and I would have quite happily settled for that, but Laura props herself up on her knees and starts to give me a very sloppy—and therefore amazing—blow job. I don't last very long and am arriving at my destination quite aggressively in no time at all. So aggressively in fact that some semen spurts into Laura's good eye, successfully blinding her for the second time in as many minutes.

The shock of semen shooting straight into the only serviceable ocular device she has left at her disposal causes Laura's hand to clench involuntarily, thus squeezing the life out of little Jamie while he's still on the cooldown lap. And thus, the evening of calamity is brought to a close. I now have a throbbing cock, toe, and back—and Laura will have bloodshot eyes for a fortnight.

Honest to God, it'll be a miracle if this baby doesn't come flying out of the womb, head butt the doctor, slide right off the table, and concuss herself on the nearest wastepaper basket.

LAURA'S DIARY

Monday, December 2

Dear Mum,

Well, this is *the* diary entry. The one you and I have been waiting on for the past nine months. I'm writing this from my hospital bed. Luckily, I'm on my own in the room right now. There are no other new mothers with me, so everything is blissfully peaceful.

It's eleven in the morning, and as I look out of the window I can see a crisp winter's day that makes the usually drab hospital grounds sparkle with frost. Clean, bright sunshine bathes the trees and grass with its weak December warmth. I can also see a couple of the hospital's patients taking constitutional walks. One has a cigarette dangling from his mouth in an act of addictive rebellion that I'm sure is doing him no favours with the nurses.

You'll note that I'm writing in a more whimsical fashion than usual. This may be due to the glow of new motherhood—but it could equally be due to the pain killers I've had pumped into my system to keep the ache in my undercarriage down to a dull throb.

My newborn baby daughter is fast asleep in a cot at the bottom of the bed. She looks serene and at peace, which gives me a warm, content feeling in my heart. All is currently well in Laura Newman's life. I am in the calm after the storm and am taking great pleasure in noticing all the little details of my placid state, making sure to soak it up while I can.

I guess it's time I told you about the storm though, isn't it?

It begins with Christmas shopping. Take the worst shopping trip you've ever experienced, and imagine it with a six-pound bag of potatoes strapped to your stomach. This will give you a fair idea of the misery I was forced to endure on Saturday afternoon. Finish by pissing yourself in front of a crowd of people, and you've pretty much provided yourself with the same experience I went through.

I didn't choose a Saturday afternoon to go Christmas shopping. I'm on maternity leave, after all, and could have gone on any weekday, when the entire population of the south coast of England wouldn't be doing the same thing. It was the only day Jamie had to spare though, and I needed him with me to nail down exactly what we were going to buy his parents. It's only been a few months since I called Jane a bitch, so I figured I'd best make an effort to purchase something big and apologetic.

We could have saved ourselves a whole lot of time and effort with a constructive hour on Amazon, but I'm one of those people who needs to give something a good feel before I buy it. After all, that cruet set may look nice in a thumbnail photo, but chances are that the photo's been touched up more times than a supermodel's, and when the set finally does arrive on your doorstep it will bear little to no resemblance to the set you actually ordered. Much better to have a look at potential presents in the flesh, even if it does mean braving the Christmas masses.

To be honest, I was glad to get out of the house because it distracted me from the fact that any time soon I was going to have to give birth to a baby. The closer you get to your due date, the more it invades all of your waking thoughts—and your dreams too, for that matter. My mind is pretty much constantly in a whirl over what's going to happen—particularly the amount of pain I'm going to be in.

Whether I like it or not, there is *nothing* I can do about the fact a baby is going to push its way out of my body sometime very soon. The absolute certainty of it is brain-freezing. Still, I'm not due until the eighth, and that's over a week away, so I should be fine right? *Yeah, right . . .*

Most women are fortunate enough to have their water break in the confines of their own home. Me, I choose to do it in front of hundreds of people, with a husband flapping around next to me like an injured crow.

We've been wandering around the gigantic shopping centre for half an hour and I'm already starting to flag. Even the rather cute red cardigan I've just picked up at GAP for half price isn't keeping my mood buoyant. My head aches, my piles itch like mad, my ankles are throbbing, and my enormous floppy tits feel red raw.

Huge floppy tits they are. Engorged with more milk than the dairy aisle at Walmart. I feel like somebody should string a cow bell around my neck and herd me into the nearest pasture.

I waddle through the shopping centre like a great barge drifting downriver surrounded by faster, more agile yachts. I see teenage girls prancing around in tiny jean shorts and leggings—and I hate them. Hate them and their young, thin healthy bodies. I'm only in my early thirties, but being pregnant makes me feel like a fifty-year-old fat man on the brink of a heart attack.

There's something exquisitely frustrating about only being able to move at a slow pace. I can understand why obese people always have red faces now. It's not because they're out of breath, it's just because they're pissed off they can't get to the doughnut stand any quicker.

Jamie is doing what all men do in situations like this: trying his hardest to contain his impatience, and failing miserably.

"Where do you want to go now?" he says, circling me like a small moon. "Do you want to look for clothes? For shoes? For hats? For DVDs?"

"I don't know! Why do you keep giving me choices? You bloody choose."

"I don't know. Wherever you want, really," he tells me, jiggling up and down on the spot and obviously chafing at my stately pace.

This is one habit of my husband's I could cheerfully beat out of him. He always leaves it to me to make the decisions about this sort of thing. I came into his life purely so he could abstain from any decision making—thus leaving more room in his brain for PlayStation 3 games and *Top Gear*.

"I guess we could look round John Lewis," I sigh and begin to change direction. I'm like one of those oil tankers that needs five miles to turn around.

"Yeah okay, that sounds good. Maybe we could get Mum and Dad a coffee machi— Oh! The Apple shop's over there!"

And there goes any chance of us finding a present in the next hour.

"Go on," I groan like a parent with an overexcited seven-year-old. "You go in and I'll catch up."

Jamie grins, kisses me on the cheek, and is lost in the never-ending crowd in an instant. I rub my back for the millionth time that day and once again change trajectory to bring my bulk on a close entry orbit with the clean, white edifice that is the Apple store.

Inside, Jamie is stroking an iPad like it's his firstborn. His soon to be real firstborn is moving around to get into a more comfy position, causing her mother to wince with discomfort as she wobbles her way past the Genius Bar. I hate going into this shop for the plain and simple reason I don't like being around objects that have been fondled by thousands of people. The buildup of bacteria and germs on each and every iPad, iPhone, and iPod in here would be enough to knock out several invading armies of Martians. If the influenza virus were going to throw a party, it would do it in the nearest Apple shop.

I look at Jamie rubbing his fingers over the iPad and resolve not to let him get near me until he's submerged his hands in bleach for ten minutes. I try not to imagine the microscopic creatures crawling all over me, so instead I concentrate on his happy little face. It doesn't take much to keep Jamie amused. Just give him a ten-inch screen and a copy of *Plants vs. Zombies* and he's as happy as a pig in—

Oh Christ. I suddenly feel very, *very* damp downstairs. *Oh shit, I've wet myself,* is my first thought. It's swiftly followed by a sensation of release that doesn't usually come with emptying your bladder.

Oh God no! Not here. I'm not due for days! But God is not listening. He's in heaven trying to get three stars on the last Angry Birds level while Steve Jobs sits next to him offering hints.

"Jamie . . ."

"Look, Laura. The zombie's wearing a traffic cone!"

"Jamie . . ."

"Where do I put this walnut?"

"Jamie . . ."

"Oh no! That one's already at the house!"

"Jamie!"

"What's the matter?"

"My water has broken," I hiss under my breath, trying to move as little as possible.

Jamie goes white. "It can't have. We're in the Apple shop," he says, as if embarrassing incidents were prevented from happening in here by some magical aura given off by a thousand touch screens.

Now I can feel liquid dripping down my leg. If we don't get out of here soon I'm going to completely ruin the lovely clean white aesthetic the shop's got going on.

"Ah . . . er . . . ah . . . eh . . ." goes Jamie, dancing a fraught jig on the spot. Several surrounding Apple fans are now looking at us, wondering what the hell is happening.

I supply them with the angriest look I can muster. "Nothing to see here people! Go back to your sodding iTunes!" I turn back to my incapacitated husband. "We have to leave Jamie, *right now*!"

I grab his arm and start pulling him towards the door. Unfortunately the idiot hasn't let go of the iPad he's holding and we're both jerked backwards by the security cable. The security alarm goes off and a chubby lad of indeterminate age trots over. He's wearing a blue T-shirt indicating he's one of the laughably named Geniuses who work in the shop. He has a look of mild panic on his face. This is one situation there definitely isn't an app for.

"What's going on?" he says.

I grab his arm as well, so now I'm propped up between husband and Genius. "What's going on," I tell him, trying to keep the dread out of my voice, "is that I'm a heavily pregnant woman whose water has just broken."

"Is that an excuse for trying to steal an iPad?" the Genius says suspiciously.

I point to the small puddle forming around my feet. "If it is, you bloody idiot, I'm really going to town on it, aren't I?"

The Genius goes as white as Jamie. I roll my eyes. "Where's your staff toilet?" I demand.

"Members of the public are not allowed to use our toilet facilities," he recites, as if he's reading from some internal teleprompter.

"Really? Are members of the public encouraged to give birth next to the iShuffle stand? Because that's what's going to happen, you cretin."

This doesn't appear to spur him into action, so I try another tack.

"My husband here may look like one of the mentally challenged at the moment, but when he isn't panicking over his wife giving birth, he is a journalist. Can you imagine how bad the PR would be if he writes a story about this?"

That does the trick. "Come this way!" the Genius wails, and creates a space in the crowd through to the rear of the store.

I go to move, but this just makes the flow of liquid from my nether regions speed up. I have to slow it down to even reach the toilet. Thus arrives the final crowning indignity of the day. Having your water break in public is bad enough, but having to stem the tide with the cute thirty quid cardigan you were planning on wearing to the work Christmas lunch next week is just *too fucking much*.

What happens in the Apple toilets is unpleasant in the extreme. Let's just say the cardigan goes in the nearest bin and the cleaner will really earn her money in the morning, and leave it at that.

The Genius stood outside the entire time repeatedly asking me if I was alright. What on earth are you supposed to reply in such circumstances? The truth would likely lead to the poor guy needing months of therapy, but to lie and say, *Yes, yes, I'm fine thank you* would stretch the legendary British sense of understated politeness way past the absolute breaking point.

Jamie used my distress as a distraction to shoplift a new USB adaptor for his iPhone. I wish he'd tucked a couple of iPads under his jacket as well, as it might have mitigated my colossal embarrassment. If you're going to drop several pints of bodily fluid onto the floor in front of a hundred complete strangers, it would be nice to have something featuring a crystal clear retina display to show for it.

The Genius, whose name is Dan, actually proves to be rather helpful in the end, partially because he shows Jamie where he can park the car at the rear of the shop so I can leave with the minimum of further embarrassment, but also because he fields the tremulous whining of his store manager. This officious little berk has the bloody cheek to moan at me for using the facilities—as if I had a choice about where my baby decided it was time to enter the world.

"This type of thing happens in the hospital, doesn't it?" he squeals as Jamie leads me to the car.

"Shut your mouth before *you* end up in hospital, pal," Jamie tells him. My husband may take a while to get in the game sometimes, but once he's there you can usually count on him for support.

In the car, my heart starts hammering. This is it. I'm going to have my baby. I've never been so terrified in all my days on earth.

First of all, we have to get to the hospital. And what a *fantastic* time we've picked for a high-speed car journey through town: Saturday afternoon a few weeks before Christmas . . .

JAMIE'S BLOG
Monday 2 December

I'd love to give you an accurate and pulse-pounding description of the drive from the Apple shop to Queen Alexandra Hospital just outside the city. I'd love to, but I can't. That's because I remember very little of it, which is probably just as well as I'm pretty sure I violated every single law of the road, apart from not driving a vehicle across the middle of a roundabout at eighty miles an hour—though to be honest, I can't even be sure about that one.

I inspected the car a little later that day when things had quietened down a bit. I discovered a two-foot-long scratch down the driver's side, a wad of grass in the front spoiler, and a passenger seat in need of immediate replacement, so I know it must have been an exciting trip, to say the least.

I do remember screaming *Breathe!* at my wife repeatedly as we hurtled northwards on the motorway. This is quite the most stupid command you can issue to another person. You might as well shout *Continue to Exist* at them for all the good it does.

The orderlies at the hospital must listen for the screech of tyres that signify the arrival of another imminently expectant mother, as I've hardly so much as flung open my car door before a genial fellow in a white jumpsuit is there with a wheelchair.

I'm somewhat disappointed. The melodramatic part of me was all ready to roll across the bonnet and scream "My wife is about to give birth! Help us!" As it is, Laura is in the wheelchair and through the lobby doors before I can say a damn thing.

"Yes Marigold, I know," she says into her mobile phone. "I *am*, Marigold, I promise." She looks at me. "No, he hasn't fainted or shit himself yet." I take great exception to that.

"Okay. We'll see you shortly, then." Laura ends the call and doubles up, gasping in pain.

"Are you alright, baby?" I ask as I hurry alongside her.

"Just peachy, thanks." The sarcasm drips from her voice. "Being in labour is such a laugh!"

I feel exquisitely useless—and will continue to do so for the next few hours. There's nothing pleasant about watching the woman you love in extreme pain, especially when you're the one responsible for it. The orderly brings us into the maternity ward, where I have never been so glad to see Marigold Ubantu in all my life.

"Aha!" she exclaims and slaps her hands together vigorously. "Time to squeeze that little bitch out, Newmans!"

All things being equal, I guess I would have preferred a homely midwife in her sixties with a calm demeanour and rosy complexion, but what we got is Marigold.

If nothing else Marigold knows what she's doing, but she never lets you forget it.

"Let's get that skinny arse up into bed, madam!" she tells Laura, who struggles out of the wheelchair and onto the bed. Once she's in position, Marigold ducks her head between my wife's legs for a quick examination.

"You're at four centimetres," she says, slapping Laura's calf. "Good girl!"

Laura tries to smile, but it's obvious she's hurting. "Can I . . . can I have an epidural for the pain?" she says.

"No," Marigold intones.

The room falls silent.

"What do you mean *no*?" Laura says.

"No anaesthetist on duty. He's off sick, girl."

"Are you telling me there's only *one* anaesthetist on duty today?" I ask incredulously.

"Only one who can give epidurals," Marigold says. "Welcome to the National Health Service!" she barks by way of explanation and then laughs.

"Can't you give me one?" Laura asks.

"Nope. Not qualified." Marigold watches Laura's face darken considerably. "Don't worry, girl! You're young and healthy. Gas and air will be fine for you today."

Something bad is happening to my wife. A tremor has started from the tips of her toes and is working its way like a tidal wave up her body. It reaches her head, which shudders briefly, before the tremor finds its voice.

"I don't want gas and air, you stupid bitch. I want a fucking epidural!"

Marigold's reaction is priceless. Until now she's only seen the cool, sweet-natured side of Laura Newman. But I know that when angered, beneath that lovely, even-tempered exterior beats the heart of a raving maniac. Seeing this dark side erupt in such a dramatic fashion stuns the six-foot African warrior woman.

Marigold looks at me. "You married that?" she asks. "You're braver than I thought, Newman." I nod my head and look a trifle sheepish.

"If you two are quite finished," Laura interrupts. "I'm trying to have a baby here and need painkillers!"

"Quit your bellyaching," Marigold bellows and wheels over the gas and air machine. She thrusts the mask at Laura. "Suck on that girl."

Laura grabs the mask and takes a deep drag. A few moments go by. "Well, that's not bloody helping at all!"

"Give it a moment," Marigold says. Sure enough, another five seconds pass and Laura's face suddenly droops into a vision of drowsy contentment.

"Fuck me on a rocking chair, this is gooooood fucking shit," she says in a dreamy voice. I've never heard Laura swear quite so much in such a short space of time.

"Just take a breath any time you need it, girl," Marigold says and turns to leave.

"Where are you fucking going?" Laura shrieks and points at me. "You can't leave me with just him!"

This sets the tone for the next seven hours of my life. Seven hours that will contain more swearing than a Quentin Tarantino movie.

"You'll be fine. Remember what I taught you about breathing, and keep taking the gas and air." Marigold also points at me. I'm starting to feel like an army private being beasted for no reason. "You look after your wife!"

I hurry to the bedside, trying to remember all the stuff from the prenatal classes—the ones at the health centre Laura eventually made me attend, I mean, not Trisha's. I wasn't about to start making whale noises and farting like a whoopee cushion. Marigold exits the room, leaving me alone with the demon that has possessed my wife.

She (it?) takes another drag on the mask and gives me the stink eye. "You know what, Newman? This is all your fault." Here we go. "If you had just bought some motherfucking condoms, I wouldn't be in this motherfucking mess."

Strike that last thought, Laura hasn't been possessed by a demon. She's been possessed by Samuel L. Jackson.

"I know. I'm sorry, dear." I figure there's no point arguing in this trying situation. Laura is about to painfully squeeze a small human from her body, so I can cut her some slack.

"Oh, you know, *do you*?" She takes a big suck on the mask. "I'll tell you what I fucking know, Jamie Newman . . ."

For the next few hours Laura proceeds to berate me for everything I've done wrong in the past nine months. This includes ruining her favourite white blouse when I stuck it in the washing machine with my bright blue T-shirt. I thought she looked quite cute in the blouse with its new blue tie-dye. She didn't feel the same way.

"I looked like a fucking hippy, Jamie. A hippy! My father would have been proud" she screams and digs her nails into my hand. "That blouse cost me a small bloody fortune!"

Then she moves on to everything I've done wrong since we met. A particular highlight of this section of the tirade includes when I got us lost on the way to a day out in Bath. "I had the bloody map, you wanker!" Laura bellows. "I knew where we had to go! But oh no! Jamie Newman doesn't need to read maps, does he? Jamie Newman knows his way *everywhere*!" The nails now draw blood. "But you don't know your way everywhere, do you Jamie? Because where did we end up?"

"Swindon."

"Swindon, Jamie, *yes*. I wanted to spend a day wandering around the picturesque Roman Baths, and instead I got to spend the afternoon hurrying past the drug addicts in the Swindon town centre."

"We had a nice meal."

"It was a fucking McDonald's, Jamie. A McDonald's."

Having reached back to the point of our first date, Laura then inexplicably moves on to everything I'd done wrong *before* we'd even met.

"I can't believe you shoplifted Wite-Out."

"I was twelve years old!"

"So you say."

"Why would I lie about that?"

"I don't know, Jamie. Why would you? You're obviously not that trustworthy, *are you*? I should never have let you anywhere near my vagina."

This journey through the errors of my past is punctuated at turns by rapidly increasing contractions, and grateful blasts of gas and air.

Each time Laura takes a hit, I'm afforded a few moments of peace from the constant character assassination. Melina walks into the room as Laura is telling me what an evil bastard I am for leaving the fridge door open last night, saving me from this cold, cold hell of my own making.

"How's the mum to be?" she says excitedly.

"Get this fucking thing out of me," Laura growls.

Melina, having been in this circumstance herself, takes a read of the sorry state of affairs and narrows her eyes. "Jamie, why don't you go and find yourself a cup of coffee?"

"Okay," I agree, and look at my wife. "Would you like some ice chips, Laura?"

"*Would you like some ice chips, Laura,*" she parrots in a high, sing-song voice. "No, Newman. I do not want ice chips. What I want is for you to have had more control over your cock nine months ago."

"Just leave for a bit," Melina tells me softly, like someone standing next to a ticking bomb.

I offer her a look of pathetic gratitude and hightail it out of there, looking back briefly to see Melina sit down next to Laura and brush hair off her forehead.

As I amble off down the corridor I wonder what it would be like to have a threesome with her. This proves—if proof were needed—that men can think about sex at the most inopportune of moments.

The worst cup of coffee I've ever had in my life was that mint monstrosity a couple of years ago during my date with Annika, the blond goddess. The one that's just defecated its way out of the hospital coffee machine runs a close second though. I nurse it for a good thirty minutes, forcing myself to drink the entire bitter contents of the Styrofoam cup. Anything is better than being called an evil bastard by your heavily pregnant wife. It's only when I get down to the dregs that I decide it's time to re-enter the dragon's lair.

When I get back to the room, Marigold is once more bent over Laura giving her an examination. Melina is sitting back in her chair nursing a bruised hand.

"Well?" Laura demands.

"Eight centimetres, girl. Your baby is getting ready to be born."

"Not fucking quick enough!" She sucks down more gas. "This shit isn't working anymore, Marigold. You told me it would help!" Laura fixes the African midwife with a dead-eyed stare of implacable hatred. "You fucking *lied* to me Marigold."

"And my cousin had his testicles blown off by a rocket launcher. Life isn't fair sometimes." Even Laura is brought up short by that one.

Marigold notices I've come back. "Where have you been, you stupid man? Your wife needs you."

"No she doesn't. She needs an exorcist."

"Get back over here, Jamie!" Laura shouts at me. "I need you to help me with my breathing, you cocksucker!"

Marigold catches my distraught look. "Man up, Newman. She's just in a lot of pain. Be thankful she doesn't have access to sharp implements."

I trot over to the chair, which Melina vacates. She retires to the couch at the back of the room, no doubt wondering whether this visit was such a good idea. Laura grips my hand like a vice and squeezes the life out of it as another contraction begins.

"Jesus, fucking shit, cunt, fucker, bastard, wanker, fucking cunt, double fuck!" screams my wife, just as my mother and father walk in.

The look on my mother's face suggests that someone invisible has just come up behind her and attempted to insert a canoe paddle.

"Is there any need for language like that?" is the first thing out of her mouth. If I don't do something about it, the second is likely to be a comment about how unattractive Laura's haircut looks. With foresight and a level of common sense I'm astounded I'm able to produce at this stage in the game, I usher Mum and Dad out of the room before Laura can launch into a diatribe about how it's their fault she's pregnant because they gave birth to me.

"I think it'd be best if you waited in the lounge," I tell them. "There's a coffee machine out there. It's very good."

They are then allowed to give perfunctory greetings to Laura, Marigold, and Melina, but I get them out of earshot before yet another foul-mouthed contraction can begin. You can tell everyone is in a heightened state of concern. Mum doesn't object when I order her out of the room, and Dad doesn't even try to look at Laura's boobs—for what must be the first time in history.

Throwing a couple of out-of-date magazines their way and promising to provide them with regular updates, I once again enter the pit of the demon.

With my hand once more turning purple and having the life crushed out of it, I try my level best to help Laura through this ordeal—willing the baby inside her to hurry up and be born.

Finally . . . *finally*, Marigold utters the words we've been desperate to hear. "It's time. You're ten centimetres dilated. Time to have a baby."

"Excellent!" I crow. "About time, too. This has been bloody awful!"

Marigold and a couple of orderlies wheel Laura out of the room and down to the birthing suite while Melina very graciously stays behind to help me off the floor where I've collapsed, having just been punched in the testicles.

LAURA'S DIARY

Monday, December 2 continued . . .

The best way I can describe labour is like being on the biggest roller coaster in the world while someone is poking your uterus with a red hot egg whisk. I know every woman's labour is different, but if yours was anything like mine Mum, can I just say a heartfelt thank you for not throwing yourself out of the nearest window, and instead successfully giving birth to me.

My labour comes in waves. At first the swell is slow and the waves high, but as the minutes and hours go by, the sea gets choppier, the waves come crashing in much harder and faster, and before you know it the coastguard is putting out severe weather warnings.

In the end, I was *extremely* lucky and had a short labour of eight hours. I have no idea how women go through twenty-plus hours of that shit. It was the most unpleasant few hours of my life—at least since we went to see *Avatar* and got stuck in a traffic jam on the way home.

I have to confess that the pain may have made me just a *tad* difficult to be around. I know that's hard to believe, but the lack of an epidural to help with the hideous contractions left me feeling somewhat *testy*. There's every chance I *may* have let a few swearwords slip. Just a few.

I can't really describe the chaotic mixture of thoughts and emotions that whirled around my head as they took me to the room where I'd deliver the baby. Terror, relief, panic, excitement, dread, exhaustion . . . and a slight worry that I may never be able to have *more* children, thanks to the knockout punch I'd just administered to Jamie's testicular region.

"Right then!" Marigold orders as I'm wheeled into place next to a series of machines I hope I'm not going to need. "Feet up, legs wide apart!"

I do as I'm bid. Where's Dr. Abbotson? I wonder. My obstetrician should be here. I know he's busy and has left much of the fun to Marigold, but I'd like him here at least as backup when this delivery occurs. As if on command, Abbotson appears, shouldering a very pained-looking Jamie Newman. My husband is leaning on the little man so much it's making him wilt. Any minute now the doctor who's supposed to bring my child into the world is going to collapse from having to haul around 170 pounds of Newman senior.

"Nearly there, Mr. Newman," Abbotson says in a soothing voice.

It's me he's supposed to be using the soothing voice on! I scream in the vaults of my mind as I go into yet another contraction.

"Let's get you over to your wife," he continues and helps Jamie—who is still clutching his groin—to a place beside my bed. "There we are. Alright there are we?"

Who cares if he's alright, you silly bastard! I'm the one about to push six pounds of humanity out of me!

"Yeah," Jamie says with a wince. "That's great doc. Thanks for your help. Maybe after this you could find me a painkiller?"

"Excuse me!" I bellow. "I hate to break this up, but I'm having a fucking baby here!"

Abbotson blinks in surprise, perhaps realising for the first time his main reason for existing. Instead of addressing me, he looks at Marigold. "How is she doing?"

"All fine," Marigold tells him with a wave of her hand. "She's ten centimetres dilated."

"Excellent!" Abbotson squats between my legs. "Okay, Mrs. Newman, I'm going to ask you to start pushing now."

This is it. I'm going to have a baby. The moment that I have been inexorably moving towards since that fateful condomless night has arrived.

Ohshitohshitohshitohshitohshitohshitohshitohshitohshitohshitohshitohshitohshit.

It is, without doubt, the worst experience of my life. I'm sure you're expecting me to follow up with something trite like, *but also the best experience of my life*, aren't you? Yeah, I don't bloody think so.

Don't get me wrong, I'm very pleased with the baby I ended up with, but I'd cheerfully forego the joy of bringing another one into this world if it means I don't need to have my vagina sewn together again—if that's okay with everybody?

I can't tell you how long the birth took. Jamie says it was no more than ten minutes. To me it felt like ten years. Ten years of burning, stinging, pressure, straining, sweating, crying, screaming, clenching, ripping, and shitting.

Yes indeed, childbirth really is a *miracle*, isn't it? I'd love to tell you that hearing my daughter cry for the first time lit up my eyes and my heart, washing away all the pain and exhaustion. The truth is I barely registered it to begin with. I was too busy crying my brains out on Jamie's shoulder.

My head stayed buried there while they took care of cutting away the umbilical cord and the afterbirth. This was the part I'd read about with horror in all the maternity books I'd devoured in the first few months of being pregnant, and I was more than happy to let them get on with it while I pretended I was on a deserted beach somewhere.

It's a very nice beach indeed—all swaying palms and glistening white sands. A gentle breeze blows through my hair, and the waves roll against the shore with a soft sigh. The extremely large glass of pinot grigio I have in my hand reflects the bright golden sunlight beautifully. Here, there is no pain, no blood, and definitely no excrement. Sadly, this is only the most temporary of vacations. I could've stayed here for at least another week, but the real world has other plans for me, the utter bastard.

Eventually, my wits start to regather themselves. The awful, awful pain is mercifully starting to recede, though I still feel like my nether regions have been run over by a combine harvester. Through the fug of bone-deep weariness I hear the high, sharp sound of a baby crying. For a second there's a complete disconnect.

Where's that baby? I think. *Can't its mother get it to shut up? I'm trying to enjoy this beach.*

Then it hits me . . . *I'm* its mother.

I'm *her* mother.

"Hey girl?" I hear Marigold say in the softest voice she's used around me. "You want to hold your baby now?"

Yes. Yes, I do.

A sudden upswell of tears rises from the depths of my being, and now I start to cry with a combination of relief, awe—and not a little pride, if I'm being honest. I take the very small package into my arms, feeling the undeniable weight of new existence through every fibre of my being.

In a second I will look at Jamie and bring him back into my life, but just for now—just for this briefest of moments—I want it to be just me and her. Me and the baby I've created. The single most important act I have accomplished in all my years on this planet. I look into her eyes and she looks into mine. We both stop crying and share a connection for the first time that will not be broken for the rest of our lives. It is, without doubt, the first time I have ever felt such peace and contentment.

"Her head's a bit lumpy," observes Jamie from beside us, "and I've seen fewer wrinkles on a wet bulldog."

I should probably be angry at my husband for ruining the moment, but I'm not. In fact, as I look up at his creased brow, I can't help but start to laugh.

"Angelica?"

"No."

"Caitlin?"

"No."

"Veronica?"

"No."

"Imelda?"

"No."

"Cathy?"

"No."

"Brunhilda?"

I know full well that my husband is trying to get a rise out of me, but I'm not having it. I only woke from a much needed three hours' sleep thirty minutes ago, and I'm determined not to have the peaceful haze in my brain washed away by his idiotic name suggestions.

"No."

"Consuela?"

"No."

"Marigold?"

"Very funny."

Jamie, sensing his attempts at ribaldry are failing miserably, lapses into silence.

I watch him pick at the bedsheet for a few seconds. Something is obviously going through that warped head of his, and I fold my arms waiting for whatever new witticism is clawing its way to the front of his cerebellum.

"Er . . ." he begins.

"Yes?" I encourage.

"I have got one sensible suggestion."

I cock my head. This is an interesting development. "Go on?"

"Well, you never knew my gran, did you?"

"No."

"No. She died six years ago."

"I know, Jamie." This calls for a softening of demeanour. I know Jamie well enough to tell when he's switched to serious mode.

"Well, I never really talked to you about her much, but I really loved my gran."

My blood runs cold. *He's going to say he wants to call our daughter after his grandmother.* This would be a lovely gesture, and one I'd be happy to get behind given that I can't think of a name for love nor money; but Jamie's gran was called Ethel. I can't have a daughter called Ethel.

Ethel Newman? Everyone will think we named her after a movie star from the thirties.

Jamie sees the look on my face. "No! I don't mean that. Give me a second to explain."

"Alright."

"Well, I used to visit gran a lot when I was a kid, and one of the things I loved to do was play with her little Jack Russell dog."

"Are you about to suggest we name our child after a bloody dog?"

"Um . . . yeah, I am."

"Jamie! Of all the stupid things I've heard you come out with—"

"The dog was called Poppy. I thought it sounded nice. Poppy Newman."

Oh crap, it's perfect. Sweet, musical, and happy. I'm going to have to name my firstborn after a small yapping mutt.

"I love it," I tell him, placing a hand on his arm.

"You do? Only I thought you'd just laugh it off 'cause it was a dog's name."

"Not anymore it's not. Now it's our daughter's."

Jamie breaks into a beautiful smile. "Brilliant! It's settled, then. Our baby's name is Poppy Lady Gaga Newman!"

He manages to skip out of the way before I can swing the bedpan across his head.

And there we have it.

Poppy Newman sleeps soundly at the end of my bed while I sit here writing in this diary—which is rapidly becoming more dog-eared than a chew toy, it has to be said.

Jamie is currently doing the rounds, letting people know about the birth, which I'm rather grateful for as it's giving me some time to cultivate and nurture the reflective mood I've been in since the birth.

I feel like I'm at a crossroads in my life. In many ways the Laura Newman who used to exist was replaced the instant I locked eyes with little Poppy for the first time in the delivery room. I went from an independent woman—one who spent far too much time worrying about what shoes go with which handbag—to a new mother, with more responsibility than she's ever had before. I also have a newfound sense of purpose to my life that's been missing since the chocolate shop closed down.

I still have my career dreams and aspirations, of course, but these ambitions are now joined by the overwhelming desire to bring up a well-rounded, stable human being who will feel loved and wanted each and every day of her life. I have no idea which one will be harder to achieve . . . but I can take a bloody good guess.

In a second I'm going to close this diary and shuffle down the bed to look at Poppy.

I find this to be an extremely satisfying pastime. I could literally stand for hours watching my daughter sleep, her tiny eyes twitching as she experiences whatever innocent dreams newborn babies have.

Poppy has a name card on the front of her cot. It has her first name and surname of course; but she also has a middle name now. The only middle name she could ever have had.

My daughter is Poppy Helen Newman. She is named for a small bouncy dog I never had the chance to meet—and for the mother who was taken from me far, far too soon.

I love you with all my heart, Mum. And even though she is barely out of the womb and still can't use her arms and legs properly, I know Poppy Newman does too.

Your tearful and hazy daughter, Laura

xxx

JAMIE'S BLOG
Tuesday 10 December

This has been the worst week of my life. I looked in the mirror just now and a ghost looked back at me.

After only two days on this earth, Poppy caught pneumonia. It was the single most terrifying thing I've ever had to endure. At first, everything was fine. She seemed healthy and happy. Laura and I took turns holding her as often as possible. In many ways she was more football than baby, the amount of times she was passed around parents, friends, relatives, and the staff of the hospital.

I can't express how scary it is to have a new born baby to deal with. There's so much to remember and none of it comes instinctively. You'd think that wouldn't be the case, wouldn't you? After all, the human race has been having babies for quite a while now. You'd imagine that after all this time we'd developed an innate sense of how to care for one the second it pops out of the womb.

This has not been the case with Laura and me. Even the simple act of holding Poppy correctly is far more complicated and odd than I expected it to be. I haven't been that nervous about holding something since I went on that God-awful clay pigeon–shooting date with Wendy. The first time I held Poppy, every time she so much as twitched in my arms, my heart started to race and I was convinced she was going to leap out of my grasp at any second and brain herself on the nearest piece of hospital furniture.

Then there's the issue of nappy changing. The process isn't that complicated, but my God it takes some getting used to. And I'm not just talking about the smell. You'd think I'd have no trouble handling a creature barely out of the womb and unable to do much more than lie on her back, but the process of getting a nappy on her still took me a good ten minutes the first time I tried it. It then took me another ten minutes to put it back on again after I'd realised it was back to front.

Laura's better at all this than me—though not by much. She still fumbles the nappy change a fair bit, and every time Poppy's head falls back on her arms she emits a hiss of terror and gives me a look filled with perplexed doubt. Neither of us felt particularly comfortable with the first forty-eight hours of baby ownership. None of the books, DVDs, or magazines prepare you for just how confusing and alien the whole thing can be. We were delighted to have a new daughter to play with, but the instructions that came with her might as well have been in Chinese and written on the back of a postage stamp.

While we were deeply unsure of ourselves, at least Poppy appeared to be healthy and suffering no adverse effects from our intrinsic lack of parenting skills. Then last Tuesday evening we noticed she'd started breathing rapidly, and there was a hoarse sound at the back of her throat that sounded quite awful. We did what any new parents would do in this situation—we panicked.

Babies are so very vulnerable at this early age that anything can be life-threatening, so even a cold could do serious damage that a baby of six months would shrug off easily. The female doctor on call examined Poppy while Laura and I held hands. I could feel Laura's nails biting into my palm.

"I'm going to get Poppy to the ICU immediately," she said in a grave voice.

"What's wrong with her?" my wife said. I've never heard Laura Newman sound so lost and scared.

"Her chest sounds congested and her breathing isn't good. There's a chance it's pneumonia," the doctor said matter-of-factly.

Ultimately, it was a diagnosis that probably saved Poppy's life.

Oh God, I'm so tired right now I can't remember the doctor's name. I'll have to ask Laura about it when she wakes up. How awful is that? I can't even remember the name of the person who saved my daughter.

Poppy was placed in the ICU in an incubator. I can't express how horrific it is to look in through a plastic box at your baby, unable to do anything to help her. All Laura and I could do was wring our hands as the hospital staff went about the business of administering as many antibiotics as was safe for a two-day-old baby.

"We'll monitor her from here," the doctor told us where we stood staring in at Poppy's still form. "With luck, the antibiotics will start to kill the infection quickly, and we'll see an improvement."

"What if there *isn't* an improvement?" I asked. The way the doctor let out a long, slow breath made me want to cry my fucking eyes out.

"We'll have to readdress the situation and decide on what further steps to take." She took another deep breath. "This is a serious condition for one so young, Mr. and Mrs. Newman. I'm not going to lie to you. But I think we caught it early, and Poppy is absolutely in the best place she can be right now."

And so began six days of utter darkness. A week in a thick, suffocating bubble, divorced from the outside world. Laura retreated into herself. I guess it was a defence mechanism and I can't blame her for it, but it left me feeling isolated from both her and my sick daughter.

Our friends rallied round to support us, of course—and we had my family as well. The absence of her mother weighed heavily on Laura, though, as I knew it would. I tried my hardest to make up for her absence, but it was no good.

I have to confess that I hated my mum a bit for her brittle relationship with Laura over the years. My wife needed maternal support, and my mother wasn't there for her thanks to the walls she'd built between them for no apparent reason—possibly other than the fact that Laura wasn't hand-picked by her to be my wife. It's at times like this I wish my mother was a bit warmer and wasn't such a control freak.

Thank God for the brilliant Melina. She and I have always had a good relationship, but we were never what you would consider close. Now, though, I would do anything for my wife's best friend. The support she gave Laura—talking with her, bringing Hayley in to play with her, sitting with her while she just stared into space—was incredible. I don't know what I would have done without her.

Also, I fostered an abject hatred of the Internet during the six days my daughter was under the shadow. The best thing about the Internet is that you can find information on any topic you desire. The *worst* thing about the Internet is that you can find information on any topic you desire . . .

I made the mistake one evening of typing "newborn baby pneumonia" into Google. The next hour was spent in an orgy of masochistic research that made me convinced my poor little baby was as good as dead. Wikipedia went from being a handy way to cheat at pub quizzes, to the Spectre of Death itself, whispering statistics and facts into my ears that tore my heart to pieces.

One failing of the human condition is that we always tend to pay more attention to the negative than the positive in dire situations like this, and I was no exception to that rule. I would gloss over the more positive articles about recovery rates in newborn babies, and dwell on the stories about how their delicate lungs cannot fight off the infection.

Never mind that these particular stories were generally about babies in third world countries, without access to the modern technology we in the UK hold so dear. Do you have any idea how hideous the term *infant mortality rate* is? Unless you've had a baby with a serious illness, you have no idea just how abhorrent those three words placed together truly are.

I should have called Marigold for a chat. She would probably have set me straight.

I was torturing myself and I knew it. It took all the strength I had to shut the laptop down and ignore the black voice at the back of my head, repeating that dreadful, dreadful phrase over and over:

Infant mortality rate. Infant mortality rate. Infant mortality rate.

The absolute low point was Friday night. Poppy had taken a turn for the worse. Her breathing was more laboured and she was barely moving in the incubator.

I'd gone to the toilet, leaving Laura standing in the ICU surrounded by the poor sick babies forced to spend the first few days and weeks of their lives in small plastic boxes. It was a stupid thing to do. Laura had been virtually silent for hours, and she hadn't eaten a thing for even longer. Leaving her even for a second in that place was a mistake I would hack off a limb to go back and rectify.

I returned to the ICU to see my wife with her hands pressed up against the incubator. She was breathing rapidly.

"Laura?" I said approaching her. "Baby? What are you doing?"

"Wake up," she said in a low voice.

"She can't hear you honey." I took her by the arms and tried to pull her away, but I couldn't move her an inch. A feverish heat boiled from her skin, and I could see the veins in her hands popping out from beneath the surface.

"Wake up!" Laura said again, this time much louder. A couple of other babies in the room started to cry in lusty voices behind me.

"You need to come away now, Laura," I said, trying to be firm, but my voice cracked with stress and worry. Laura pushed me away and returned to stare at Poppy.

"Wake up, Poppy! Wake up now!" she virtually screamed.

I started to cry. "Please, Laura. Please calm down, baby. She can't hear you."

"For God's sake, Poppy, wake up!" Laura cried and hammered on the incubator. Poppy didn't stir.

Then she said something that shattered what was left of my heart.

"Don't die, honey. Please don't die, Poppy."

Jesus Christ, this is hard to write.

"Stay with me, Poppy." Laura's voice had dropped to barely a whisper. She turned to look at me. "What are we going to do, Jamie? What are we going to do?"

I had no words. Do you know how exquisitely painful that is? To not have any words of comfort for your distraught wife? The person you love more than anything else in the world? All I could do was put my arms around her and hope that would be enough. She cried then. For the first time since the diagnosis, she cried in my arms. In long, ragged, hitching breaths she let out the pain that had built inside her over the past few days.

I cried too, as I have never cried before. With our dear, sweet baby lying next to us, we cried for her, feared for her . . . and hoped for her. Looking back on it now I know it was a cathartic experience and a necessary one. But dear God, if you are up there, please never make me go through anything like that again.

Twenty-four hours later Poppy started to show signs of improvement. The fever was down, her breathing was becoming more regular, and there was a better flush of pink to her complexion.

People say a week is a long time in politics. These people have no *fucking idea* what they are talking about. They should try twenty-four hours with a sick baby. With Poppy's recovery came the recovery of her parents as well. We both managed to sleep properly for the first time in days. I was out for a full twelve hours—and awoke to be told that Poppy was also awake, and not bloody happy about being imprisoned in a big plastic box. The turnaround was quite remarkable. From a listless grey shape, to a vibrating pink ball of anger, my daughter was proving the effectiveness of modern antibiotics in no uncertain terms.

Have you ever sat round with a bunch of friends and completed one of those personality quizzes? You know the sort: What's your favourite place in the world? What's your favourite time of day? What's your favourite swear word? That kind of crap. Well, I can safely say that if I ever have to answer the question: What's your favourite sound? I will be able to answer very easily, by simply stating, "My daughter crying after a bout of pneumonia."

By Monday it was like she'd never had an infection at all.

"It's quite incredible," Dr. Abbotson said to us after a routine examination. "Poppy's recovery has been lightning fast. You have a very special little girl here."

And that's when the "dad gene" kicked in for the first time. This is the part of a man's genetic make-up that convinces him his child is leagues above anyone else's. If the child in question is male, this sense of overweening pride usually kicks in when the little sod starts playing football (if he's any good at it, of course). If the kid is female, it can be a little harder for a man to judge his daughter's worth against other girls, considering he has no idea what the rules of netball are. Therefore, a father must grasp any indication of his daughter's brilliance whenever he can find it—at whatever age.

Well, yeah! Of course she recovered quickly. She's my *daughter!*

Chest puffed out with ridiculous pride I looked in at Poppy . . . who gave me the finger. I kid you not. I looked at one podgy little hand and I could swear that just for a second she curled her fingers up bar the middle one and flipped her father the bird. It appears that from now on I will have not one but two women ready, willing, and able to deflate my pomposity at a moment's notice.

"Did she just flip you off?" Laura asked incredulously, before erupting into laughter . . . which, it turns out, is the second best sound in the world.

So here I sit, a few hours after Poppy gave me the finger, having recovered from what could have been a fatal bout of pneumonia. Life is never *ever* predictable, no matter what the movies try to tell you. I really should be asleep again. The twelve hours obviously weren't enough and I'm finding it very hard to type, but I knew I had to get all this down as quickly as possible while it's raw. I have a tendency to sugarcoat the hard stuff if I'm given enough time to think about it, and the past week deserves to be retold in all its unvarnished glory. Otherwise I'd feel like I was somehow cheating my daughter.

Does that make any sense at all, or am I just so messed up at the moment I'm coming out with complete rubbish? That's how I feel, though. Poppy went through hell the past few days, so the least I can do is pour out my pain on the page properly.

Now that horrible job is done, I have a warm, soft wife sleeping peacefully by my side, so I'm ending this post with a hearty thank you for sparing Poppy to whatever gods may be out there. I would have been beyond devastated to lose her, even if she does like flipping me the bird.

Judith Searle. That was the doctor's name who saved my daughter's life. I asked Laura this morning. I can safely say that I owe her my life. She is one of the most important people in the world, and I thank her from the bottom of my heart.

LAURA'S DIARY
Monday, January 13

Dear Mum,

There are times—not very often, but every once in a while—when I despair for the future of the human race. With Poppy now in my life, I wonder why I took the decision to bring a child into this world, which is so chock-a-block with complete idiots it's hard to see how anything gets done.

My latest chance to revel in the stupidity of my fellow man came a couple of days ago when I opened a letter that had just dropped onto the doormat. Jamie was still fast asleep upstairs, thanks to the promise he made to himself all week to sleep in on Saturday morning, and I was preparing to give Poppy her first feed after dawn, when the letterbox rattled. I was quite startled as the Saturday morning post has been coming later and later recently, as if the postman was seeing how annoyed he could make his customers without getting a complaint levelled against him.

Shuffling down the hall yawning my head off, I pick up the long, brown envelope and look at the back. It's from the Registrar of Births & Deaths, so either a distant relative has fallen off this mortal coil and left me a load of cash (highly unlikely) or Poppy's birth certificate has finally arrived. Jamie was meant to sort this out weeks ago, but as ever his sieve-like memory let him down time and time again. I was forced to hide his PlayStation 3 controller until he got off his arse and drove down to the registry office.

This is a rather unlovely aspect of having a baby that doesn't occur to you at first—the bloody paperwork. There're forms to fill out for the doctors, the hospital, the local government—and any other organisation or person that has a vested interest in keeping tabs on your newborn baby. I've always hated filling in forms, so getting Poppy officially registered as a human being required the patience of Job.

With another huge yawn I open the letter, and with bleary eyes begin to read the certificate.

Ten seconds later I'm storming up the stairs, waving the certificate in front of me and shouting my gormless husband's name at the top of my voice.

"What? What?" he exclaims in a sluggish voice as I sit myself down on the bed, ready to sally forth with a ticking off of no uncertain proportions.

I suddenly remember I have a baby in the house and look over to where Poppy is blissfully unaware of her mother's newfound apocalyptic rage and is sleeping like a log. I throw back the bed clothes and grab Jamie under one arm.

"Downstairs . . . now!" I hiss in his ear.

Giving him no time to reply—or scratch his balls, a morning ritual I will never get used to seeing—I heave him out of the bedroom and down into the lounge.

"Read!" I command, thrusting the certificate at his puffy face.

"What?" he repeats, brain not entirely caught up with his body yet. I stand and tap my foot while he stretches, yawns, and scratches his balls. This appears to kick start his cerebral cortex. "Why do you want me to read this now, woman? I need a piss."

"Just read it, Jamie," I seethe.

"Alright, alright." He takes the certificate and scans down it. "Seems fine to me."

"Read it again," I say in clipped, even tones.

He does so, brow knitted in concentration. Getting to the end he shrugs his shoulders. "Nothing wrong with it as far as I can see. What's your problem?"

I let out a huff of exasperated air. "For a guy who writes for a living, you're not great at proofreading are you?" I stab the part where our daughter's name is recorded. "Read *that bit* again."

Jamie does so, and I am rewarded with his face turning ashen.

"You see the bloody problem now, Captain Observant?"

He looks up with wide eyes and nods slowly.

The reason for Jamie's shock and my towering rage is quite simple. Where Poppy Helen Newman's name should be written in clear, legible font, it instead reads POOPY HELEN NEWMAN. A small mistake in terms of lettering—an enormous one for my daughter's future if we can't get it rectified.

"They got the name wrong," Jamie says.

"You fucking think so?" I rage. "I give you one simple task Jamie Newman, and you still messed that up!"

"It's not my fault!"

"The kids at school will call her Shitty Newman, you know that don't you?"

"I said it's not my fault!"

"Or Poo-head. They'll call her Poo-head." I point a finger. "Is that what you want Jamie? Our daughter to be called Poo-head until she reaches college?"

"I filled the form in right Laura!"

"Did you?"

"Yes!" Jamie pantomimes writing something down. "Poppy Helen Newman, I wrote. I even double-checked it."

"And yet, Jamie, we now appear to have a daughter named after the act of taking a dump."

"They must have fucked it up at the office."

"You think that's likely, do you? You think it's more likely that a government organisation has made a gigantic fuckup than you have?"

I realise what I'm saying. *Of course* it's more likely a government organisation has fucked up. This is Britain!

"Yeah . . . you see it wasn't me!" Jamie says triumphantly.

I offer him the pointy finger again. "You're not off the hook yet, pal," I tell him and stalk over to the phone. Then I remember it's Saturday and there will be no bugger answering for two days.

For two whole days my poor little baby—who has already been through a bout of life-threatening illness—will have the indignity of being called Poopy Newman. I know her parents are no strangers to embarrassing toilet-related incidents thanks to some chicken well past its sell-by date, but I hardly think that warrants being named after the disastrous night in question.

We should have just called her Fajita Newman and been done with it.

Needless to say I was on the phone at precisely one second past nine this morning:

"Good morning, Registrar of Births & Deaths."

"Morning. I want to speak to somebody about a fuckup."

"Pardon me?"

"A fuckup, madam."

"Can I have your name please?"

"Laura Newman. Please make sure you write that down carefully. I don't want people thinking my name is Paula."

"Excuse me?"

"Never mind. I'm calling about a mistake on my baby's birth certificate."

"What kind of mistake?"

"Her name is Poppy. You have called her Poopy."

"What?"

"Poopy. For some reason known only to you and your colleagues, you have decided to brand my innocent little baby with the name Poopy for the rest of her natural days. Why would you do that?"

"I can assure you we wouldn't, Mrs. Newman."

"Oh really? The only other explanation is that your office is run by a bunch of lazy incompetent morons. Surely *that* can't be true, though, so I can assume you're out to get my daughter?"

"No one is out to get your daughter, Mrs. Newman."

"So you are a bunch of incompetents then?"

"That's not what I said. Look, I'll have to put you on hold for a moment."

You don't need money, don't take fame, don't need a credit card to ride this train. It's strong and it's sudden and it can be cruel at times. But it might just save your life. That's the power of love! Oooh, that's the powwwwer of love!

"Hello, Mrs. Newman?"

"Yes."

"My name is Peter Neville, I'm the senior clerk here. You say you have a problem with your baby's birth certificate?"

"Yep. Her name is Poopy. Why is she called Poopy, Mr. Neville? Was it your idea? Do you get some thrill at naming children after bodily functions? Is there perhaps another poor unfortunate wandering around with the name Jizzum Bloggs? Or possibly Mucus Jones?"

"Come now, Mrs. Newman."

"No, *you* come now, Mr. Neville . . . er, I didn't mean that. Look, my daughter's name is wrong on her birth certificate and I want it changed!"

"That's impossible, Mrs. Newman. We are very careful with names here. Whatever was put on the form is the name that is registered."

"Then my husband is a pillock."

"That may be the case, Mrs. Newman."

"It may be, but I don't think I'm quite willing to let things go at your end, Mr. Neville. Can you find the original form my husband filled out? It's important for the future of my marriage and his genitals."

"Already being located, Mrs. Newman. My associate Miss Penrose is looking for it as we speak."

"Good. I'd like this cleared up as soon as possible. I can hear Poopy waking up and I need to go change her."

"Aha! Here we are. Here is the form your husband filled out and I can see that—"

"Mr. Neville?"

"I am so very, very sorry, Mrs. Newman. It does appear that the error has been made by one of our staff. I'll just need to put you on hold again for a moment."

It's hip to be square . . . Here, there, and everywhere . . . Hip, hip, so hip to be square. Here, there, and everywhere . . . Hip, hip, soooo hip to be square—

"Hello, Mrs. Newman?"

"Is that the Huey Lewis greatest hits album? Only I meant to buy it for Jamie last month and I can't find it anywhere."

"I'm sorry?"

"Never mind, what have you got to tell me, Mr. Neville?"

"As I said, I'm so very sorry for the error and the inconvenience. We'll make sure the name is changed on Poopy's certificate—"

"*Poppy's* certificate."

"Indeed! Poppy's certificate, and we'll have a new one sent out to you immediately. I'm so sorry for the inconvenience. This really is something that shouldn't be allowed, Mrs. Newman. In all the years I've been senior clerk, nothing like this has ever happened before."

"Are you crying, Mr. Neville?"

"No, no. I have hay fever."

"In January?"

"Yes. It's a very rare type."

"It must be. Perhaps you're allergic to snow."

"I really am most definitely sorry for the inconvenience, Mrs. Newman."

"You already said that, but thank you very much Mr. Neville. With any luck I won't need to call you again. Unless I have another child and you end up changing its name to Urine."

So we now wait for the second birth certificate to come through. This one had better be correct or I'll be sending a harshly worded letter to my local politician. Delivered via Peter Neville's rectal passage.

Love and miss you, Mum.

Your still quite irate daughter, Paula

xxx

JAMIE'S BLOG

Friday 28 March

Sleep. Dear, sweet sleep.

Once you were my constant companion, there for me whenever I needed you. I would be tired, and you would take me in your warm embrace, ushering me into a wonderful land of dreams from which I would awake refreshed and ready to go about my day. But you have deserted me, sleep. No longer constantly at my side, no longer there whenever I need you. I have another companion now. Her name is Poppy Newman, and there is every chance she is going to drive me crazy.

We were lulled into a false sense of security at the hospital and in the first few days of having Poppy at home. All she seemed to do was sleep. We got through nights with barely a peep out of her. Oh, she would wake up and Laura would breastfeed her, but it was only once every five or six hours—and we were still bathed in the novelty of the whole thing, anyway.

Her gentle cries would wake us from slumber and Laura would take care of it. This meant I didn't have to do a damn thing, plus I got a look at my wife's enormous boobs. Such was the novelty of having Poppy that we'd often conduct random checks of her during the night anyway, just to have an excuse to look down at her. There we'd stand at one in the morning—arms wrapped around one another and doe-eyed expressions on our faces as we watched Poppy dream her little baby dreams. I look back on those days now, and it takes a great deal of self-control not to throw up on myself.

All in all, then, things were going just *fine*. They continued to be that way well after the initial novelty of being a parent had worn off a tad. It looked like Poppy was going to be one of those babies who slept a lot and went through the night on a regular basis.

Then a few days ago, Laura stopped breastfeeding. This was very early in Poppy's life but also quite necessary. "She's ripping my nipples to shreds," Laura said last week. "It's uncomfortable, painful, and I'm sick of having to flop a tit out in public. I keep expecting either to be arrested or perved on at any moment. I'm fed up with it." And that was that. Boobs out, bottles in.

This is when my life became a living nightmare. My daughter was not going to be the type of baby that slept calmly through the night. Not by a fucking long shot. Poppy did not take kindly to being taken off the breast. Not kindly at all.

She's started to wake more frequently at night and lets you know about it in no uncertain terms. I have to share the job of feeding her as well, now, thanks to Laura deciding to go the bottle route. Any last lingering doe-eyed happiness about being a parent was blasted into the ether the first night we put Poppy to bed after bottle–feeding her.

Poppy usually waits until we are both asleep before turning herself into a mini-air-raid siren. This is the signal for a bleary-eyed in-bed argument to begin.

"Is your turn, Jamie."

"No. No. Sleepin'. Your turn."

"I did . . . last one."

"Liar. Ow! Don' kick me inner balls, woman!"

"Ge' Poppy or I'll do it again."

Depending on who wins the argument (usually Laura as my extremities are more delicate than hers), one of us will then shuffle out of bed and over to Poppy's crib . . . where the little cow will instantly shut up. The second she sees your face looming over the side of the cot, the tears dry up and she gives you a look of beatific innocence. You stand there and wait for her to start crying again, but after a good thirty seconds it seems she's shut up for good.

Until you turn your back and head to bed, that is. As soon as the duvet is wrapped around your freezing body, the screaming starts again. It's as if Poppy is conducting some kind of horrific social experiment that will likely result in me losing my mind and bludgeoning myself to death with the nearest feeding bottle.

What generally follows is anything between ten minutes and three hours of walking up and down and patting a grizzling baby while trying not to trip over the furniture and the plethora of brightly coloured plastic crap that is Poppy's collection of baby toys. From the amount of time Laura and I spend doing this, I'm starting to believe my daughter is actually the next step in human evolution.

We are now evolving into a species that no longer needs sleep, one that can function quite happily without all that bother of having to get their heads down for a kip. As far as I can tell, in the last week Poppy has slept for about forty-three minutes in total. That's what it feels like to me, anyway, as I stand in the half-light of dawn, looking out of the patio doors, and wishing a massive aneurism would strike me down just so I could get some decent rest.

If the zombie apocalypse ever does occur, the undead will have a problem differentiating me from their rotting brethren, given the state I'm in these days. I look and feel like hammered shit. It only took seven days—seven days!—of my daughter's nightly screaming sessions to reduce me from a productive member of society to a shambling misfit barely able to tie his own shoelaces.

Laura is handling it better than me, but then Laura hasn't come to the end of her maternity leave yet and can take naps during the day when the baby is asleep. Me? I get the pleasure of going to work each and every day on about two hours' sleep. You can imagine how enjoyable that is.

I can't be sure, but I think the lack of decent rest may be affecting my work. For instance, I spent a quarter of an hour on Wednesday trying to spell the word *collision*. I just could not remember how many *l*'s it has in it. Or *i*'s for that matter. It didn't once occur to me to look at a dictionary, so I took half-hearted stabs at it, hoping my subconscious would break through the murk of exhaustion and throw up the correct spelling. I came up with *collusion*, *collection*, *collegic*, and *collagen* before settling for *colllisiion* and moving on before my right eye burst in its socket.

Yesterday, in another example of my shattered state—this one featuring expensive damage to property—I arrived twenty minutes late at the office, even though I'd driven into the parking lot at work on time. The reason for the long delay between parking lot and desk was quite simple: I crashed the bloody car.

That may be going overboard somewhat, but I definitely did damage to the poor old Ford, which was already sporting several dents and scratches thanks to the headlong rush to the hospital when Poopy was born.

Yes, I know her name is Poppy, but ever since that fuckup with the birth certificate I'm finding it very hard to shake calling her Poopy. It just seems so apt. All she does all day is poop. I'll have to get out of the habit soon, though, otherwise I'll be calling her Poopy at her university graduation, which I assume won't go down well at all.

The car crash was the direct result of my lack of sleep, needless to say.

The brain (especially mine) needs that eight hours a night to recharge its batteries. Not getting the required amount of slumber can leave you as fuzzy-headed as if you'd just smoked three joints in a row. I'd been driving to work every day, feeling more spaced-out than Captain Kirk, but until yesterday I'd managed it without causing me or anyone else any harm. Having Radio 1 blaring at top volume helps. There's nothing like the grating screech of Lady Gaga singing about her vagina to keep you wide awake at seven thirty in the morning.

On this particular morning, though, I'd had a week of this lack of sleep and my batteries were dead. Not even Gaga, Rihanna, and Kesha all singing about their vaginas could have kept me alert as I swung the car into the lot and drove to my parking space.

Space. That's the key word we have to think about at this juncture. More specifically, Jamie Newman's ability to comprehend space (and indeed distance) accurately on a total of nine hours' sleep over the past five days.

My parking space at the paper is towards the back of the parking lot (naturally) and backs up to an abandoned building, where they used to store the huge rolls of paper. It's now used by the local rats as a brothel. Usually, it's very easy to pull my car into the space, leaving an adequate distance between bumper and wall. Not today, though.

From where I sit, hands clenched on the steering wheel and brow creased, the idea of completing this simple task—one that I've easily managed hundreds of times before—seems totally beyond me. The space looks *tiny*. There doesn't seem to be any way I can get the Ford parked without scraping it down the side of the Smart car to one side and the Nissan Juke to the other. I edge the car forward as slowly as possible, a grimace on my face. Tectonic plates have shifted faster than I'm moving the Ford into position. It's frankly amazing that moss doesn't start to grow on the dashboard in the time it takes me to park the bloody thing.

I put the handbrake on very carefully, and for a moment I think I've done a good job. The Ford is in its space and all is well. Except when I get out of the car I discover that there's actually a good three feet between bumper and wall, with the arse end sticking out so far into the lane it would be impossible for anyone to get past. It takes me a few seconds to digest this. How could I have parked so badly? It took me six months to do it, after all. I get back in and gingerly start to move the car forward again, slowly moving closer to the wall and—

Smash!

What I thought was *gingerly* in fact turns out to be *far too fucking fast, you moron*. What I thought was a delicate touch on the accelerator turns out to be the kind of foot to the floor aggression that Lewis Hamilton uses every time the red lights go out. The Ford comes to an immediate halt with a crunch, and my head jerks painfully forward. Then the airbag goes off, punching me in the face just as I've come to terms with my new whiplash.

"Ohhfurglebassacunn!" I muffle into the airbag before it deflates. I put a hand up to what is now a lovely new nosebleed and try to staunch the flow. Luckily, there are some tissues in the glove box, and I roll a couple up, sticking them in my nostrils to prevent the blood from escaping, while I get out and survey the damage to the car. It sounded worse than it actually was, thank goodness, and while there will be an expensive trip to the garage to fix the bumper and replace the airbag, the grill, lights, and front of the car have escaped relatively unscathed. This is good, as I'm running pretty low on money right now thanks to Poopy's never-ending demand for nappies.

Picture the scene in your head, if you will: Jamie Newman, standing by his crumpled car, hair in a messy thatch, suit creased to high heaven, shirt untucked, shoes unpolished, face of haggard aspect thanks to no sleep, and two long strands of man-sized tissue emanating from each nostril—both going a healthy shade of red from the top down.

Now I have a multiple-choice question for you: Who do you think appears on the scene right at this moment to confront Newman in his current state?

A) Janice, the friendly parking lot attendant, who is always nice to Newman every time he sees her and is able to render much needed assistance and sympathy at this trying time?

B) Pete, a passing paramedic, who—by massive coincidence—is coming out of the newspaper building and is able to render much needed assistance and sympathy at this trying time?

C) Megan Fox, who—by *unbelievable* coincidence—is coming out of the newspaper building and is able to render much needed assistance, sympathy, and a sloppy, teeth-rattling blow job at this trying time?

D) David Keene, owner and CEO of the newspaper, who—by incredibly unlucky coincidence—is coming out of the newspaper building and is able to render a completely unneeded dressing down in the middle of the parking lot to one of his employees—whose had a car crash and no sleep for a week, and now has a throbbing headache thanks to the deployed airbag.

Those of you who have been reading my musings for some time will have automatically—and correctly—dismissed the first three choices as being the kind of things that only happen to other, more fortunate people.

"Good morning, Mr. Keene," I say from behind my man-sized tissue tusks when he's finally stopped berating me for looking so scruffy.

"What the bloody hell are you doing, Newman?"

My brain, already taxed to its limit by exhaustion, simply cannot conjure up a feasible excuse for this sorry scene, so I just stand there and make fish faces at Keene for a few seconds.

"Why have you got that stuff stuck up your nose?" he asks.

I struggle to think of the answer. "I . . . I didn't get that much sleep last night, sir." I tell him, completely out of context.

"Really? Is that because you kept jamming things up your nose?"

"What? Er . . . no, sir. My baby."

"Your *baby* kept jamming things up your nose?"

"No, no. I'm just . . . very, *very* tired, Mr. Keene."

I look a pathetic sight. Even David Keene, a man known for his cut-throat business practises and hard-nosed approach to every problem he encounters, can't stay angry at me. It would be like kicking a three-legged puppy with weepy eyes. His countenance softens and he puts a hand on my arm. "It's alright, Newman. I was a new father once as well. Is the little one keeping you up much?"

"Yes. She screams all the time at night. It's like living with an insomniac banshee."

Keene nods sympathetically. "Are you okay to work today, my boy?"

My bottom lip trembles. I'm a fully grown career professional, with an extensive client portfolio—and I'm about to start crying in front of my boss's boss. "I think so, sir. I just need some coffee and an aspirin."

Keene rifles in his pocket and produces a blister pack. "Here's some Advil. I can't help with the coffee, but the machine's working in the foyer."

I take the gift of painkillers with heartfelt gratitude. "Thank you."

"Not a problem."

Keene starts to walk away, back in the direction of his own car.

"Mr. Keene?" I call to him and he turns back. "Does it get any easier? Bringing up kids I mean?"

He responds with a snort of laughter. "*Easier*? Trust me, Newman. This *is* the easy part. You just wait until the little bastard starts moving around under its own steam. That's when your problems really begin!" He chuckles again and turns away for the final time.

I am left with the secure knowledge that I'm going to have to kill myself. Poopy's reign of terror is only just beginning.

Here's a tip if you're planning on having children any time in the near future: sleep as much as possible. Whenever and wherever you can. Luxuriate in your bed. Have enormous, satisfying lie-ins. If you think you've slept too much, just roll over for another half an hour and pull the covers over your head. Believe me; these pleasant memories will keep you going at three in the morning, when you're standing butt naked in the front room with a baby in your arms, rocking her gently to stop her from screaming the house down.

LAURA'S DIARY
Thursday, June 5

Dear Mum,

Believe it or not, it's actually possible to see the inside of your own eyelids—no, it really is. All you need to do is give birth to a baby who never sleeps for more than thirty-eight seconds at a time and spend six months in her company.

I can close my eyes now and see patterns swirling in the darkness. It's quite hypnotic. A lot of people say that when you're deprived of sleep over a long period of time it can lead to hallucinations. I can't say I've experienced this as yet. I even said as much to my new friend Barnabas the purple troll, who lives in the cupboard under the sink and drinks the bleach.

After Jamie's little accident at work I started to take on more of the nightly feeds. I felt it a better idea for me to walk around like one of the undead instead of him, considering I don't have to sit at a computer monitor all day to earn money. I get my maternity pay whether I'm awake or fast asleep, so it seemed the logical solution.

This, of course, makes me a complete *idiot*. I went from being able to function quite well on approximately six hours sleep to malfunctioning like a submerged toaster on three. Then Poppy started teething. It's quite amazing how you can think a baby has reached the absolute limits of her abilities to drive you insane but can then ramp it up another entire level thanks to the emergence of teeth.

I am quite sure my daughter is going to grow up to sing in a heavy metal band. I believe this partly due to her father's horrific taste in music, and partly because when she screams it sounds like the gates of hell have opened in the next room. I looked out of the window the other day to see a whole flock of starlings crash-land on the garden in a collective fit. The gargantuan sound waves coming from Poppy had scrambled their poor bird brains with disastrous consequences.

There must be ways of making money off my daughter's superhuman decibel levels, but I'm way too tired to think of any right now. I'm too tired to do much of anything other than sit and stare at walls until they become transparent.

Other than my new friend Barnabas and the ability to see through solid objects, I'm discovering that a marked lack of sleep leads to near apocalyptic levels of indecisiveness. I've always prided myself on being able to make a quick and well-informed decision about most things, but even this faculty has deserted me since I became the one in charge of getting up to service our maddened daughter's every whim at four in the morning. For instance, you would think that choosing between baked beans and minestrone soup for lunch would be easy. After all, it is merely a decision to either eat beans stewed in tomato sauce or a thick soup of Italian origin featuring a variety of vegetables and pasta. Simple, yes?

No. It transpires that this is a problem more complex and profound than the search for a unified theory of the universe. It is an issue of such magnitude that the argument over whether God exists is merely a trivial waste of time and effort by comparison. The beans, you see, have high fibre, which is good for my digestive system. However, they also give me chronic wind. The minestrone soup is probably the tastier choice, but it will probably contain thick chunks of onion. I don't like the texture of onion in my mouth, especially when it's in big chunks. Then we have the whole thorny issue of the bread that will be involved in either meal. On the one hand, if I have the beans I will have to toast the bread. Now I love a bit of toast, but I once read in the *Daily Mail* that burnt toast contains carcinogens. I also read that the country is falling apart thanks to Polish people being better at plumbing, so I'm not entirely sure of the article's accuracy, but I have a baby and shouldn't probably take any chances. On the other hand, I only like bread with lots of butter on it when I have minestrone soup. Butter contains a lot of calories and will make me fat. It probably causes cancer as well somehow, I'm sure—everything does these days. Up to and including breathing.

And thus, Laura Newman, university graduate, woman of the world, and twenty-first-century mother, spends nearly *an hour* agonising over whether to have baked beans or soup for lunch.

Governments have been toppled in less time than that. Thousands of people have been born or died. Stars are born in nebulas on the other side of the galaxy, creating magnificent firework displays that stretch across a million light years of space. Major and cataclysmic events that have shaped the world we live in have taken place over a shorter period of time than it takes me to decide whether I wanted to have the chronic farts or onion breath for the rest of the day. In the end panic overwhelmed me and I dumped both tins into a mixing bowl and ate the contents cold during two episodes of *Escape to the Country*. By the time the fat, rich couple from Milton Keynes had decided the seven-bedroom mansion by the river was the right house for them, I was farting merrily and my breath could peel wallpaper.

My common sense has also gone out the window thanks to the lack of rest and effective ear plugs. So much so, I made a dreadful mistake on Tuesday—and inadvertently stumbled on to something quite, quite horrific.

It was about ten thirty in the morning, and I was enjoying a cup of coffee during the thirty-eight seconds Poppy would be sleeping. I'm still not used to this lifestyle. Everyone I know is at work. I have no idea what to do with myself when not dealing with my incandescently angry daughter. I could watch some television, but the only thing on at this time of day is the kind of programming reserved for the mentally retarded. A host of insincere television presenters take turns poking a variety people from council housing estates until they explode and start eating the set. It's either that or a collection of mildly unattractive middle-aged women sitting around a coffee table complaining about something trivial.

I have no idea who watches this tripe, but I certainly wouldn't want to bump into them in the kitchenware aisle at Walmart any time soon. The only other viewing choice I have is the news, which is too depressing to contemplate. I don't need any more evidence of the failing economy than the closure of my lovely chocolate shop; and being the secular type, the situation in the Middle East just seems baffling and idiotic to me.

My only recourse of action during the day therefore, is to snatch a few moments of sleep here and there. This would work out fine were it not for the fact that Poppy is psychic. As soon as I slip into a temporary dreamless slumber, she's awake and bawling the house down again with her aching gums.

Such is the case on Tuesday, when I snap awake to the sound of my daughter screaming the house down, spilling coffee on my pyjamas. I stumble upstairs to the bedroom and pick up Poppy, wincing as she delivers an eardrum-splitting shriek right in my face. I start to massage her gums in the hope it might cool her down a bit, but with no luck. Then I try the teething gel I'd bought from the pharmacist. This doesn't seem to have any appreciable effect, either. If anything, having a gob full of nasty-tasting gel makes Poppy even angrier—and therefore even louder.

My only other choice at this point is to just rock her and hope she cries herself out.

Ha! Fat chance. Nearly an hour later she's still going for it in a big way. I now think that as well as a heavy metal singer, Poppy will also be a long-distance marathon runner, given her seemingly inexhaustible supplies of energy.

I have completely run out of options. My sleep-deprived brain cannot think of anything else to stop her. As it's mid-morning on a Tuesday, all the friends I would ring and ask for help are at work. Even Melina—the person I always turn to first on baby matters—isn't available. She's on holiday in Tenerife for the week, the utter bitch. I'm definitely not going to the doctor for advice. I just couldn't bear the humiliation. There's no one I can ask for help!

Then one name springs to mind, making me grimace. *Jane*. Jamie's mother. Without you here, Mum, she's the only parental unit who might be able to offer some advice. After all, she's raised three kids of her own, so she must have some nuggets of useful information tucked in that bear trap that passes for her mind.

My relationship with Jane has been incredibly strained ever since the night we announced the pregnancy. Jamie tried his best to mend fences for a while, but he gave up eventually, once he realised he was unlikely to succeed. The simple fact of the matter is some women just don't get on—and never will. There's no rhyme or reason to it; we just have the ability to rub each other the wrong way and create animosity that can never be overcome.

Jane is the second such person I've encountered in my life. The first being Susan Bleakley, who I first developed an instant dislike to at preschool. We ended up following each other right through to the end of our college years, and I still want to punch her in the face if ever I catch sight of her when I'm out shopping. The thing is, if you asked me to give a reason why we hate each other, I couldn't give you one—and neither could she. A similar situation exists between Jamie's mother and me. My calling her a bitch probably didn't help the situation, I have to admit. Nevertheless, on this particular Tuesday morning I'm desperate, so I pick up the phone and call her.

Bugger. No answer. Jane doesn't work, and Jamie's moaned on several occasions about her relaxed, carefree lifestyle courtesy of his father, so I have to wonder where she might be. As their house is only a ten-minute drive away (unfortunate in other circumstances, but handy today) I elect to take the gamble that Jane didn't hear the phone and strap Poppy into her car seat, intent on driving round to find her.

The car engine makes Poppy scream even more, so I spend ten minutes with my teeth gritted during the drive to the palatial five-bedroom house Jamie's mum and dad own near the waterfront, just outside the city. I pull into the driveway and am relieved to see Jane's car.

"Poppy?" I say to my red-faced daughter. "You stay here for a moment while Mummy just checks to see if Grandma's home, okay?" She can't understand a word I say, of course, but she responds anyway with a fresh bout of screaming. I'd never normally leave her in the car like this, but it'll take me mere moments to ring the bell—and I could frankly do with a few seconds of peace, if I'm honest.

At the front door there's no answer when I press the doorbell. I rattle the letterbox, with similar negative results. It seems very strange that Jane's car would be in the driveway but she would not be home. Jane drives everywhere. Michael Newman earns a damn good wage as a chiropractor, and she intends to spend every penny of it she can, damn it.

I trot round to the side of the house, open the gate, and wander through into the garden. I can still hear Poppy—and the driveway is very secluded—so I'm not worried about her being kidnapped by one of the hordes of paedophiles the papers keep telling us are hiding behind every bush in the neighbourhood.

"Jane?" I call, passing the heated swimming pool and rounding one corner of the massive house extension.

"Jane?" I repeat and reach the double doors. "Jane? Are you ho—"

Oh my God. Oh my actual God . . .

There are sights no person is meant to see. Visions of such magnificent terror it would quail the hearts of the gods themselves. A

German soldier sitting on the beach in Normandy on June 6, 1944, for instance, seeing the five thousand ships of the allied assault descending on him like the wrath of mankind. Or a Japanese woman tending her garden on March 11, 2011, seeing the wall of water created by the awful tsunami coming straight at her. How about an American businessman buying a bagel on a New York street on September 11, 2001, looking up to see a plane fly into the World Trade Center building? Or, the most horrific event of all, one that the world may never truly recover from: *Sex and the City 2.*

To these awful moments in human history please add Laura Newman looking through a patio door on this very day in history, seeing her sixty-three-year-old mother-in-law bent over a rattan sofa—her wrinkly arse exposed for the world to see, while a man twenty years her junior and dressed in neon Lycra thrusts into her from behind with a look of aggressive delight on his face.

I feel the universe shift on its axis. Existence itself teeters on the brink of an abyss. I must stop looking. I must turn away and run for my very life. I must leave before Jane looks up and sees me standing—

Oh fuck it, she already has.

I've never seen a woman move so fast. With a shriek that would rival one of Poppy's finest, Jane jerks upward. This produces an equally loud squeal of agony from her paramour, thanks no doubt to the fact his penis is bent back painfully as she does so.

Jane then pushes herself backwards, sending the muscle-bound squealer stumbling. He falls, crashing into the forty-inch plasma screen TV Michael Newman had bought as a treat to himself, because Jane hogs the fifty-inch LCD in the living room. Jane pulls up her trousers, her eyes never leaving my shocked, ashen face. She ignores Lycra boy's wholesale destruction of the conservatory and rushes in my direction.

My heart hammers in my chest. *She's going to murder me.* Without a doubt, Jane Newman is going to throw open her patio doors and come at me like an enraged honey badger. She does indeed throw open the patio doors, but I'm spared a hideous mauling. Instead, Jane tries to smile. She fails miserably. It looks more like someone's electrocuting her.

"Hello Laura!" she says in a voice several octaves above the norm.

"Jane," I answer warily. "What's going on?"

This is a bloody stupid thing to ask. It's obvious what's going on. Jane has been getting rather too friendly with her gym instructor. In fact, to borrow a rather unattractive phrase Jamie seems to enjoy trotting out just to irritate me every once in a while, the gym instructor was "balls deep and going for gold" in my mother-in-law—of this there is no doubt. I know it. Jane knows it. The gym instructor—whose penis I can still see poking out from the zipper in his Lycra shorts—knows it too.

Jane's face drops. "Oh God, Laura. Please don't tell Michael!" Her face drops even further. "*Please* don't tell Jamie! I beg you!"

Most of me is in deep shock. I'm still trying to process what I've just stumbled across, and the fact that Jane is begging me for mercy doesn't register for a few moments. I stare at her dumbfounded, trying to marshal my thoughts. I'm disgusted, repulsed, and horrified in equal measure. I'm also entirely unsurprised.

The whole situation borders on the clichéd: bored older woman married to successful-but-dull man has affair with attractive younger gym instructor. It's a bloody miracle the guy isn't the pool cleaner, really.

"I don't know what to say, Jane. This is a pretty upsetting thing to see." I grimace and look at Jane's love monkey. "And so is your penis, matey-boy. You want to tuck the little champ away now?"

"Nigel!" Jane shrieks.

Nigel looks down and realises his penis is still waggling freely in the wind. I have to grudgingly admit that from the size of it Jane has chosen her partner in this sordid little exchange quite well. Once

Nigel junior is safely stowed away, his owner looks up at me with a sheepish expression on his face.

"I'm very sorry about this."

"Not as sorry as you're going to be if you don't sod off right now, Nigel," I order with a stern expression.

"Yes, you'd better go, Nigel," Jane says in a meek tone of voice. I have to say it's one I thoroughly approve of.

Nigel rushes past me, turning as he leaves. "Will I see you at the gym tomorrow, sweetheart?" he says to Jamie's mother.

It's all I can do not to throw up my breakfast.

Jane has the decency to turn bright red. "I don't know, Nigel. After this, I doubt it. Just go away will you!" The waspish tone with which she dismisses him is far more the Jane I've come to know and loathe. The gym instructor does as he is bid.

Once he's gone I turn back to my mother-in-law. Now the initial shock has passed, I'm formulating some opinions that Jane Newman isn't going to like one little bit but sure as hell is going to listen to. What she's done here is awful. I like Michael a lot, despite his apparent obsession with looking at my breasts. He's a hard-working man who's always done his best for his kids and he certainly doesn't deserve this kind of treatment. And what kind of mother does this to her son as well? Jamie's going to be heartbroken when I tell—

Poppy! I've left Poppy in the fucking car! Here I am mentally berating Jane for being a bad parent and I've left my baby in the car like a dog.

"You stay right there!" I bark at Jane.

Five seconds later I'm opening the car door to find my daughter fast asleep. There's not a paedophile in sight. I carefully unbuckle her and carry her back to the rear of the house. Jane starts to babble as I return, but I silence her with a finger to my mouth, holding the car seat up for her to see her sleeping granddaughter.

What follows is a strange pantomime of me asking Jane where I can put the baby, her eventually understanding what I'm saying, and me tiptoeing to a downstairs guest room, where I leave Poppy sound asleep. I close the door as quietly as possible and slowly walk back through to the conservatory, where Jane awaits. With the baby safely squared away for the time being I can deal with the horrors I've just witnessed.

"What the hell are you playing at Jane?"

She sinks into the couch she was so recently being penetrated over and looks at the broken TV. Then something deeply distressing happens. Jane begins to cry. It's rather like seeing a sabre-toothed tiger playing with a ball of string.

"I don't know why I did it, Laura!" she wails. "Michael doesn't come near me anymore. All he cares about is that bloody thing!" She stabs a finger at the television. "Nigel just showed me some attention. One thing led to another, and . . ."

"He's slipping you a mid-morning length?"

"Yes!" She starts to cry again. "I haven't felt wanted in years! He . . . he made me feel *special*. Can't you understand that, Laura?"

I had intended to launch into a verbose attack on Jamie's mum, having been on the end of many a barbed comment and throw-away insult over the years. I was looking forward to getting some payback for all her self-obsessed, holier-than-thou bullshit.

This isn't that Jane Newman, though. This is a sad, lost, and lonely woman, rapidly descending into her dotage. It's quite pathetic—and it takes the wind out of my sails completely. I sit beside her.

"Yes, I understand. Though he could have made you feel special with a meal and a bottle of wine, Jane. You didn't have to go straight for the hardcore doggy-style antics."

"I'm such a fool!" Jane punches the couch armrest. "I've ruined everything. You'll tell Michael and Jamie and everyone's lives will be destroyed."

Aaah . . . So the real Jane Newman starts to reassert herself. Laying this at my door is a masterpiece of deflection. I'm not having it.

"Don't bring me into this, Jane. This is your doing. I won't say anything, but I expect you to have the guts to tell them yourself."

I'm not really sure if that's the right way to play this, but I'm not letting this manipulative harridan paint me into a corner, where I have to be the one to decide whether the truth comes out or not. Her eyes narrow. She can see I've got her pegged. It's wrong, but a small part of me does an exultant back flip of pride.

"You can't expect me to tell them."

"I can and I bloody do. This is your mistake . . . you deal with it."

I want to leave now. The quicker I can get away from here the quicker I can start drinking to blot out the last ten minutes of my life. I could drink if I didn't have a baby to look after, that is. Damn Jamie and his stupid healthy sperm! I get up off the couch and stalk towards the guest room to retrieve Poppy.

"Why did you come here in the first place, Laura?" Jane asks.

"I wanted your advice on teething. Poppy's being a nightmare."

"You wanted *my* advice?" Jane sounds incredulous.

"Yes. Yes I did," I reply, my voice softening traitorously.

"Oh." She actually looks quite touched.

What a fucking bitch!

"Try putting the pacifier in the fridge before giving it to her. That always seemed to work for Jamie."

"Did it? Okay. I'll give it a try."

I gather up my sleeping baby and open the front door.

"Are you going to say anything to Jamie?" Jane asks forlornly as I cross the threshold.

"I don't know. I'll wait to see what *you* do, Jane." I can't leave without a final comment. This is, after all, a woman I don't really like. "Just try not to shag anyone else in the meantime."

I don't wait for a response. I'm off down the driveway and into the car before she can say a damn thing. As I back away, I look back briefly to see her standing on the doorstep looking very small and lost. Jane Newman has always been a frightening spectre in my life, but now I see her in a totally different light. She's gone from a stone-faced mother-in-law, standing over me in judgement and disapproval, to a woman with her knickers around her ankles and an expression of deep sexual pleasure on her face while a gym instructor rams her from behind. I really don't know which image is worse.

So there you have it, Mum. I am now faced with a dilemma. Do I tell Jamie? Or do I keep it to myself? I know if Jane says nothing I'll be harbouring an awful secret—but should I really say something to Jamie that might deeply upset him?

Also, do you want to know the *worst* part? Jane's advice about the dummy worked. Poppy's been quiet for hours.

What a fucking bitch!

Love you, Mum.

Your confused daughter, Laura

xxx

JAMIE'S BLOG

Sunday 13 July

Something is going on with my wife. I'm about as astute when it comes to the female mind as Sherlock Holmes after a lobotomy, but even I can tell something's up. For the past few weeks her behaviour has been quite strange. Not all the time, but enough for me to notice. I've questioned her about it. This was, as ever, a colossal mistake.

The first time I asked what was wrong, she just said "nothing." The second time I got, "honestly, Jamie, nothing." The third occasion resulted in, "Will you leave me alone, you twat! I said there was nothing wrong!"

I should have ended it there, but a couple of hours later I asked again . . . and she ignored me for the rest of the evening. I know there's something funny going on, though, and I'm itching to find out what it is. I'm almost 100 percent sure Laura's not having an affair. What with looking after Poppy every minute of the day, she'd have to buy a time machine to make time to cheat on me. I keep telling myself that over and over, anyway. The mere idea of her gallivanting around with another man makes my blood freeze in my veins. She's displaying all the hallmarks of a partner up to no good, though. It's undeniable.

I'm actually glad I'm so knackered thanks to work and Poppy. I don't have enough time to properly chew over the concept of my wife cheating on me, so it doesn't get a chance to grab a foothold in my subconscious. Even if she isn't cheating, there must be a rational (and less soul-destroying) reason for her strange behaviour.

To find out the truth, I will have to exercise patience—which I've never been very good at, mainly because when I have a problem on my mind, I can get very distracted from day-to-day activities. This can lead to disaster.

Dwelling on what might be wrong with my wife (and indeed my marriage) led to a mortifying experience the other day, one that might also have led to a lengthy prison sentence if I hadn't done some very fast talking—and if Captain Coincidence hadn't reared his head to save the day.

For the first time in the seven months since Poppy was born, I was allowed out of the house with her on my own. Due to subsequent events, however, it was probably the *last* time as well. Laura is naturally the parent Poppy has been alone with more, given the fact that I have to go out to work every day. This has given them time to bond as mother and daughter, as is right and proper. When it comes to *my* relationship with my daughter, it largely consists of me pleading with her to shut up and ramming a bottle into her mouth, so I doubt she thinks of me as a vital part of her existence right now. In fact, Poppy probably groans inwardly whenever she sees me coming.

In an attempt to rectify this imbalance and prove that I have what it takes to be a father, I suggested to Laura yesterday afternoon that I be allowed to take Poppy out on my own while she had some girlie time with Melina. It's Mel's birthday, and she had a spa day planned for her and her friends. This seemed like the perfect opportunity to take Poppy off Laura's hands for a few hours.

"I don't know," Laura says in a very uncertain voice. "You are Jamie, after all."

"What's that supposed to mean?"

"Honey, you can be a bit absent-minded now and again."

"If you're going to bring up me forgetting to buy condoms again, I'll—"

"I didn't mean that. But you have to admit you can be a little scatter-brained."

"Laura, please," I say, voice dripping with honey. "This is our baby we're talking about. I'll be very careful." I stroke her arm. "It'll give you and Melina a chance to have some fun together."

That seems to do the trick. "Okay . . . you can have her this afternoon. Just be careful, okay?"

"Of course! Everything will be fine."

And it was for about three hours. Then I lost Poppy.

I waved good-bye to Laura from the doorstep and went to get my daughter ready for our big day out. There were a few things I wanted to buy in town, so I'd decided to take Poppy to the shops for a walk about. When I told her this was the plan, she smiled. This may have been genuine pleasure or just a natural female reaction to the word *shopping*, I couldn't quite tell.

I spent twenty minutes making sure I'd packed everything. Babies are tiny things, but they come with a half ton of baby equipment that you need to have with you at all times. It took a few minutes of grunting and swearing to get it all in the trunk, especially the bloody stroller, which cost me about as much as the car did.

With Poppy strapped into her car seat with a minimum of fuss, I drove away safe in the knowledge I'd successfully packed everything for the trip. Three minutes later I drove back to pick up Poppy's bottle . . . then drove away safe in the knowledge I'd successfully packed everything for the trip. Two minutes later I drove back to pick up the nappies . . . then drove away safe in the knowledge I was a fucking idiot.

We arrive in town about half past two. About five to three I finally manoeuvre Poppy's stroller out of the parking lot lift and we begin our relaxed walk around town.

Except it's a Saturday afternoon, so it's about as relaxing as nuclear haemorrhoids. There are people everywhere. I had planned to spend a couple of hours here, but as I try to negotiate the enormous stroller around the vast amount of foot traffic, I decide to cut the shopping trip short and take Poppy to the park.

In fact, the only store I now intend to tackle is Macy's, because Laura has asked me to pop in and pick up a present for a wedding we're going to in a couple of weeks. I'm under strict instructions to buy a Macy's reading lamp. Not just *any* Macy's reading lamp, though; I must purchase an Elenora reading lamp in silver. Quite why they feel the need to give a lamp a woman's name is beyond me, but I didn't argue the point knowing it would be an argument I would most definitely lose.

Into the store I go and thus begins a nightmare of epic proportions. First of all, I have to find the lighting department. Initially this appears to be on the first floor, so I head there in the lift. Ten minutes wandering around proves otherwise—there are no lamps to be seen anywhere. I'm becoming increasingly annoyed as the stroller, a bugger to control at the best of times, is almost impossible to negotiate along the narrow corridors between ladies hosiery and knitwear. Luckily, Poppy is sound asleep through all of this. I think the addition of a wailing baby may have sent me over the edge.

"Oh, sorry, the sign hasn't been changed yet," a skinny shopgirl tells me by way of explanation when I ask her where the lighting department has gone. "We're being refurbished. It's now on the third floor."

Of course it is. The third floor is right at the top of the building and will force me back into the lift again, with its inevitable slight smell of piss.

We eventually reach the third floor, and off I go again, trying my hardest not to crash the stroller into the myriad linen and glassware displays ranged in front of me like an obstacle course. Poppy and I finally reach the lighting department. It's *enormous*. How many different types of lighting does a person need? They all do the same thing, don't they? I spend the next ten minutes in a fruitless effort to find the bloody reading lamp. Elenora proves more elusive than the Scarlet Pimpernel. I accost another skinny shopgirl (they produce them in a factory somewhere, I believe) and ask her where I can find one.

"Two aisles up sir, on your left." She points a bored finger. "Close to where that lady with the stroller is."

I follow her finger to see a small Asian lady also negotiating a large stroller along the aisles. I feel a pang of empathy for her. "Thanks very much," I tell the shopgirl and make my way towards my goal.

Reaching what looks like the right aisle at last, I park Poppy and quickly beetle off down the narrow passageway between the lighting displays.

There's no bloody Elenora reading lamp to be found, naturally. Not immediately anyway. I have to take a right, a left, and another right before I find the right area. Cursing under my breath I pick up one of the lamps (which doesn't come in a box, of course—that'd be far too handy) and make my way back to where I've left my daughter. Still muttering all sorts of dark opinions about the layout of the twenty-first-century department store, I grab Poppy's stroller and start to make my way back to the payment counter. When I get there, I have cause to swear once again as there's a sign over it that reads: "Please use payment counter on second floor. We apologise for any inconvenience while we upgrade our store for you."

I bet you don't really.

I turn the awkward stroller back to the lift, carrying the tall, heavy reading lamp in the other hand. I reach the lift and mercifully it opens to reveal an empty carriage. I reverse into it, press the button for the second floor, put the reading lamp down, and put my head back against the wall and expel a loud sigh. I only have to pay for the lamp and get out of here now with Poppy. She's still very quiet, so I pull back the hood of her stroller to check if she's okay.

Yep, Poppy seems absolutely fine . . . apart from the fact she now appears to be Chinese. *My baby has turned Chinese!* I scream incomprehensibly in the vaults of my mind. *Why is my baby Chinese?* I move quickly round the stroller and bend down to take a closer look. Maybe my eyes are going. Maybe I just need a closer look at her to—

Nope, she's still fucking Chinese. Icy cold panic overwhelms me. For a moment the sheer impossibility of it renders me immobile. How can this have happened? Is this some kind of bizarre disease I wasn't aware of? *Chinesechangeitis*? Is Poppy a mutant, like in *X-Men*? If so, what kind of superpower is the ability to turn Asian? It's not going to help you much unless you're playing hide-and-seek in the middle of Kowloon Bay.

Then rationality does a great job of reasserting itself. It doesn't make the situation any less terrible, but at least it helps make it more plausible. *You grabbed the wrong stroller, you twat.* I remember the small Chinese lady also in the lighting section—who *also* had a baby in a stroller. I've left my daughter on her own in the middle of a busy department store while simultaneously kidnapping a Chinese baby. I frantically bash the stop button on the lift, which comes grinding to a halt. I then hammer the third floor button so hard it splits my fingernail. Sucking on my painful digit I hop from one foot to the other as the lift crawls back up to the third floor.

The door eventually pings open. I grab the Elenora reading lamp again (because now I've found the sodding thing, I'm not letting it go no matter what) and rush the stroller out of the lift. Sadly the reading lamp is unbalanced, tips over to one side and slams up against the walls of the lift, knocking me back on my arse. Chinese baby continues to roll out onto the shop floor as the lift doors begin to close on me. *Oh great, now I've lost another fucking baby.* That's two in the space of as many minutes.

I stagger to my feet, still holding the now hopelessly bent reading lamp, and throw my arm between the doors before they fully close. I wrench them open, catching the Chinese baby before he or she is lost in the small crowd of people waiting for the lift. "Sorry! Sorry!" I wail and push between them as fast as I can, taking off in the direction of the lighting department. Chinese baby has had enough of this little adventure and is crying his or her bastard head off now, attracting even more attention. God knows what I must look like pushing a screaming Asian child along, bumping into everything in my way, and brandishing a bent reading lamp, which is swinging around everyone's heads in an extremely dangerous fashion.

As I reach the lighting section my heart leaps and drops at the same time, in all defiance of the physical universe. It leaps because I see Poppy, still sound asleep in her stroller. It drops because standing behind her is a Chinese woman in tears and a burly security guard speaking into a walkie-talkie.

"Wait! Wait!" I scream. "Everything's fine!"

Everything is obviously *not* fine. As far as the poor Chinese woman is concerned, the man who kidnapped her baby is now thundering back towards her, using her poor screaming child as a battering ram and wielding a massive metal lamp with which he no doubt intends to strike her mightily about the head.

"He got my baby!" the woman shrieks and points at me, jumping up and down.

I come grinding to a halt in front of both of them, fling down the stupid reading lamp and begin to babble my apologies, attempting to explain what has happened.

The legendary crowd of gawping onlookers forms around us. The security guard listens, digests everything I have to say . . . and tells me he's still going to call the police because my story is obviously far too outlandish to be true. I simply must be some kind of evil sexual predator, who has decided he's had enough of one baby and fancies a Chinese. My salvation comes from the distraught mother, who, throughout my convoluted explanation, has been looking at me in a very funny way.

"I know you!" she exclaims. "You Jamie!"

I am, needless to say, completely fucking nonplussed.

How the hell does this woman know me?

"Yeah! You Jamie. You with Laura!"

She knows my wife, too! I look around the store, trying to spot the hidden cameras. When none are in evidence I turn back to her. "How do you know my name?" How do you know my *wife*?"

"You at Trish's class!"

Visions of whales being sexually molested fill my brain. "It's Lolly, right?"

"Yeah! Yeah!"

"You know this man?" the security guard asks her.

"Oh yeah! He funny guy. I hear him fart out loud once!"

The guard looks at me with an expression that suggests his sanity is rapidly failing. "So . . . you two know each other, then?"

"Apparently," I tell him, putting my head in my hands.

"Yeah! Yeah! He make joke about whale fucking!"

I have to shut this woman up. Her voice is carrying over the crowd of massively entertained onlookers, and she's making me sound like a bloody lunatic.

"I'm sorry about the mix-up with the babies, Lolly."

She waves a hand at me. "It don't matter. Now I know you, I don't think you a big, fat, old sex grandad anymore." She points at me. "You whale-fart man!" This makes her collapse into giggles again. Her Chinese baby (sex still undetermined) joins in with its mother.

Poppy remains fast asleep. Great . . . the girl wakes up in the middle of the night if a mouse farts two doors away, but in a noisy department store where her father's just avoided a kidnapping charge she's dead to the world. I suppose I should be grateful. The guard speaks into his walkie-talkie, assuring his colleague that there is no reason to call the police. The nearest mental hospital *maybe*, but not the police.

"Well, now that's all cleared up, I think Poppy and I will be leaving," I say, trying to bring this horrible episode to a close.

"No! No! You come have coffee with me and Ling!" Lolly screeches. "He like your kid. What you say her name was? Poopy?"

"Poppy. It's *Poppy*."

"Ha ha! Poppy and whale-fart man. You come get coffee, we chat about babies."

I have to go, of course. The spectre of my baby theft still hangs over us, and I feel guilty for making Lolly panic. The fact that she also apparently took care of Poppy in the few minutes I was gone makes it even worse. I simply have to spend half an hour drinking awful Macy's coffee with this woman, there's no way out of it. I nod and smile at the guard, who gives me the stink eye and walks off towards the bathroom section with a swagger his position doesn't really justify. Lolly and I each take our babies (the right ones this time) across the shop floor to the restaurant at the back.

We sit and chat for about an hour. It turns out that while Lolly's grasp of the English language is a tad fragmented, she also has a degree in biochemistry from one of China's leading universities and only came to England after falling in love with Brian while he was over there on a fact-finding mission for GlaxoSmithKline. There was me thinking she was some kind of mail-order bride when in actual fact she's better paid and far more educated than I'll ever be. I end up promising that Laura and I will have dinner with her and Brian at the nearest opportunity and finally leave Macy's just as the heavens open, soaking me to the skin as I run back to the parking lot. I didn't try to find another reading lamp. The bastards can have vouchers.

Just as I think the worst of this stupid trip into town is over, Poppy wakes up and starts screaming the house down.

For many reasons, this will be the last time Jamie and Poppy go out together on their own—until she's fifteen and can carry the fucking reading lamp for me.

LAURA'S DIARY
Friday, July 25

Dear Mum,

It's no good. I'm going to have to say something to Jamie about his mother.

It's been well over a month since I caught her in flagrante delicto with the Lycra-clad penis, and she still hasn't had the guts to say anything to her husband or children. I haven't seen Jane to speak to her about this—and frankly I don't really want to. Her cowardice annoys the crap out of me, and I don't intend to hold my counsel any longer.

I've tried to hide my dirty little secret from Jamie, and by and large I've been successful. Whenever he mentions his mother, though, it's a different story. I am *terrible* at keeping secrets, as you know, and being forced to do so makes me awkward, embarrassed, and angry—emotions I am not well equipped to deal with. Therefore, I end up being mad at Jane for putting me in this position, and inexplicably mad at Jamie for talking about her. I then stay mad at him for the rest of the day. It's horrible and wrong but I can't help myself.

To make matters worse, every time we try to get down to some naughty business when Poppy is asleep, visions of Jane's naked arse being hammered by Nigel and his big, waggly penis spring into my head, ruining my mood completely. So now Jamie thinks I don't want to have sex with him either. The poor guy is walking round in a daze. Jamie doesn't react well when something's amiss. He tends to make silly mistakes when he's distracted. Take, for instance, the other day when I was visiting Dan and Tim. I'd asked him to get some baby food out of the freezer for Poppy's lunch, reheat it, and give it to her. He ended up thawing out two Chicago Town pepperoni pizzas and liquidising them. I came home to a wailing daughter with chronic heartburn. Her nappies were even more horrific than usual the next day.

Then there was the business with Jamie stealing Lolly's baby in Macy's last month. Okay, it eventually led to a very pleasant meal and a newfound friendship, but I'd rather avoid Jamie doing anything else that might wind up with him being able to see his wife and daughter only during prison visiting hours.

This problem with Jane is starting to affect my marriage, so it's time to come clean and end it once and for all. If I don't say something soon, the secret is bound to drive a wedge between Jamie and me, and that's the last thing I want. When he does discover his mother's infidelity, he's going to need me for moral support. I simply have to tell him before it gets to the point where he'll resent me for holding on to what I know for too long.

Not tonight, though. Tonight Jamie and I are going out on our first date since Poppy's birth, and I don't intend to let my dirty little secret ruin it. It can wait at least another twenty-four hours. We've had so little quality time together recently that's it's worth the delay. The date was Jamie's idea. He very romantically suggested a meal in the newly refurbished Barley Corn pub, scene of our first ever date, which sounded lovely. I agreed straight away. Melina, bless her, has volunteered to take Poppy for the evening. This will be the first time both Jamie and I will be away from the baby for any length of time.

The whole thing makes me very nervous, but I'm going along with it as Jamie and I need some time alone—and I need some alcohol in me, dammit. I've almost forgotten what it feels like to have a good time with a glass of pinot grigio. Also, it's nice to get dressed up for a change, especially because I can just about fit back into my little black dress, thanks to the treadmill Jamie bought me for Christmas. I've walked three hundred miles on the bloody thing, and my reward is being able to slip into my favourite evening wear.

Okay, there's a bit of a bulge in the stomach region that wasn't there before, and I won't be eating a big meal, but I'm in the bloody thing—and that's what counts. Mel has my phone number on speed dial and a list of emergency numbers. She had all these anyway being a mother herself but thankfully resists the urge to punch me in the face as I go through the list with her for the fourth time.

"It's all fine, hun," she tells me in a soothing voice. "Poppy will be okay with me for a few hours. You two go and have a nice time."

"Okay, but any problems . . ."

"Yes, I know. I'll call you straight away. Don't worry!"

I am worried, though. I know Poppy's illness at birth has probably made me overprotective, but I can't help it. As I sit here writing this, I can feel a gnawing sensation in the pit of my stomach that won't go away no matter how much I tell it to. I'm not going to change our plans, though. Mel is a great mother, and Poppy will be fine, I'm sure. Jamie and I are going to have a lovely dinner together, and I'm going to forget all about his cheating mother for the evening.

I may even give him a blow job later, just to make up for the grief I've put him through recently.

Oh boy. It's four hours later and I'm pleased to report that pinot grigio has once again become my bestest friend in the whole wide world. I'm not shit-faced or anything—I have a baby to look after and there's no way I'd be able to write all this down if I were. This is a good thing, as I want to get the events of the evening down on the page before heading off to bed.

Jamie is already snoring his head off upstairs, thanks to the epic sloppy blow job I've just administered. Poppy is likewise fast asleep in the cot next to him, thanks to a warm bottle of milk. The combination of wine and the espresso coffee I had at the end of the meal means I've got a real buzz going on at the moment and won't be sleeping for a while yet.

Here're the highlights of this evening, then—an evening that started with me full of nervous anxiety and ended with me being extremely surprised by my husband.

"You look lovely," Jamie says from the doorway as I pose in my little black dress.

I've really gone to town with the make-up tonight. Given that I haven't been dressed up for months, I've probably gone overboard, but Jamie thinks I look good, so I'm happy.

"You look very smart," I reply. And he does. Jamie is wearing his best suit, the one that gets trotted out only for weddings and job interviews. He's even ironed his shirt and combed his hair. I'm once again reminded what a very attractive man my husband is when he puts in a bit of effort. Jamie comes up to me and delivers a lingering kiss that makes my knees a bit shaky.

"Shall we go?" he asks.

"Yeah, let's go eat!" I reply happily. What I'm really looking forward to is that lovely tall glass of pinot, though.

We get to the car. Jamie jumps in and I'm opening the passenger door when I catch sight of one of Poppy's dummies in her car seat behind me.

"Er . . . I'm just going to ring Mel and check that I gave her a dummy for Pops."

Jamie sighs and nods. He knows better than to argue. Mel does indeed have a dummy, so I put the phone away and we drive to the Barley Corn. Halfway there I spot a sign by the road advertising fresh vegetables for sale. This reminds me about Poppy's carrot and leek baby food, so I ring Mel again to check that I've given her some to feed Poppy with during the evening. Mel says yes—in a voice betraying only a little of her understandable exasperation—and I put the phone away as we park outside the pub.

Once inside we're shown to a secluded table at the back of the refurbished restaurant section. It's very nicely decked out, with some pretty paintings on the wall of what looks like the surrounding countryside. There's one particularly good painting of a field full of gambolling lambs that catches my eye.

Ten seconds later I'm on the phone to ask Mel if I packed Poppy's bib. The one with the fluffy sheep on it. This time Mel doesn't bother to keep the exasperation out of her voice and assures me that she does indeed have the bib in question. I put the phone away as the waiter walks up to take our order.

I have the lasagne and Jamie orders a big, fat juicy steak. Then, nirvana approaches in the shape of another waiter with my large glass of pinot. How lovely it sparkles in the soft light of the restaurant. I snatch the glass off the waiter's tray and take a long, wonderful gulp. Yes I know you're supposed to savour wine, but I'm a new mother who hasn't fed her pinot addiction for months, so gulping was the only option at this point.

It tastes *marvellous.* A symphony of flavours on my tongue. The fantasies I'd enjoyed earlier in the day about this glass have been well and truly realised. Then it dawns on me that the wine has made me temporarily forget about Poppy. It's only been a few seconds, but I already feel like the most neglectful parent on the planet. There she is, without her mother in a strange place, and here I am feeding my alcoholic tendencies with not a thought for her dire situation. It's a wonder they don't call social services.

I figure a call to Mel just to check up can't hurt. This time she cuts through the chitchat and tells me to fuck off. Quite understandable under the circumstances. It takes all of Jamie's strength to wrestle the mobile phone from my grip, but he eventually succeeds and pops it away in his jacket pocket.

"Poppy's fine, Laura. Mel knows what she's bloody doing."

"Does she, Jamie? *Does she*? For all we know she's left Poppy in the kitchen with the dog while she watches soap operas in the living room!"

"Don't be so bloody stupid. Mel is your best friend, for Christ's sakes. Just relax. The kid couldn't have a better babysitter."

Jamie is right, of course. I'm being ridiculous. If anything, Mel is probably a better mother than me, after all she's been doing it longer. So why won't that nagging fear that Poppy is being neglected leave me? Why do I want to smash the wine bottle over Jamie's head and grab the phone from his jacket while he bleeds out on the floor?

Get a grip, girl. How? How do I get a bloody grip? *The wine. The wine is the answer and our salvation.* My brain is, as ever, one step ahead of me and is absolutely right. I take another gulp of the lovely liquid. Then another. Then I refill my glass, right to the top, and take another gulp.

By the time our meals arrive, I've already got quite a buzz on and am feeling much more relaxed about the whole Poppy situation. Even if Mel has left her in the kitchen, she can tie a pork chop round her neck so the dog will play with her. I giggle.

"What's funny?" Jamie says over his enormous steak.

"Nothing, husband of mine. Eat your big old bit of meat." *Slosh.* Giggle.

Jamie returns to his mastication. I fork some lasagne into my mouth. It tastes quite nice, but nothing can compare right now to the orchestra of flavours the wine is playing on my taste buds.

Oh dear, I might be getting a bit tipsy here. I have to get a grip! *Drink more wine, that's the ticket.* You're utterly right, brain! More wine it is! *Slosh*. Giggle. By the time our meals are over I'm soaring on the wings of inebriation.

"You're pissed," Jamie says as I hurl wine over the tablecloth. Thankfully I'm not drunk enough just yet to want to suck the liquid out of the cotton.

"Don' be so . . . so bloody silly, Jamie. I am a mother and have responsibililies. Big, fat responsibililies." To show how big and fat they are I hold my arms out wide, nearly punching a passing waiter in the genitals.

"Yeah . . . maybe I'll put Poppy down later, eh?"

"What's that suppos' to mean?" I am indignant! How dare Jamie cast aspersions on my parenting abilities! "Are you sayin' I'm norra a good mother, so-called Jamie Newman?"

"No . . . I'm just saying it might be wise if I took care of her while you're in your present state."

"Presen' state! What d'you mean by presen' state, cackface?"

"Well, you're drunk enough to call me cackface, how's that?"

"Bollocks. I'm a fantastic mother. Not like yours!"

Oh shit. I hate you wine, you utter, utter bastard. Jamie sits back in his seat. A mixture of confusion and hurt crosses his face. My heart sinks.

"What do you mean by that, Laura?" He says it in such a lost little voice that my heart decides sinking isn't enough and tries to implode as well.

"I'm sorry baby," I slur. "I shouldn't have said that."

"No, you shouldn't." He sits forward and leans his elbows on the table.

"Jus' ignore me. I've had too much to drink," I say, trying to wave the conversation away.

"What's going on, Laura? Why can't you just tell me what the problem is?" Jamie pleads.

This is going from bad to worse. All I wanted was a nice night out and this has to happen.

"It's really nothing," I say—but it's so obvious I'm lying, it's surprising my nose doesn't shoot out and knock over the wine bottle.

"You've been acting weird for a few weeks, now," Jamie continues. "I keep trying to ignore it, but something's up. You're so busy with

Poppy it's been impossible to bring it up, but I'm really sick of it and just want some answers."

I fiddle with the stem of the wine glass. "Nothing's wrong, Jamie."

"That's a load of crap. I know you too well." Now he sounds angry—and can I really blame him? This is the first time I've willfully held anything back in our relationship. We've built a marriage on a foundation of honest communication, and here I am keeping secrets and being dishonest. Jamie takes a long swig of his one beer for the evening and stares at me with his eyes narrowed.

"Are you having an affair, Laura? You might as well tell me."

"Of course I'm not! That's just stupid."

"Is it? You get in moods with me for no reason, you don't want . . . *you don't want to have sex*," he whispers. "Every time I suggest seeing my family, you act like I'm asking you to do something horrendous."

"I . . . I . . ."

"What?"

Oh God, I'm going to have to tell him.

I wanted to wait, but if I don't say something now, this evening—and possibly my marriage—will be completely ruined.

"Please don't be mad at me."

He takes a deep breath. "I won't be, honey. Just tell me what the problem is. *Please*."

"Well, last month Poppy was teething really badly and I had no one to ask for help, so I went round to your mother's—"

"You went to *Mum*? Christ, it must have been bad."

"It was." I glug my wine. This probably isn't the wisest decision, but Dutch courage and all that.

"She didn't answer the door when I got there," I continue, "so I went round the back to find her, and . . . and . . ."

"And what?"

Just take the plunge you silly bitch.

"I saw her being screwed over the sofa in the conservatory by Nigel the gym instructor!"

Hmmm. I could have perhaps used a better turn of phrase to break the news to my husband that his mother is an adulteress. I sound like I'm summing up a particularly bad game of Clue. We'll blame it on the wine. Jamie's face goes slack.

Oh my, this is very bad. We came out tonight to try and reconnect with one another over a nice meal and some alcoholic refreshments. Instead, the evening has become a de facto confessional for me, and I've just destroyed Jamie's family unit in one fell swoop. This was the last thing I wanted to do tonight, but the evil pinot has led me astray once again. *Damn you, my glorious liquid friend. Damn you and everything you stand for.*

Then something quite unexpected happens. Jamie, who I thought would be distraught at this news, starts to laugh. It's one of those laughs that begins as a quiet chuckle before rapidly ascending into a full-blown guffaw. I knew I'd make him cry when I told him about his mother's adultery, but I didn't think it would be with tears of *laughter*.

"What's so funny, Jamie?" I ask. Maybe the terrible news has driven him instantly insane. I start to move the forks out of his reach just in case he's about to grab one and stab himself in the genitals.

"Sc . . . screwed over the sofa?" he repeats and goes off into another gale of laughter. The people sitting near us are starting to look over and wonder what's going on. I cringe with inebriated embarrassment.

"Yes!" I hiss under my breath.

"By . . . by a gym instructor?"

"Yes! Called Nigel." I try to think of something else to say. "He had a big willy. I saw it when he fell over."

"He fell . . . he fell . . ." Jamie can't get the words out. He's now holding his sides and his face has gone the red of a fire engine.

I have to try and salvage this situation. I have to say something to mitigate the awfulness of my dirty secret coming out in such a fashion. I mentally grasp for the right silver lining. Sadly, pinot is still in control of my speech centre and comes out with this fucking zinger:

"Your mother has a very peachy bottom for a woman of her age."

For a second Jamie stops as still as a statue. His eyes become saucers as he stares at me, digesting this latest piece of information. Then he lets out the loudest laugh so far and starts banging the table.

"Oh God, no more . . . please, no more. I don't think I can take it."

"Why is this so funny, Jamie? Your mother is *cheating* on your father!"

Jamie wipes his eyes and takes a deep breath, trying to regain some composure. He looks at me. "Yes Laura, I know. We *all* know. She's been doing it for years. I nearly caught her at it once myself."

I'm amazed. No, I'm bloody *flabbergasted.*

"Does your dad know?"

"He's the one who originally told me, Chris, and Sarah about it ten years ago," Jamie confides, wiping his eyes with a shirt sleeve.

"And he doesn't *mind*?"

"Mum's and Dad's marriage has been a bit of a sham for a long time. I'm pretty sure he's knocking off one of the women who works at his golf course, actually."

"But your mother doesn't realise that you all know what she's doing?"

"Good God, no." Jamie offers me one of his trademark lopsided smiles. "Where would the fun be in that?"

And there is all the revenge I could ever want for the way haughty Jane Newman has treated me. The fact she runs around terrified of anyone knowing she's banging different men left, right, and centre when it's common knowledge among her entire family is just too rich for words. Something else occurs to me.

"I've been walking around for weeks worrying about this," I say in a very dark voice. He might find the whole thing hilarious, but the stress of thinking I knew something that could destroy Jamie's family has been awful.

"I know, baby. Why didn't you just tell me?" There's a look of such relief on my poor husband's face that the anger I can feel bubbling upwards is immediately taken off the boil.

I take another swig of wine. "You know what, Jamie?"

He takes my hands in his across the table. "What, my gorgeous wife?"

"There have been times when I've been jealous of you because you have a family. Now, though, I've decided I'm bloody glad I don't."

"But, baby," Jamie gives me a mock serious face. "They're *your* family too now."

I fling one arm in the air. "Waiter!" I screech.

"What are you doing?"

"Ordering another bottle of wine."

The rest of the evening went very well. I moderated my alcohol consumption to a level that kept me just at the mildly pissed stage, I'm pleased to say. This was helped by the gigantic chocolate pudding we ate between us as the time rapidly sank towards eleven o'clock. The amount of starch and fat in the flaming thing would be enough to soak up all the alcohol in a brewery.

Poppy was absolutely fine in Mel's company, of course. In fact, when we picked her up she was fast asleep with a content look on her face. I may have to leave her with my friend more often . . . say for a couple of months or so.

What a very strange but equally cathartic night this has been, Mum. When you marry a man, you don't realise what baggage comes with him until something like this happens. You do marry into the whole family, after all, whether you want to or not. I suppose that's why Jane's behaviour towards me in the past has bothered me so much. She wouldn't have chosen me as a wife for her son, and that shows in our every encounter. My social standing, bank account, and lack of a double-barrelled surname account for most of that attitude, I'm sure.

I probably should be angrier about that, but I can understand a mother's desire to see her child do well by marrying into money. When Pops reaches adulthood, I'd certainly like her to find a rich, successful man to spend the rest of her life with. Where I differ from Jamie's mother, though, is that I won't be that bothered if she *doesn't*. As long as he loves her and takes care of her, I won't actually care whether he's rich or not. It just isn't that important to me. I can see that it is to Jane Newman though, so I guess she'll never be entirely happy with Jamie's choice of bride—unless I win the lottery or discover I'm thirty-eighth in line to the throne.

I have a feeling that whatever her feelings are towards me, she's going to be a *lot* more polite to me from now on, thanks to Nigel and his big willy. This gives me a nice *warm* feeling inside.

On the flip side of my tempestuous relationship with Jamie's mother, I have to confess it does make me feel good to know that I now have a brother, sister, and father in my life. Jamie may have shocked me by pointing that out to me, but the more I think about it, the more it makes me smile. No one could replace you of course, Mum, but having the void of other family members filled makes me very happy indeed . . . even if Michael does keep staring at my tits.

Love you, miss you, and am very glad you never had a thing for gym instructors, Mum.

Your tired and still ever so slightly drunk daughter, Laura

xxx

JAMIE'S BLOG
Wednesday 3 September

In the name of all that is holy, in the sight of all that is divine and righteous in this universe, why the hell did I think it would be a good idea to go camping on a bank holiday with a nine-month-old baby?

I mean, come on. This is *me* we're talking about, right? Jamie Newman. A man who has a near alchemic ability to turn any minor drama into a crisis of monumental proportions. In what plane of reality did I think it was a good idea to take my wriggling ball of mucus and noise to a field in the middle of nowhere and stick her in a hot canvas tent for the weekend?

"Are you *joking*?" said Laura when I suggested the idea last Thursday.

"No. It'll be lovely. We could get in the car on Saturday morning and go spend the weekend somewhere nice. The weather's looking good for it."

"We haven't got a tent, you maniac."

"Mum and Dad bought an enormous new one last year. We can borrow that. They won't mind."

"I'm not sure this is a good idea. Us camping? I get the feeling it could end with me slapping you repeatedly about the head."

"Very funny. I think it's a great idea. We haven't been away anywhere in *ages*. Everything's been so stressful recently. A bit of time away will be good for us."

Right, you see the above sentence, do you? If you're ever in a situation where you find yourself saying something similar, do not under *any circumstances* actually go on holiday. Vacations, day trips, and weekends away are things to be conducted only when your life is stress free. Don't fall under the illusion that buggering off for a few days will relax you in any way whatsoever and make you forget your worries back home. If anything, it'll actually make things *worse*. You'll spend the entire holiday safe in the knowledge that all that crap is still waiting for you back home. In fact, it will no doubt be even crappier when you do get back, thanks to you sodding off to another country and not keeping on top of it for a week.

My advice is to book a holiday at least six months in advance—and then do everything you can in those six months to reduce your stress level to zero. You can then cheerfully fly off to Tenerife for a week without a care in the world and actually *enjoy yourself*. I wish I had a time machine so I could go back four days and remind myself of those salient facts before embarking on our camping weekend away.

At one o'clock in the afternoon on Saturday, I'm driving up the M27 with a tent the size of the Vatican strapped to the roof. Laura is staring out the window with a look of deep worry on her face, and Poppy is happily filling her nappy in the baby seat behind us with a grin on her little face as she does so.

The weather is unseasonably hot once again for September. This has been the norm for Great Britain in recent years. We get wet Julys, cold Augusts, and Septembers with at least one week of temperatures in the high seventies. This is due to something called the jet stream that is apparently being mightily confused by all the cars they're driving in China. I don't quite know how a man going to buy rice across the other side of the world contributes to it being almost eighty degrees in September in the south of England, but I'm going to take it at face value until someone convinces me otherwise. I roll down my window wishing I'd got the air-con fixed at the last service.

And what exciting destination is family Newman heading for on this sunny bank holiday weekend, you may ask? Are we perhaps on our way to the dramatic Lake District? Or driving to the spectacular landscapes of Dartmoor? Surely I'd come up with a suitably exciting and attractive destination for our trip? One worth all the time and effort?

Nope. We're going to Wookey Hole, which, as you may have deduced already, is a hole called Wookey. Yes I know it sounds like a particularly nasty medical condition, but it is in fact a series of interesting and spooky caves in the West Country. It derives its name from a roughly human-shaped bit of rock that may or may not have once been an evil witch frozen in place by a passing monk on his way to Glastonbury for a party.

It's a place I have fond memories of visiting as a small boy. I also have fond memories of picking my nose and wiping it on my sister, but that is neither here nor there at this present moment as I turn off the motorway and hit the twisty-turny A and B roads of the West Country. There are more dramatic and user-friendly attractions in England to be sure, but Wookey Hole is fairly close to home and quite easy to get to, so it seemed like the best choice for our weekend away. It's also a pretty undemanding place to visit, which suits me fine. Theme parks are all well and good when you're fourteen and out of your mind on sugar, but as a man in his thirties with a wife and child, give me a slow stroll around a big hole in the ground any day of the week.

Yes, I have lost my mind at this point. I'm well aware of this and you don't need to remind me. The very concept of camping on a bank holiday weekend is as insane as sticking your penis into a passing grizzly bear. I can only blame a heavy workload, interrupted sleep patterns, and an unhealthy diet for the massive lapse in judgement.

We arrive at the campsite only two hours late. This is quite good going for a visit to the West Country. They seem to have a pathological aversion to motorways in this part of the world, so tailbacks and choked, single-lane roads are a common sight. As are motorists being rushed to hospital suffering from ruptured stomach ulcers. At the campsite—unimaginatively named Witch Field—I even find the pitch we'd booked in only a few minutes.

"Is this big enough? It doesn't look it," Laura says, surveying the small patch of grass lying between a huge caravan and the fence that designates the edge of the campsite. A gentle babbling brook lies on the other side of the fence, surrounded by the low-hanging branches of a number of beech trees.

"Yeah! It's fine," I say, pulling the tent off the roof rack and dragging it over to the centre of the grassy square we'll call home for the next two nights.

I'm only just about right. We end up with about a foot of clearance to the caravan, and the other side of the tent rests against the rickety fence, but the canvas monstrosity does just about fit, so I'm able to stand back with a look of pride on my face, having successfully tied off the last rope to the nearest ground peg. I'm sweating like a pig thanks to the heat, but I've managed to put up a tent all on my own—something I've never attempted before.

"Well done," Laura says from the car where she's rocking Poppy to sleep. "I was worried you might impale yourself on something there for a while."

"Oh ye of little faith, woman."

By six o'clock everything else is unpacked, including Poppy's travel cot and our sleeping bags. The tent fairly bulges with our stuff. A quick tour of the campsite shows that Trip Advisor got it just about right; there are indeed clean toilet, shower and baby-changing facilities, and the campsite staff seem friendly and happy to see us.

We spend a very pleasant balmy evening in the beer garden of the nearest pub and by ten o'clock all three of the Newman clan are relaxed and ready for a good night's sleep. As I pull back the tent door flap I'm actually thinking this camping idea may not have been a bad one after all.

"Bloody hell!" exclaims Laura as a wall of heat wafts across our faces.

The tent is boiling hot inside, thanks to being lightly cooked in the high September temperatures. I hadn't planned for this. I was expecting it to be cold at night, so had packed a multitude of blankets to keep us toasty and warm. It was obvious we wouldn't be needing any of them.

"Leave the door open for a bit Jamie," Laura tells me as she ducks into the tent and puts a fast asleep Poppy in her travel cot. I do so, and then flop myself down onto the inflatable mattress, ready for a healthy eight hours in bed. Laura joins me and gives me a lingering kiss.

"On second thought," she says, nibbling my ear, "maybe you should close it."

It's the best sex we've had in a long time. We're quiet—a sleeping child and thin canvas demands it—but by God, it's *good*. We're in no rush, we don't have to be anywhere tomorrow, we've just had a very relaxing evening, and it's a balmy late summer night. We're also a good sixty miles away from Astrid and her cat Mittens, so I'm confident I'm not going to be interrupted. By midnight we're both in postcoital bliss and lying in each other's sweaty arms. It's the perfect way to end a good day in our lives. I close my eyes and smile as I look forward to dropping into a deep, tranquil sleep.

I would have done so as well, if it weren't for the fact that our lovemaking had turned up the ambient temperature in the tent to stifling proportions. I try to ignore it and roll over on my side. This doesn't work, so I roll onto my back again. Then my front. Then my side again, then my back again. Laura is having similar problems and is thrashing around next to me like a dolphin on crack.

"I can't sleep." she drones.

"I know. It's too hot."

"Open the flap again."

"I can't! We're both naked."

"Oh God."

I'm perspiring so much now that my skin is sticking to the sheet that we'd thrown over the inflatable mattress. My testicles are swimming in a pool of sweat. My mouth is dryer than a judge's wit, and my tongue feels like sandpaper. Every time Laura shifts and her skin touches mine, we both flinch involuntarily at the feel of the other's clammy body. And we have at least another six hours of this before dawn.

Then Poppy, who has up until now been sleeping quite contentedly, realises how hot it is, too, and emits a blatting scream that probably wakes the entire campsite. In the end, I sleep for about two hours max.

By the time the sun creeps over the horizon, I'd drunk an entire two pints of water from one of the bottles I keep in the trunk in case the radiator goes again. This just about replaced the gallons of sweat I'd excreted overnight. Laura got a similar amount of sleep and had to drink a similar amount of liquid. Only Poppy managed more sleep, because babies can pretty much sleep through an earthquake if they're tired enough.

Over a cup of the strongest coffee I could make on our tiny Campingaz stove, I gaze out at what looks to be another roasting-hot day in the making.

"I'm so tired, Jamie," Laura says from where she is still prostrate on the mattress. "I don't think I can move."

"Come on, have a coffee and get up. We want to get to the caves before they get too busy."

"Fuck the caves. I just want to sleep."

"Laura!" I whine. "We have to go see them. They're really spooky. I loved them when I was a kid. Poppy will like it."

"Poppy is nine months old, Jamie. We could be standing on the edge of the Grand Canyon and she wouldn't give a damn."

My brow knits in indignation. "Look, I want us to have a nice family day out today and have some fun."

"I'm all for that, but can it be in the bed department at the nearest Ikea?"

This isn't going well. If I don't get Laura on my side we may be travelling back home sooner than planned.

"The caves are very cool, you know," I tempt. "Like they've got their own air-conditioning."

This perks her up a bit. "Oh alright. Anything's better than staying in this sweatbox."

The caves themselves are a couple of miles away, but there's a free minibus (with working air-con) provided by the campsite management, so I don't have to worry about driving—which is very handy. We arrive to find Wookey Hole crawling with sightseers. Children clad in witches' hats run amok while their long-suffering parents look on in dismay. Portly Americans wobble around in Bermuda shorts and sunglasses, talking loudly and eating a variety of snack foods.

Wookey must have had some money injected into it since the last time I was here, as a theme park has grown around the caves themselves. There's a mini-golf course, a park full of gigantic plastic dinosaurs, a mirror maze, a penny arcade. In fact, there's a whole range of entertainment measures laid on to help you forget that what you're essentially visiting is a big fucking hole in the ground.

"This had better be worth it, Newman," Laura says darkly as she narrowly avoids being mown down by a gaggle of ten-year-olds dressed like rejects from Harry Potter.

"It will be!" I say confidently, striding in the direction of the main cave entrance.

Poppy gives a little shout of happiness from just behind my shoulder, indicating that she has more faith in her father than his wife does. I've got our cheerful little daughter in one of those baby carriers that are popular these days. I like to avoid the stroller after the

Lolly incident, and these "baby backpacks" are a great alternative. Besides, it makes me feel like Luke Skywalker with Yoda on his back during the second act of *The Empire Strikes Back*, which is no bad thing in my book.

It turns out my optimism is justified. The caves are blissfully cool. Such is the pleasure derived from this simple drop in temperature that we temporarily forget how exhausted we are and spend a happy hour wandering around Wookey Hole, marvelling at the interesting rock strata and eating ice lollies. Laura doesn't even mind too much when I start doing bad impressions of Chewbacca. The similarity between the name of where we are and Han Solo's hairy sidekick is just too good to pass up.

"Rrrraaawwwwlll," I gurgle.

"Stop it, Jamie, you sound broken."

"Haarrrlll raaawwwlll."

"Give it a bloody rest, you're embarrassing me."

"Annoying I am," I say, now attempting Yoda. "Divorcing me you are, if I don't shut up, yes?"

"Quite possibly."

I look back at Poppy.

"You like my Chewbacca impression don't you, gorgeous?"

"Hrbbleggrrrll," she replies.

"Nearly, honey, you just need to work on the growl a bit more."

By two o'clock I'm dead on my feet. The lack of sleep and heat have really started to take their toll. We've pretty much covered all the fun Wookey Hole has to offer. The caves have been thoroughly investigated. The unrealistic plastic dinosaurs have been laughed at. The mirror maze has been solved, and Laura has soundly beaten me at mini-golf. Poppy has become a dead weight on my chest and shoulders. I'm carrying her in front of me in the baby carrier and she's nodded off, obviously satisfied that the excitement of the day is well and truly over.

We trudge back to the pickup point for the minibus that goes to the campsite. There is supposed to be one leaving at two fifteen—i.e., *now*—but as we plonk ourselves onto a nearby bench to rest our weary feet no bus is in sight.

"You won't be getting that bus from 'ere for a while," a voice says from just behind us. I turn to find an old man in what looks like a suit from the 1940s giving us the squint eye.

"What do you mean?" Laura asks him.

"Bugger broke down about half an hour ago. Feller driving managed to get it going, but it didn't look none too healthy to me. Said 'e was gonna nurse her back to the campsite and fix it."

"Then maybe he'll be back soon with it," Laura says hopefully.

"Maybe. But I know a broken head gasket when I sees one, madam. I reckon you'll be waitin' a while for that bugger to come back."

"Thanks very much," I tell him, not meaning a word of it.

"I guess we'll just have to wait," Laura sighs and fans her face with the Wookey Hole visitor's guide.

This is obviously the right course of action at this point. All three of us are dog-tired, the temperature is somewhere in the high seventies, and I have a headache forming above my right eye from too much sun.

"I think we should walk it," I suggest.

"What?"

"We should walk it. There's no telling how long it'll be before the bus comes back, and it's only two miles back to the campsite."

"No Jamie."

"It'll be easy! In fact, I think we could probably cut some time off the walk by going across that field. I'm sure that's the direction the camp is in. I remember from this morning."

"No Jamie," Laura repeats, somewhat more emphatically.

"Oh come on! It's definitely over there."

"You folks stayin' over at Witch Field, are ya?" the old man asks.

"Yep."

"Ar. It is over in that direction, young man. You'd be right about that one."

I look at Laura smugly. "See? Told you."

I stand up.

"No Jamie!" Laura says for the third and final time.

"Yes Laura. I'm not going to sit here and get piles waiting for a bus that's never coming. I can find the campsite, no problem."

I take off across the road and over the low stile that allows access to the fields beyond. Determination carries me over it in moments, and I'm marching off in the direction of the large copse at the other end of the field before Laura reaches the stile, climbing over it with weary resignation.

"If we get lost, Jamie, I'm going to kill you!"

"We're not going to get lost!" I call back with supreme confidence.

Forty minutes later and we're more *Lost* than Jack, Kate, Hurley, and the hobbit bloke from *Lord of the Rings*. The English countryside is very picturesque but consists of more or less the same thing repeated ad infinitum: green fields, long hedgerows, leafy trees, shady copses, babbling brooks, dozing cows, frolicking sheep. In my defence, it's quite easy to get turned around. Take a left when you should take a right and all that repetitive scenery can swallow you up in no time at all.

"I think we should have gone left back in the field with the cross-eyed cow," I tell Laura. "That's where I went wrong."

"You know where I went wrong, Jamie? I didn't kill you with that bloody moped," Laura retorts. "If I had, I wouldn't currently be standing here being eaten alive by every sodding midge and mosquito in Somerset!"

"It's fine. I just think we need to go across this field and we'll be back on course. The campsite is definitely over there."

Naturally it isn't, and another half an hour goes by spent trudging up copse and down brook, getting increasingly more and more frustrated with every step.

We're navigating what suspiciously looks like the same shady copse we entered an hour ago, when Laura's patience finally gives out.

"That's it!" I hear in a high-pitched screech from behind me. "I've had enough!"

I turn to see my exhausted wife sit down hard on a tree stump and thump her back against another tree behind it. She folds her arms and scowls at me. "I'm not taking another step with you in charge of this stupid expedition, Jamie. You have less sense of direction than a herd of blind roller-skating elephants in Antarctica."

Oh dear. Laura really is pissed off. When she starts coming out with esoteric crap like that I know I'm in trouble.

"It's just a little further, baby."

"Just a little further? What exactly is your definition of *a little further*? A few hundred fucking miles?"

"Look, I'm sorry. I thought this would be a good idea."

"Oh yes, a really good idea! We would have been back at the camp quicker if we'd have let Poppy lead the way. This really is typical of you, Jamie. You just don't listen to me and now we're—*Ow*! *Bastard*!"

Laura jumps to her feet in a split second.

"What's the matter?" I cry and move towards her.

Then I hear it. A sound that in our current situation is probably the last one you want hear. *Buzzing*. Laura is rubbing at her left elbow and grimacing with pain. Then I feel something jab into my left eye lid. The pain is instantly excruciating. My hand flies up to my eye and I let out what I can only shame-facedly describe as the girliest scream this side of a One Direction gig.

"Bees!" Laura screams. "Bees! Bees!" she repeats, pointing her reddened elbow at me as if this is all my fault, which I suppose it is.

"Run!" I cry, shielding Poppy's unprotected head from the swarm of angry black and yellow insects that are pouring out from the trees behind Laura. She must have disturbed the nest when she sat down.

Laura doesn't need telling twice and is off as fast as her legs will carry her. I'm slower, because I have Poppy and have to be more careful. Her welfare is more important than mine. As such, I am stung a total of seven times. Twice on my forehead to join the one on my eye lid, once on the back of the neck, twice on the back of my right arm, and once on my right testicle. The little bugger must've flown up my shorts leg and headed straight for the crown jewels like a fucking Luftwaffe pilot zeroing in on a dockyard. I slap at my crotch to try and kill the little sod and only succeed in punching myself hard in the nuts.

I burst from the copse into an open field. Still protecting Poppy—who is now crying like a maniac—I stumble forward away from the bee-strike zone. My genitals are a giant ball of agony, so I have to run in a bowlegged sideways crab motion to avoid adding to the pain with friction. Laura, having been bitten only once—is having no such problems and is fairly sprinting away, shrieking and slapping at her head like a crazy woman. Trying to calm Poppy with some soothing words, I look up at Laura running away and am therefore treated to the sight of her hitting an enormous pile of fresh cow dung and sliding a good three feet on its slick surface before plummeting earthwards with a loud squawk that echoes across the field, signalling the end to this latest epic tale of woe.

LAURA'S DIARY

Sunday, August 31

Dear Mum,

I am covered in cow shit.

That is all.

Laura

xx

LAURA'S DIARY
Thursday, September 4

Dear Mum,

Right now, Jamie Newman is not my favourite person in the world. Call me oversensitive, but if someone is responsible for me having to clean excrement out from under my nails with a plastic spork, I'm not likely to have them in my good books for a bloody long time.

We haven't spoken to one another in four days now. This is not just because of my cow shit bath, I hasten to add. If our disastrous weekend away camping had ended there, some forgiveness may have been in the cards by now. After all, I married the idiot, so I know how colossally stupid he can be if you don't keep him on a tight rein. It really was my fault for following him into that field—and once again putting my faith in his awful sense of direction. I think Poppy's welfare had a lot to do with it. If I'd have let him go off with her alone, there's every chance I wouldn't have seen her again until her eighteenth birthday, when I would finally track them both down to an opium den in Cairo.

Sadly, the attack of the killer bees heralded only the beginning of the most uncomfortable twelve hours of my life—labour and pregnancy excluded.

"I am giving the directions from now on," I tell my husband from where I sit in the cow flop.

"Understood," he replies in a very small voice.

"Help me up." I extend my dirty hand.

Jamie wrinkles his nose.

"If you don't help me to my feet, Jamie," I say in a low growl, "I will make your life such a living hell that getting some smelly cow shit on your hand will seem like a day trip to paradise by comparison."

Common sense prevails in the Newman skull, and he takes my hand, pulling me to my feet and immediately backing away, wiping his hand on his shorts. "I don't want to get any on Poppy," he says when he catches my expression.

"Poppy probably filled her nappy the second the bees started coming. I'm sure a little cow poo won't bother her."

I try to ignore the stench wafting up from all three of us and look across the field to a gap that shows a narrow road beyond. I point at it. "We're going that way."

"But didn't we just come from over—"

"We're going that way."

"Okay, baby," Jamie says sheepishly.

Without another word I walk towards the road. Jamie dutifully follows. Poppy, the excitement now over, has nodded off again against his chest. Thankfully my olfactory membrane packs up due to the stink rising from my body, so I'm spared the constant smell of cow manure as I guide us back to the campsite. It takes me less than ten minutes to get back to the main road and within twenty we're walking down the gravel path that leads to our tent.

"I could've found it alright," Jamie mumbles to himself just loud enough for me to hear. I ignore him.

At the tent, I command Jamie to retrieve my shower gel, sponge, towel, and dressing gown. He does so wordlessly, passing them over like a humble servant.

"I'm going to clean this shit off now. Have a cup of tea waiting when I get back."

"Okay, baby."

Yes, I am being imperious, childish, and demanding, but I'm covered from head to toe in manure, and my elbow is throbbing like mad with bee venom. I'm making no apologies for my attitude.

I spend a calming twenty minutes in the shower. By the time I turn it off, the manure is washed away and the elbow is less painful. If I don't bend it, I can hardly feel the sting at all now. My mood would have lifted were it not for the fact that the cow shit has ruined both my new jeans and the cute floral vest top I'd bought in April and had been looking forward to wearing all summer. Both went in the nearest bin. You just can't get rid of dry cow crap once it's ground itself in.

I wrap myself up in my dressing gown and amble back to the tent as slowly as possible, enjoying the hot sun and trying not to think about the phantom smell of cow excrement still lingering in my nostrils.

"Well, I certainly feel better for that," I say as I pull back the tent flap. "You should probably go and have a shower yourself, Jamie. It might help your—oh good God, what's happened to your face?"

Jamie looks like he's been punched by Mike Tyson. His upper left eye has swollen into a puffy red ball and closed over itself. Two more bee stings are swelling on his forehead as well, one on either side. He looks like he's growing horns. You can imagine how delighted Poppy is to have this grizzly visage peering down at her from over the travel cot she's lying in. I instinctively know that the sharp wail emitting from the cot translates as: *aaaaargggh! aaaaargggh! A monster has possessed Daddy. Why is his face like that? Save me, Mummy, save me!*

Jamie looks up at me. "I don't think bee stings agree with me," he slurs. I wholeheartedly concur.

"Come and sit down," I tell him and help him over to the mattress. I'm still irritated with him for getting us lost, but my anger is being quelled by his current sorry state. Any punishment I could pile on

Jamie now couldn't compete with the swelling bee stings that are rapidly turning him into Joseph Merrick.

I root around in the first aid kit for the tweezers and set about removing bee stingers from various parts of Jamie's anatomy.

"Ow!"

"Don't be a baby."

"Aaaaargggh!"

"Stop moving your head."

"Oooo!"

"The more you struggle, the longer it will take."

"Aaah!"

"Oh for crying out loud, you've been stung by a few bees. You haven't been stabbed by Freddy Krueger."

"Ooosshh!"

"Jamie, why are you unzipping your shorts? This is hardly the right time for that kind of thing; I can't believe you're horny—oh, you're not horny, you just have a stinger in your ball. Looks nasty. I'll leave you to do that one, I think. Here're the tweezers."

"Acchhhh. Errrcchh. Aaaaargggh!"

"Well stop poking yourself in the penis, then! You're supposed to be getting the stinger out, not delivering an intravenous injection. Give them here."

"Aah! Aaah! Aaaah! Aaaaah!"

"There you go. I'll rub some sting-relief cream on as well, that should ease the pain."

"Haaaaaaaaaaaaaaa."

"There you go. Feeling better?"

"Hrrrmmm."

"Oh bloody hell, Jamie, I don't believe you!"

Jamie barely moves for the next three hours. It's only when my stomach starts to rumble that I manage to get him off the mattress and down to the pub for a meal.

Men. How they became the dominant half of our species is still way beyond me. As I sit watching my husband acting like he's contracted the plague—rather than been bitten by a few annoyed bees—I can't help but wonder how any of them fought all those wars that led to our current civilisation. If the average man reacts to the mild pain of insect venom like this, how the hell any of them managed to wade their way across blood-soaked battlefields with their arms shot off defies belief. If the women of the world had gotten together and threatened the men with irritating skin conditions and mild head colds, we'd have probably taken over thousands of years ago. Religion would be a lot bloody different, that's for sure. Jesusina and Mohammedess would've sat down over a cup of tea and sorted their differences out in no time at all. Then all that money wasted on guns and explosives could have been spent on chocolate, spa days, and erecting a thirty-foot-high statue to the glory of Bradley Cooper. These idle thoughts roll around my head as Jamie winces over his T-bone steak and gently prods his cream-covered forehead.

"Just leave it alone," I tell him as I spoon-feed Poppy another mouthful of mashed potato.

"I can't. It's agony."

"I can tell. You're handling it very well, though." This sentence is so heavy with sarcasm it's a wonder its gravitational pull doesn't suck us all into a black hole.

"Thanks, baby."

Good Lord.

Having put a snoring Poppy down for the night, I climb into bed (sorry, slightly deflated mattress) at just after nine o'clock with the safe and secure knowledge that it could be a bed of nails and I'd still nod off in less than a minute. This has been one of the most ridiculous days of my life, and I want it to be over as quickly as possible. If nothing else, I'm still so colossally irritated at my husband that it's probably a good idea we go to sleep and don't try to communicate anymore. Maybe things will settle down a bit by morning, and I won't have the overwhelming urge to kick him in his bee-stung testicles.

The temperature is a lot lower than last night, thank God. A gentle wind is blowing outside, and light rain is falling on the campsite, providing grateful relief from the stifling heat. The rain patters against the tent canvas—an almost soothing sound to my ears. Hell, a jumbo jet aircraft taking off would be a soothing sound right now, given how knackered I am.

"Night, baby," Jamie says, still prodding at the bee stings on his head.

"Night," I grunt and roll over onto one side away from him.

I get the impression Jamie looks at me for a few moments trying to think of something else to say, but eventually he decides discretion is the better part of valour and lies back without another word. I close my eyes and drift off into sweet, sweet slumber.

I'm awoken not by dawn's light but by the sound of rain now hammering against the side of the tent. This is not a soothing sound in the slightest and is loud enough to bring me out of a very pleasant dream about Bradley Cooper dressed as Jesus, offering me herb tea and a free massage. The weather has taken a decided turn for the worse. Jamie continues to snore by my side, but I can't drift off again, so I spend the next hour listening to the rain come down, waiting for Poppy to wake up and inevitably start crying. Miraculously, this doesn't happen, and I eventually do nod off again, my tiredness overcoming even the heavy raindrops that have turned our tent into a giant bass drum.

I fall into another dream. This one is even better than the one with Bradley as it involves me floating down a Venetian canal in a gondola. I have a glass of pinot grigio in my hand. I'm wearing that gorgeous blue Gucci dress I saw online a few weeks ago that I could never afford in a million years. The gondolier poling me along the canal is Jamie—only this Jamie has spent at least six months in the gym weightlifting, and his face is not covered in angry red welts that make him look like a lumpy strawberry.

"This is the life, isn't it baby?" he says and manfully thrusts the pole into the river, his arms glistening with sweat.

I take another sip of my cool wine and nod, "It is indeed."

I tip my head back and look up at the blue sky above. A few bright white clouds scud across my field of vision, and I follow them as the gondola floats down the canal. My eyes close and I sigh happily, floating along without a care in the world. Floating, floating . . .

I wake up, opening my eyes to the grey of predawn light. I look up at the roof of our tent, which inexplicably is moving across my field of vision, much like the clouds in my dream. I must still be half-asleep. The tent isn't moving, of course. I just haven't yet shaken off the relaxing feeling of floating along without a care in the world. I rub my eyes to bring myself out of it some more and wake up properly.

Nope. The tent is still moving.

I turn my head and am surprised to see that I am gently sliding towards Poppy's travel cot. We set it up a good four feet away from the mattress, but now it's less than six inches from my nose.

The human brain never functions at its best first thing in the morning, but mine is now starting to fire on more than one cylinder and is coming to some fairly alarming conclusions very quickly: Heavy rain, plus inflatable mattress, plus babbling brook next to tent, plus idiot husband's decision to take us camping equals *big fucking problem*.

I drop my hand down along the side of the mattress. *Splosh!* I sit bolt upright, causing the mattress (raft?) to wallow in the pool of water that now fills the entire floor of the tent. I look past Jamie to see more water sluicing in from under the canvas wall that rests against the wire fence outside.

I grab Jamie's shoulder and shake it. "Jamie!"

He snorts but doesn't wake up.

"Jamie!" I shout louder and shake him again.

"Go 'way Mum. Don' wanna go to Grandma's."

"Jamie! Wake the fuck up!"

"No, no. You get off the boat. I'll stay here and watch the dolphins. They need some maracas."

Right, last resort time. I poke one finger into one of his forehead bee stings.

"Aaaaargggh!" he cries and both eyes fly open. "Wha' did you bloody do that for?" he says and scowls at me, rubbing his head.

"Oh, I don't know, Jamie. I just thought I should wake you up to tell you we're about to drown!"

"Wha' you talkin' about? Drown? We're in a tent." He rubs one eye. "I'm really tired, Laura. Lemme go back t' sleep, will you?"

Unbelievably, Jamie shuts his eyes again, putting his head back on the pillow. Within a minute he's snoring again like a chainsaw. I sit in stunned silence for a moment. Then, with grim and dark determination I swivel off the mattress and stand up in the cold water that reaches past my ankles. I then bend and search for the air plug. I find it and hook it out. Air instantly starts to whistle out of the hole. I stand up, fold my arms across my chest, and await developments.

The mattress starts to sink. The first parts of Jamie's anatomy to touch the water are his toes. He instinctively draws them up onto the mattress.

"Iss cold, Mum. Why you makin' me take a bath in Sainsbury's?"

The water creeps slowly over the top of the bed. Some of it trickles between his legs.

"Hrrrmmm. I wee'd m'self," Jamie says. "Prince Harry won' wanna go skiing wi' me now, Captain."

How much longer can he possibly stay asleep? I'm given the answer when the weight of his body finally overcomes the inflatable's ability to stay afloat. Water engulfs my husband completely.

"Aaaaargggh!" he wails and starts to thrash around. "Drownin'!" he screams. "Help me Mum, I'm drownin'!"

His arms and legs fly about like a break-dancer having an epileptic fit in a kiddie pool. I should probably just shake him out of it, but the memory of being covered in cow shit is still strong, so I leave him to it. If he starts to show signs of being in genuine trouble I'll intervene. My help is not needed, though, as Jamie now rolls over and sits up, arms still splashing around maniacally. I'm reminded of Poppy in the bath.

He looks up at me. "What the fuck is going on, woman?"

"Oh, not much. We've just been flooded out, that's all." I deliver a slap to the back of his head. "You see, Jamie?" I say calmly, administering another slap, "I told you this would end with me slapping you around. You just don't listen to me, do you?" The final slap is delivered with gusto—its impact heightened by the fact that I catch him on a bee sting.

"Stop hitting me!" he shouts, getting to his feet.

Having done so, he looks around the flooded tent at all our possessions, some of which are now floating under one wall and out into the open, probably never to be seen again. Poppy, who has so far been blissfully unaware of this latest development thanks to the height at which her cot sits, now wakes up and starts crying for her morning feed.

Having surveyed the damage, Jamie looks back at me with a look of resignation. I stare back at him, the irritation still writ large across my face.

He sighs and bends his head towards me. "Oh alright. One more then. Just try to avoid the sting on my eye."

I do avoid the sting—and end up hurting my hand more than the back of his head, it has to be said. The pain is worth it for the enormously satisfying *clunk* noise it makes as it rebounds off of my husband's skull. I'd suspected that Jamie's head was completely hollow the second he suggested a camping trip to me. It's nice to have it scientifically confirmed.

We're not the only ones to bear the brunt of the overnight downpour, but our proximity to the brook ensures we come off worst. By eight o'clock we've salvaged everything we can. Jamie has lost his sunglasses and one of my bras is probably making its way swiftly towards the Irish Sea, but apart from that there's no damage done that a tumble dryer won't be able to fix.

The water level drops as quickly as it rose, which greatly helps the cleanup operation. I have to thank the staff of the campsite at this point. They took the stupid tent down for us and pushed the car clear of the muddy field so we could get out. I'd like to think they were just going above and beyond the call of duty, but it equally may have been because they were terrified of the review we could leave on Trip Advisor. They were probably taking steps to improve their rating beyond a resolute one star.

It is with huge relief that I spy the sign by the side of the road that tells us we are a scant three miles from the motorway. This weekend has been such a nightmare that I'm actually looking forward to going back to work on Monday. I have resolved that from now on I will never again agree to anything Jamie suggests, even if it's a free spa day with complimentary chocolate followed by a threesome with Bradley Cooper. It would only end with Jamie suffering a hideous allergic reaction to the mud pack facial, me choking on a strawberry fondant, and Brad sticking it in the wrong hole.

Reading back over the bulk of this diary entry, I'm aware that I'm being very unkind to Jamie. Yes it was a silly idea to suggest a camping trip on a bank holiday, but at least he was making an effort. Jamie's heart is always in the right place, and that's always stopped me short of losing my temper with him for very long. Not this time, though. I *still* feel incredibly annoyed with him, even several days later. This worries me greatly.

More and more recently, we seem to be arguing, not communicating properly, and generally getting on each other's nerves. Every time I sit down to think of a way to solve this problem, I draw a total blank. Life is just so stressful at the moment, and it's really taking a toll on our relationship.

To be frank, I'm a little scared, Mum. This is the first time I've ever felt like this, and I don't like it one bit. I hope something happens soon to lighten the load, otherwise my marriage could be in real trouble.

Love you and miss you, Mum.

Your worried daughter, Laura

xx

JAMIE'S BLOG
Tuesday 4 November

The following is a direct transcript of a conversation recently held between Jamie Newman and his eleven-month-old daughter, Poppy:

"Morning Poppy!"

"Ufurgul gurglke munna."

"Did you sleep well?"

"Murble turble munna dadda meeooowww purb."

"That's wonderful to hear. And are you making any progress with your neutronium death ray?"

"Pibble fluurmy wobba yadda dadda munna."

"Excellent. The world will soon tremble with fear at your dainty pink feet."

Burp.

"I couldn't have said it better myself, daughter of mine."

"Meeeble."

"What would her highness for breakfast this morning?"

"Keeow! Keeow!"

"Ah, so you'd prefer the thick, green sludgy stuff out of a jar rather than the thick, red sludgy stuff out of a jar, would you? A superb decision."

"Mibble daada munna hooble daada munna muuuna weeble flurble dadda!"

"Exactly, I wholeheartedly agree. The Middle Eastern peace process won't progress until both sides are ready to get round the table and make real, comprehensive changes in their attitudes towards one another. Now open wide! Here comes the horrible red sludge!"

The sad thing is this probably represents one of the most sensible conversations I've had with another human being in years.

Pops has reached that stage in her development when things are really starting to get interesting. When I say interesting, I mean bloody terrifying. She's now crawling like a special forces soldier under heavy fire. The turn of speed she can achieve is amazing. I put her down the other day for a second in the hallway as I had a massive sneeze building. By the time it had made its seventy-mile-an-hour way out of my nostrils, my daughter had already reached the kitchen door and was about to hightail it down the garden path into the stinging nettles.

As each day goes by, the contents of our house move upwards, thanks to her ability to stand and reach. We can't leave a damn thing at Poppy height otherwise it's in her mouth quicker than food snatched by a starving fat man going to town on an all-you-can-eat-buffet.

I caught her behind the TV dismantling the TiVo box the other day. She'd already pulled out the cable running to the dish and was having a real go at ripping out the power cable as well. I would have put it down to a random act of baby vandalism were it not for the fact that *The Only Way Is Essex* was on the TV at the time. Her reaction, therefore, was perfectly understandable.

Another thing Poppy now does, which cracks me up, is move along on her wobbly little feet from couch to chair and back again. It really is quite amazing how similar an eleven-month-old baby is to a twenty-year-old media student after ten pints. Both are incredibly uncertain on their feet, both have to use every available handhold to prevent themselves crashing to the floor, both have an expression of intense but unfocused concentration on their faces, and both have a similar chance of getting a decent job in the next three years.

In babies, this moving about from one piece of furniture to another is called cruising. Now I don't know about you, but I thought cruising was an occupation primarily carried out by homosexual men dressed in brightly coloured clothing that's too tight for them. I'm giving what Poppy does a new name to divorce it from the seedy activity of looking for sex with other brightly coloured gentlemen in the local public conveniences.

From now on it shall be called wobble grabbing, which has a far nicer ring to it. It's probably the name of a small village in the Lake District as well, but I'm sticking with it regardless.

"Look, Laura! Pops is wobble grabbing again!" I exclaim happily to my wife, who gives me a disparaging look from over the top of her Kindle before returning to whatever chick lit ebook she's got on the go that evening.

Poppy's not quite walking yet, though. We've got the digital camera on standby up on the sideboard, but thus far all attempts at walking unaided have resulted in a very one-sided argument with the carpet.

Not everything's adorable. I'm afraid we've fallen prey to the age-old problem of mimicry. Poppy is at the stage where she babbles incomprehensibly most of the time, but occasionally she does come out with full words. We've had *Mamma* and *Dadda* for a while, now, which makes Laura all misty-eyed. I just collapse in heaps of laughter every time she says them. There's something delightfully silly about proper words coming from her tiny little mouth. I've been so used to Poppy being a wriggling lump of scream, babble, and poop that for her to be using proper human behaviour tickles my funny bone in no uncertain terms.

"I do wish you'd stop laughing at her, Jamie. You're going to give her a complex," Laura chides every time I so much as chuckle when she says something funny. I personally think I'm just going to push her into a career in stand-up comedy, but I try to restrain my chucklesome ways whenever the wife is around. As I said, though, it's not all adorable. You may have heard many stories about babies picking up swear words and repeating them, to the embarrassment of the parents and the hilarity of passers-by. I read a book recently where the guy's kid wouldn't stop saying *fuck* in loud, clear tones over and over again.

If only.

No, Poppy Newman decided to go one further and use the brass ring of swearwords—in front of the worst person imaginable.

Now, I'm not saying my daughter began shouting the rudest term for a lady's parts at the top of her voice one day for no reason. That would just be silly. No, it was a slow, drawn out process that started three weeks ago.

Here is another Jamie/Poppy conversation transcript by way of explanation:

"Peekaboo, Poppy!"

"Murble."

"Peekaboo!"

"Heh heh! Meefle! Meeooowwwn meefle dadda!"

"Where's Poppy's nose? Where's Poppy's nose?"

"Gurnal me forble gurna dadda mibble pew."

"There's Poppy's nose!"

"Heeble! Meeble turble curble dibble dadda munna neeble."

"Peekaboo!"

"Hee! Meefle moooeeeble cun deeble."

"Poppy!"

"Cuuuunnnn daa."

"What?"

"Dadda purble meeble cunnn da."

"Did you just say what I thought you just said?"

"Munna heeble arble peeble cunnn da. Cun-da! Cund!"

"Poppy, language!"

You see? Not really *that* word, but pretty damn close to it. Babies are basically learning how to form words every second of every day, and as they develop the ability to use new inflections, sounds, and letters, they like to get in a lot of practise. Poppy has caught on how to form the hard pronunciation of *C* and wants the world to know about it.

Over the next few days she continues to practise the hard *C* whenever possible. I am the only one who picks up on the fact that she's virtually saying the worst swear of all, though. Maybe it's just my filthy imagination, but I seem to be the only one who hears it. Every time we're in company and Poppy gives off a good *cuuunnnn da*, I pause with a fearful look on my face, waiting for the person I'm with to point at my daughter, call her the devil's child, and run away screaming. Thankfully this never happens, and I make the mistake of relaxing, thinking it's probably all in my mind and nothing to concern myself with.

As I'm writing about this in a blog post, you can appreciate this proves not to be the case. The problem gets worse when Poppy also discovers how to pronounce the letter *T* for the first time. To begin with, all we get is *teeble*, *turble*, *taaargle*, and variations on the same theme. Then she hits on the fact you can stick *T* at the end of a word as well: *heebblleet*, *munnannat*, *ooort*, and so on. The sheer joy of combining *C* and *T* with the appropriate vowel in between only occurs to my daughter when Laura and I are on a day trip to Bath, on one of the very, very rare days we actually get to spend some quality time together.

It's another fun-filled multiple-choice question, folks. See if you can guess from the following options who Poppy says the c-word in front of while on the streets of the historic Roman town:

A) A German tourist who doesn't understand English all that well and misses the word completely.

B) A deaf elderly lady, who doesn't hear her say it.

C) A child behavioural psychologist, who knows all about this kind of thing and offers some sage advice on how to break Poppy of the habit.

Or . . . wait for it . . .

D) A bad-tempered police officer who we make the mistake of stopping in order to ask directions to the Crescent building.

"You need to go back the way you came, sir," he tells me, shielding his eyes from the unseasonable November sun.

"Teeeble heeeertle daaaa," comments my daughter from behind my back, where she's safely ensconced in the baby carrier.

The copper notices her peeking out from over my shoulder. "Cute kid," he says with a grunt.

"Thanks very much."

"Do we need to go all the way back to the park?" Laura asks.

"Yes, you do," the copper says bluntly. Looks like we've stumbled on a policeman who missed the people skills part of his training.

"Cuunnn meeee dadda munna cun," says Poppy helpfully.

"Do we go left or right when we get there?" I enquire.

The policeman sighs. "Right sir, the other way goes down to the town."

"Thank you."

"Is that everything, sir?"

"Yes, I think so. Thank you for your help."

"Not a problem, sir. I'm happy to—"

"Cunt!"

Silence erupts. I know silence doesn't technically know how to erupt, but by God it chooses to have a good go at it now.

"I'm sorry?" the copper says to my daughter, who is still peeking out from behind me in the cutest fashion possible, her eyes fixed on the incredulous bobby.

"Cuunnn ta!" she repeats.

Then, to compound matters, she points at him. Poppy loves to point. It's her favourite hobby. The world around her doesn't exist until she's had a good point at it, it seems.

Laura has gone red. I have gone puce.

"Did your . . ." he begins, not knowing how to word the enquiry properly. "Did your daughter just call me the c-word?"

I give him full marks for not swearing back at us. He might have attended the people skills course after all.

"No! Oh good grief, no." I assure him, shaking my head like a dog with a rag in its mouth.

"She's just at that age." Laura adds.

Just at what age, darling? The difficult age between first word and first steps commonly known as the get Daddy arrested for public disorder age?

"Meefle! Hee beeble munna dadda CUUUN TA!" *Point, point, point.*

It appears I'm carrying a future career criminal on my back.

"I'm really very sorry," I tell my new policeman friend. "She doesn't know what she's saying, of course."

The suspicion in his eyes suggests he doesn't believe a word of it. He probably thinks I spend hours at home with my daughter strapped to a chair while I show her endless police procedural TV shows and a flip chart covered with obscenities.

"You might want to get her to stop, sir," he says, eyebrow raised.

"Cuunnn ta!"

"Certainly officer."

Laura is rapidly un-Velcroing Poppy from the backpack.

"Baddle! Maaggle! Meeee munna dadda cuuunnnnn da!"

He's going to throw us all in handcuffs any minute.

I start backing away, pulling Laura with me. "Thank you for your help officer," I squeal.

Poppy wriggles in Laura's arms like she's not finished and wants to go back to call the policeman a fascist pig fucker as well. Thankfully the officer takes no steps to follow us. With one hand resting on his utility belt and a slight look of disgust on his face, he watches us with a beady eye until we've disappeared around a conveniently placed hedge.

That was a week ago. Poppy has not repeated the c-word again as far as I can tell. She literally picked it up for a minute in front of one of Her Majesty's finest and dropped it again the moment we were out of sight. It is the most inexplicable thing to happen in nearly two years of inexplicable things. My daughter has kept me awake all night, worried me to tears with illness, forced me to drink coffee with a Chinese lunatic, and made me fork out for a new TiVo box. But all of those pale in insignificance alongside the fact she's barely out of the womb and already a card-carrying member of the criminal fraternity.

LAURA'S DIARY

Monday, November 10

Dear Mum,

I have entered a world I am ill-prepared to deal with: the world of the competitive mother. It's a cut-throat place where otherwise sane and rational women become deranged, capable of such hate- and bile-filled behaviour it's a wonder they're not arrested and sectioned on sight. It all comes down to whose baby is better. Better looking, better behaved, more advanced, happier, brighter, more alert, better dressed, better equipped, taller, hairier, cleaner, prettier, stronger, livelier, and cuter. The list goes on and on. And on.

I've done my level best to avoid these women, but they smell you coming, and before you know it you're being accosted in the middle of the park when you're trying to enjoy a nice walk.

"Hello there!" a voice hails me as I sit moving Pops back and forth in her stroller while idly checking out the arses on the blokes playing football across the park. Into my field of vision—and interrupting a particularly peachy bottom as it's about to take a penalty—is a tall, skinny brunette with an expression usually found on the face of one of those clipboard-carrying charity folk who ambush you on the way out of a high street shop.

"Morning," I say warily. She's pushing what looks like a vastly overpriced stroller.

I know what's coming and mentally roll my eyes.

"Lovely day for taking them to the park, isn't it?

Actually, I'm the one enjoying the park, sweetheart. Pops doesn't really have a choice in the matter.

"Yes."

She sits down next to me, pulling her baby alongside mine. She leans over to look at Pops, who gives her a blank stare. "How old is your little one?"

"Nearly a year."

"Oh! Lovely. Mine's eleven months and already talking properly!"

"That's nice for you."

The brunette leans over her own baby and gives the poor bastard a bug-eyed stare. "Izn't that wight ickle Philpot?"

Philpot? The kid's name is fucking Philpot?

"That's an unusual name," I say, trying hard not to laugh.

"My late grandmother's maiden name. She was deputy mayor. We wanted to honour her appropriately."

And make your son the target of every bully on God's green earth, no doubt.

Philpot, as if trained to do so in some Pavlovian-style experiment, looks up at me and speaks. "'Ello!" he says in a clear, crisp voice.

The brunette's eyes light up.

Shit. Now I have to get Pops to perform for me, otherwise she's going to look more backwards than the West Country in front of this brown-haired monster and her experiment in parenting.

"Say hello, Poppy!" I tell my daughter, with no appreciable response. "Say hello!" This elicits no more than a dribble and a lopsided smile. The brunette gives me one of those smiles people aim at the homeless. "Say hello to the lady, Poppy!" This time Poppy lets out a sonorous, heavy fart that indicates I'll be finding the nearest baby-changing room in a few minutes.

The brunette, whose name I'm pleased to say I never discovered, sits back and puts her hands in her lap. "Well, all babies develop at different rates, don't they?"

What an insufferable bitch. Here I was, quite happily perving over some footballer's bottom, and she comes along interrupting my happy mood with her stupid talking Philpot. What makes women think this is okay behaviour? You wouldn't walk up to another woman at random and start comparing handbags or shoes, would you? No, you'd carry out the comparison covertly from afar with a sneer on your face, as is right and proper. Why is it different with children?

I stand up. "I have to go and change her. It was nice to meet you." I look down at Pops. "Say good-bye to the lady, Poppy," I say, hoping she'll mistake this bitch for a policeman and come out with her favourite word. No joy, though, I just get another fart and a slight look of desperation.

"It was nice to meet you, too. Say good-bye Philpot."

"'oodbye 'hilpot."

What a little twat.

This is why I maintain only one close relationship with another mother, the one I have with Melina. We've been friends far too long to let competitiveness get in the way. The fact that Poppy is developing at the same rate as Hayley did a few years ago is the saving grace. If Mel's kid could have recited Shakespeare and tied a reef knot one-handed at one-year-old we may have had more of a problem.

"I got that too," Mel tells me when I recite the tale of Philpot and his mother. "Still do. Your kid becomes such an all-encompassing part of your life that it's difficult not to treat the whole thing as a contest. Hayley's the biggest contribution I've made to the world, so of course I want her to be better than the other kids."

This was disturbing. Mel is normally as level-headed and sensible as me. The idea of her succumbing to this ridiculous game of one-upmanship means I might, too. But I can't spend the next few years avoiding my fellow mothers, can I? I'll become a recluse, and Pops will grow up weird and socially inept. Just like her father.

"Swim classes," Mel says.

"What?"

"The best thing I did when Hayley was little was take her to swim classes. It's very popular these days and a good way to get to know other mothers with babies the same age."

"I don't know, Mel, it sounds awful."

"Put it this way Loz, it'll give you a chance to wear a swimsuit and show off how well you've lost your baby weight."

This is all the convincing I need. Mel knows me so well. All those walks with Pops and sessions on the treadmill have (more or less) returned me to my pre-pregnancy weight—with the added bonus of larger boobs. Even if Poppy isn't streets ahead of the other babies, I should be able to outdo the other mothers in the swimsuit department. This is both hideously egotistical and poor parenting in the extreme, but it would take extreme measures to get me out of the house at eight on a Monday morning and down to the leisure centre. The class is called Aquababes, which sounds like a top-shelf DVD full of bikini models to me, but who am I to judge?

It's certainly well attended. There are a lot of cars parked at the leisure centre at this ungodly hour. Most of them sport a variety of those idiotic Baby on Board stickers.

I pull into the parking lot a good ten minutes late and rush Poppy through to the changing rooms as quickly as possible. I change us both into our swim clothes and head for the pool.

We have come prepared to dazzle. Poppy is resplendent in a brand-new ten-quid baby swimsuit, and I am rocking the gorgeous cut-out number with the scalloped edges I bought on my honeymoon. As we head out past the footbath into the main pool area, I feel a little strut in my step coming on.

Look at me. I have a child and also shapely hips. Look how my stomach is flat—providing I hold my breath in slightly. My hair is gold-

en and flowing, my baby is well nourished and happy. Tremble in my presence!

Yes, I am being utterly ridiculous, but being a mother isn't all that conducive to feeling sexy and confident most of the time. You're always knackered and pretty much consumed with taking care of your child twenty-four hours a day. There's not a lot of time left over for dressing to impress. A girl likes to feel good about herself, and I'm determined not to let this opportunity go by.

"You're late!" an irritated voice snaps, ruining my ego-trip.

I look into the pool to see a trim, tanned, black-haired woman standing in front of a group of mothers holding babies. All look at me with a mixture of curiosity, veiled contempt, and (hopefully) jealousy.

"Sorry! I'm new. Where do I go?"

The woman in charge points to a spot about halfway along the shallow end of the pool where the class is taking place.

"Just there, next to our other new lady today."

I nod and gingerly enter the water, carrying Poppy awkwardly as I lower myself into the gratefully warm pool to join my fellow newbie.

"Hi, I'm Samantha and this is Mickey," she says, holding up her baby boy.

"Hi there. I'm Laura and this is Poppy."

"Nice to meet you."

"Ladies, please!" the instructor snaps, silencing us. I swallow hard. This is looking unpleasant. The tall woman is built like a drill instructor and looks like she was born with a whistle in her mouth. I await further instructions.

"All of you are only one or two sessions in, so we're still introducing our babies to the water. Today is all about getting your child used to being immersed in water and submerged above their heads once comfortable."

Submerged? I had visions of holding Poppy while she flails her arms and legs around on the surface, not putting her under the bloody water. I raise my hand.

"Yes?" the instructor asks.

"Erm. What do you mean by *submerged*? I thought this was about them having a splash about wearing cute little armbands?"

"Splash about?" she parrots in a tone verging on disgust. "Armbands?"

"Well, yeah." I turn to Samantha, who nods briefly in agreement. She must feel the same way.

"That is *not* how this class operates," the instructor says with hands on hips. "Didn't you read the pamphlet?"

I *never* read the sodding pamphlet. That's what usually gets me into trouble in the first place.

"This class is about promoting the natural mammalian reflex inherent in all babies," she informs me.

"Come again?"

"All babies are born with the ability to swim. They spend the first nine months of life immersed in utero. We are here simply to encourage the development of that intrinsic skill."

Well, there was me thinking I just needed a cute swimsuit to come to this class, not a degree in biology. The stern instructor looks back at the whole group again.

"We're going to start with gently placing baby into the water to get him or her used to it." She turns to another woman behind her holding a robust looking dark-haired boy. "Can I have Francis now, Helen?" The baby is duly passed and held up in a tableau that disturbingly reminds me of a sacrifice scene from a horror movie. "Gently lower baby into the water . . ."

I try to copy her movements with Poppy. Initially, my baby squirms as the water immerses her legs and bum. Then, miraculously, she calms down and starts to waggle her arms and legs. Poppy lets out a cry of delight. This is *wonderful*! I smile at Sam, who seems to be having a little more trouble convincing Mickey that the water is a nice place to be. Around me the other mothers are having a variety of success with the task as well, but no baby appears to be as happy in the wet stuff as mine.

A small, warm glow of self-satisfaction passes through me. I try to suppress it . . . and fail. I have become that which I detest: a smug mother.

"Excellent!" the black-haired instructor says, looking at me. I beam with newfound pride. "Now, lower the baby further if they are happy. If you feel confident enough, loosen your grip and allow them to float on their own."

I do so, and Poppy giggles in delight once again. She appears to be a happy little water baby. *Maybe she'll go to the Olympics*, I think, getting way ahead of myself, Poppy, and the universe as a whole. I take one hand away and still Poppy splashes about with no trouble. *This is amazing. This is brilliant. My daughter is a real talent!* I confidently take my other hand away.

Poppy, relieved of all motherly support, drops like a fucking stone. I screech in panic as my poor baby's shocked face drops away into the watery depths. Everyone turns to stare at me. My idiotic hubris is going to get my firstborn drowned!

With another wail I plunge into the water, grab Poppy around the waist, and stand up. The entire incident couldn't have lasted more than three or four seconds, but to me it's a lifetime. Poppy starts to cough loudly. I pat her on the back and she produces a belch of magnificent proportions.

"I'm sorry Pops! I'm so, so sorry." I tell her, hugging her close.

"Never mind, dear." the instructor says. "That's fairly common. She's perfectly fine."

Oh sod off, you muscle-bound cow.

I'm expecting a torrent of tears from my daughter, but once the coughing fit passes she just starts to babble at me in her usual baby talk. "Meeble! Herflurgle me booble nodda munna mumma weeble."

"I know Poppy, I'm sorry for letting you go."

She points a dainty finger at me. "Merble tooble munna bunna wabba." Her little eyebrows lower into a frown. "Cuuunn ta!"

For the rest of the session, I control my competitive streak and let Poppy progress at a slower pace. I'm pleased to say that my foray into overconfidence doesn't appear to have dented Poppy's. She is still more than happy in the water, and by the time the thirty minutes are up, she's happily bobbing around, pointing at things and laughing her head off. It's quite magical to watch a baby paddling about. There's such an intense sense of *rightness* about it that I find hard to put down in words. Maybe the instructor is correct—there is something in babies, and in all of us, that makes us comfortable in the water. A subconscious remembrance of what it was like to be in the womb.

After we've all changed, a few of us remain behind for a coffee in the leisure centre café. Sam is a nice girl and Mickey is a well-behaved little boy. Not once does she compare his progress with Poppy's, and not once do I feel like I'm in competition with her. It's nice to have a new friend. We spend a happy hour slagging off every other mother and baby at the session, and we both decide our friendly instructor is probably a lesbian. If there's one thing worse than one woman in competition with another, it's *two* women who share similar opinions ganging up on the others.

I must introduce Sam to Mel. Between the three of us we should be able to look down on the entire female population of the planet.

The main thing I'm learning is that being a parent brings out both the best and the worst in you. As each day passes, the fierce love I hold for my daughter grows ever stronger. I know that I would do anything for her, sacrifice anything to keep her safe. This is quite a noble feeling, which makes me feel pretty good about myself. On the other hand I'd throw everyone I know—including Jamie, probably—under a train to protect her. This is not a noble feeling in the slightest. The next time I meet someone who has trouble expressing their emotions, I'm going to recommend they give birth as soon as possible. There's nothing like a string of sleepless nights and a sense of protectiveness bordering on the psychopathic to open your emotional floodgates.

Love you, miss you—and am grateful you didn't take me to baby swim classes, Mum. I would have drowned in seconds.

Your thoughtful daughter, Laura

xxx

JAMIE'S BLOG
Sunday 30 November

Tempus, as people insist on telling me, has a distinct habit of fugiting when you least suspect it. Life may be the thing that happens while you're busy making other plans, but time is the thing that decides how long you get to do it.

Today was Poppy's first birthday. It's hard to believe an entire year has passed since Laura made a mess of the Apple store and I did a serious amount of damage to the car—none of which has been fixed properly yet. It has been, without a doubt, the hardest, silliest, most brutal, and most amazing year of my life. And this is coming from the person who nearly murdered his future wife with a fajita, got sexually molested by a drunk lunatic, and bawled his eyes out in front of a chubby lass dressed as Lara Croft—all in the space of twelve months.

There's been a lot of strain on my relationship with Laura since the birth of our daughter, of that there is no doubt. I'm fairly sure she still hasn't completely forgiven me for nearly drowning her in Wookey Hole, for starters. Thanks to how tired we've been for the past year, our marriage now consists more of arguments than sex. This is a troubling turn of events neither of us was prepared for. I knew having a baby would be stressful but forgot that bringing a child into this world just adds to all the existing stresses and strains you have to deal with anyway. Working forty hours a week, dodging my insane mother, and maintaining any kind of feasible social life is only made all the harder once you introduce a miniature human being into the equation.

And I'm not the one who has to do most of the caring for Poppy. Laura has to cope with a majority of the day-to-day stuff—fitting it in round her part-time hours at Morton & Slacks, arranging for babysitters when she can—and on the odd occasion actually taking Poppy into work with her when she can't.

All of that jumbled together means there's not been a lot of Jamie and Laura time in the past year, which is no doubt the source of our current difficulties. We've always had quite a fiery relationship, but in the past there was always enough time to make up with one another after any argument—usually in bed and naked. All we seem to have time for these days is the argument, with none left for the making up afterwards.

Such was the case on this particularly special morning. Last night had ended with yet another row over money, one of the really unpleasant ones when you thank your lucky stars you made it out with no internal injuries. Opening the water bill at half past ten at night was a mistake I won't be making again anytime soon. We'd gone to bed angry with the issue unresolved, which all the relationship books and magazines delight in telling us is a very bad thing, indeed. We'd both woken up in the same bad mood the next day, barely able to spit out a civil good morning to one another as we climbed out of bed.

"Let's just try to forget about last night," Laura eventually says as she slips on her dressing gown. "This day is supposed to be about Poppy. I don't want her upset."

"I won't say anything, don't worry," I grunt and shuffle out of the bedroom without even attempting to give my wife a morning kiss.

Not the best way to begin your daughter's first birthday, is it?

Thank God I have a very special child who seems to have an innate sense of timing—one which will no doubt see her on the stage in the future. I'm now thoroughly convinced she'll have a successful career as a stand-up comedian. This is due to the fact that a year to the day since she popped into the world from her mother's ravaged lady bits (from what I've been told, I didn't have the guts to look), Poppy Helen Newman took her first unaided steps across the lounge floor and showed Laura and me why all the crap we'd been through this year has been absolutely worth it. It's quite incredible really.

As it was her first birthday, we decided to go to town and purchase Poppy as many birthday presents as we could with our current unhealthy bank balance (the credit cards took a pounding as well, I can tell you). She's not old enough to appreciate any of them properly, but what the hell; your firstborn doesn't turn one year old every day of the week. This is the rather silly mentality that keeps the major baby toy companies in Porsches and expensive champagne—but I digress.

Laura and I argued about what to buy Poppy, of course. We can always find something to vocally disagree with one another about, even the supposedly pleasurable pastime of buying presents for our daughter. I was all for buying the big, beefy trike I spotted in Toys "R" Us, until Laura handily pointed out that it was obviously meant for a child much older than ours, and if we tried to put her on it, she'd wobble about for a few seconds before falling off in a screaming, nappy-filled heap.

When a baby is one year old, everything worth purchasing is plastic, brightly coloured to the point of stupidity, and (naturally) hideously pricey. Never mind that said baby is endlessly entertained by a set of car keys being jangled in front of her. If the brightly coloured plastic piece of rubbish has buttons on it that when pressed play an out-of-tune rendition of "Twinkle, Twinkle Little Star," you're onto a real winner. Poppy will receive many of these for her first birthday.

So much so that half of them will no doubt end up on eBay at some point.

Our main present is an enormous playhouse that Laura fell in love with the second she laid eyes on it. I tried to point out in the shop that our daughter is only two feet long, whereas this monstrosity is nearly tall enough for me to stand up in. The wife is having none of it, though. She's completely enamoured with the cute flower boxes and little arched windows. Laura is sure that Poppy will love it, too, in spite of her diminutive size, and will treasure it from the first moment she lays eyes on the silly thing. Which is all very well, but I'm the one who's going to have to put the fucking thing up, aren't I?

Baby's first birthday also gives friends and relatives the chance to celebrate, and in certain cases a chance to alleviate the guilt of avoiding you like the plague for the past year because you now have a screaming ball of mucus and poo with you at all times. Our lounge is veritably *stuffed* with expensive plastic brightly coloured crap when we bring Pops down at seven in the morning.

"Ooh! Look Poppy! Look at all the lovely presents!" Laura says in as excited a voice as she can muster at this hour. Naturally Poppy couldn't give a monkey's about any of it, and is far more interested in the water stain on the ceiling I've been meaning to paint over for months. Her little finger points at it imperiously—a damning indictment of my DIY skills.

"I'm making coffee," I say and shuffle off into the kitchen.

By the time I've put together two cups of awful brown instant and shuffled back into the lounge, Poppy is cruising—sorry, wobble grabbing—her way around the room while her mother desperately tries to elicit some kind of interest regarding the hundreds of pounds' worth of baby toys now littering every surface.

"Look at this, Poppy!" Laura waggles a badly wrapped stuffed giraffe in Poppy's face. "You want to open it with Mummy?"

Not a fucking chance. Poppy's far more interested in the bloody TiVo box again. I hustle over to stop her from electrocuting herself.

Laura then takes it upon herself to open the giraffe and hand it to Poppy, who gives it a squeeze, points at the water stain again, and goes in search of more mischief, abandoning the poor stuffed giraffe to its own devices behind the fish tank.

For the next twenty minutes, Laura and I unwrap everything while Poppy ignores us. She means to wobble grab her way around the room at least five times this morning, dammit—and there's not a thing we can do to stop her. It's like she's decided on her daily workout regime and intends to stick to it come hell or high water. I eventually give up on trying to interest her and start unwrapping presents on the sofa. Poppy is across the other side of the room with Laura, pointing up at the fish tank and calling the clown fish a cunt.

We're really going to have to wean her off that word at some point.

I'm down to the last present. It's a small one from my idiot brother Chris. It's amazing we even have a gift from him. He's missed my birthday six years in a row, now. He must have felt *really* guilty about not visiting us more this year.

It's a ball of some kind. Even Chris's hideous attempt at wrapping can't disguise the spherical nature of the present within. I open it and give it a once-over. It's purple and squishy, and when you whack it with your hand a light comes on at its centre and it plays a tinkly little tune. I give the thing a half-hearted wallop and hold it out while it glows and sings to itself.

"Jamie look," I hear Laura say.

I gaze over and see Poppy absolutely transfixed. Gone are thoughts of water stains and TiVo boxes. If the clown fish is a cunt, my daughter no longer cares. The purple squishy ball is her entire life now. From where she stands leaning against the television, Poppy takes a step towards me. Laura's arms shoot out.

"Hang on! Let's see what happens," I say.

"I don't want her to hurt herself."

"This baby has survived a bout of pneumonia, being abandoned in a department store, and a near drowning. I'm sure she'll be fine."

Laura sits back on her heels.

"Poppy!" I call. "You want this?" I hold out the ball. "Come and get it, Poppy."

She's not sure. You can see the cogs in her brain whirring. She wants the ball, but there's nothing between her and it. It will require walking without a handy couch or TV to lean on.

"C'mon, Poppy!" I repeat, vaguely aware that I sound like I'm calling a dog.

"Go on, Pops. Go to Daddy," Laura says, getting into the spirit of it.

"Munna wobba mummy dadda," Poppy tells us in a serious voice.

I waggle the ball again. Poppy holds out one hand . . . and then, ever so carefully, ever so *daintily*, my gorgeous, glorious, wonderful daughter—the centre of my universe—takes her first step forward.

LAURA'S DIARY
Sunday, November 30

It was incredible, Mum. One second she was clinging to the telly for support, the next she was walking. It was wobbly, slightly unsure and threatened to send her into the fireplace at any moment, but they were Poppy's first true steps. And what a day for it to happen!

My heart leapt into my mouth, and I could see Jamie trembling as Poppy reached out one podgy little hand and tottered towards her father, eyes fixed on the weird little purple ball Jamie's brother had bought. As I watched her cross the room, tears filled my eyes. Mostly tears of happiness, of course, but I think there was a part of me that felt a slight sense of loss in those brief moments between television and sofa. Everything would change now. Poppy would no longer be a baby, she was entering into the uncertain—but wholly fascinating—world of the toddler. This no doubt means my stress level is about to rise even higher, but that's par for the course when you have children, I suppose.

The most beautiful part of Poppy's first walk is when she reaches Jamie. I am expecting her to simply grab the ball and bounce into the sofa next to him, but instead her pace actually slows as she reaches him. One gentle hand goes onto the ball and she looks up at him, face full of wonder.

"Daddy," she says in the sweetest, clearest tone I'd ever heard her use.

"Yes honey, it's Daddy." Jamie's voice is thick with emotion. "You want the ball?"

Her other hand reaches out and she lifts the ball from his grasp, staring at it intently.

Jamie looks at me over her. It's the same look he had on his face when he asked me to marry him. I wish—*oh God, I only wish*—that I will see that look on his face a thousand more times in my life.

All of the pain, frustration, anger, and worry of the last year disappears in that split second. It's like the greatest magic trick ever performed—and one that only my year-old daughter could have pulled off. Jamie and I share a look that contains a thousand apologies for all the trivial, spiteful, stupid things we've said to one another since I fell pregnant. The look is also filled with the unconditional love that still binds us together after all this time.

What I feared may have been fading away from our relationship was merely trapped behind a wall built out of all the stresses and strains of everyday life. A wall that my little girl has just utterly destroyed with a few wobbling steps across the living room carpet.

Poppy simply stands studying her new toy, oblivious to the silent act of joint forgiveness going on over her head. The ball probably cost all of a fiver but is providing her with more joy than the plethora of expensive gifts that surround us—and is providing Jamie and me with an extremely cheap and effective form of marriage counselling to boot.

"Poppy," I say in a quiet voice. "Why don't you show Mummy the ball?"

Jamie is standing slowly and reaching for the digital camera. I put my arms out. Tears are rolling down my face, so I smile broadly. I don't want my newly ambulant daughter to think I'm upset.

"Come here, Poppy. Come and show Mummy."

"Mummy!" Poppy cries and giggles, holding the ball towards me.

Now I'm shaking. It's all a bit too much for this girl. We expected to be giving Poppy presents today, but she's given us the best gift imaginable. Pops starts to make a move back over to me. It seems that with each and every step she gets stronger, her gait steadier. Not for the first time I am reminded of how fast babies develop, of how quickly they change.

Jamie knows this too, as he snaps away with the camera like a man possessed. We end up taking over one hundred pictures of Poppy walking on her birthday. Our Facebook profiles will not know what's hit them.

Although it takes her but a few seconds to toddle back to my waiting arms, I savour each and every moment, each and every detail—burning them into my brain: the bright, innocent smile on her face; the minute wobble in her knees; her hair lifting from her forehead as she moves; the way the purple ball pulses gently, lighting her perfect little fingers as she grasps its rubbery surface; and, above all, the sublime, high, happy laugh that seems to emanate from every part of her. If a baby's heartbeat is the sound of the universe, then her laughter is surely the sound of its creator.

I take my giggling daughter in my arms and wrap her tightly in them. Jamie joins us, crouches down, and puts one arm around me. The camera is forgotten for the moment.

As Poppy plays with her new toy, Jamie kisses my forehead. "I think we did alright sweetheart," he says in a soft voice.

"Yeah." I offer him a lopsided smile. "So far, anyway."

I believe it, too. We *have* done alright. In fact, we've done *better* than alright in my book. For two people completely ill-equipped to bring a baby into the world, we've negotiated ourselves to this point where our daughter is healthy, happy, and loved.

Through illness, calamity, embarrassment, argument, and exhaustion, we've stayed together—all three of us—keeping smiles on our faces for as long as is humanly possible.

I don't know what lies in the future. There are bound to be more hiccups along the way. Given how ridiculously her parents have behaved in the past, I'm sure Poppy will make her fair share of mistakes. But that's okay, because Jamie and I will always be there for her. That's what we do now.

And knowing that—more than anything else—makes me love and miss you harder and deeper than ever before, Mum. If I can do half as good a job of loving Poppy as you did with me, I'll be the best mother in the world.

To the future, to the past, and to this wonderful moment with the sound of my daughter's laughter ringing in my ears.

Your happy daughter—and an even happier mother—Laura.

xxx

POPPY'S iTALK
December 02, 2031

OMG!

I'm spacing, Hayles.

Full-on weirded out here . . .

The units gave me this messed up present for the b-day.

On a flash drive, I got Dad's blog he used to write way back in the day. Mum scanned her old diary onto it as well.

When they give it to me, they tell me it's all about me being born. *Literal.*

I read it coz it sounded kinda cool.

Wish I hadn't now . . .

My units are soooo embarrassing. There's all this stuff about Mum getting preggers—which is far, far gross.

Would you believe Dad lost me in some ancient real-world shop when I was only a few months old?

Then there's all the stuff about Grandma. That freaked me out, too. Can't see how the little old lady we go see every week could have been like that. Mind you, she does look at the pool guy funny whenever he comes over.

You know how I keep saying I don't feel like I'm normal? Like I'm kinda "outside" everyone else?

Now I *know* it.

You only have to read this stuff for a few pages to be sure.

You get a mensh, chick. Your Mum does, too. Seems like she babysat me when the units went out on a date. Never knew Mum was such a booze hound back in the day!

Dad blogged about me having pneumonia. Didn't know how bad it was. Guess I know why Mum always bugs me large about dressing warm when it's cold out.

It's not all bad, I guess. Some of it's kinda sweet. Clear they love each other—and me.

Eeerggh . . .

You have *no* idea how much my skin crawls thinking of the units as being *sweet*. I'm used to them either being bossy, boring, or embarrassing.

Reading about when they were young and still had it? *Terrifying*, chick. Dead terrifying.

Next time I crash I'll bring it with. You can have a read yourself.

I could go on about it here, but better you see with your own spheres. You wouldn't believe half of it if I just told you.

The blog and diary only go up to my first birthday, though . . .

I was kinda bummed coz I wanted to read about what happened after. From what they've told me in the past, that's when things *really* started to get good!

Okes, gonna flip out now chick, gotta do an essay for tomorrow.

Loves ya, misses ya, and can't wait to kick it with you on Sats.

Your mate,

Poopy.

The End

ABOUT THE AUTHOR

Nick Spalding is the bestselling author of six novels and two memoirs: *Life... With No Breaks* and *Life... On a High*. Nick worked in media and marketing for most of his life before turning his energy to his genre-spanning writing. He lives in the south of England with his fiancée.